SHADOWQUEEN

Debbie Tanner Federici was born and raised in rural southeastern Arizona. She and her husband now live with their three sons in a large metropolitan Sanctuary called Phoenix.

Susan Vaught is a writer and a psychologist in private practice. She lives with her son and daughter in Westmoreland, a small Sanctuary in present-day Tennessee.

C.1

SHADOWQUEEN

DEBBIE FEDERICI
SUSAN VAUGHT

Llewellyn Publications
Woodbury, Minnesota

First Edition
First Printing, 2005

Book design by Megan Atwood and Andrew Karre
Cover design by Ellen Dahl
Cover image © 2005 by PhotoAlto
Editing by Rhiannon Ross and Megan Atwood

Library of Congress Cataloging-in-Publication Data
Federici, Debbie Tanner, 1965-
ShadowQueen: the L.O.S.T. story continues--/Debbie Federici, Susan Vaught.
p. cm.
Summary: Now the King of the Witches, Brenden tries to rescue Jazz while battling the evil Erkling, a fearsome shapeshifter, and his enchantress daughters.
ISBN 0-7387-0827-5
[1. Magic--Fiction. 2. Witches--Fiction. 3. Space and time--Fiction.] I. Vaught, Susan, 1965-II. Title

PZ7.F3133Sh2005
[Fic]--dc22

Llewellyn Publications
A Division of Llewellyn Worldwide, Ltd.
2143 Wooddale Drive, Dept. 0-7387-0827-5
Woodbury, MN 55125-2989, U.S.A.
www.llewellyn.com

Printed in the United States of America

To my three sons, Tony, Kyle, and Matthew.
You guys mean the world to me.

—Debbie

To my sweet aunts Judy, Carol, Gloria, and Sylvia,
and my beloved grandmothers Nell and Gert.
Never underestimate strong women.
You have mastered shadows. You have changed the world.

—Susan

Acknowledgments

We'd like to offer loud, annoying gratitude to Sheri Gilbert, our intrepid critique partner, who was brave enough to read this (really fast); to our agent, Erin Murphy, who was brave enough to sell this (really fast); and to Megan Atwood, Llewellyn's Acquisitions Editor, who was brave enough to buy this (really fast). Equally loud, annoying gratitude to Rhiannon Ross, who was brave enough to edit us and who went the extra mile to preserve our oh-so-tender writerly integrity. Last but definitely not least, quite calm, gentle, appropriate, and absolutely non-annoying gratitude to Ellen Dahl for another amazing cover (sssshhhh, great artist at work).

Thanks!

Tho Shadowe stands defeated,
Darke shall come to fynde yts vengeance,
Ande yf yts hand be fyrm,
Ande yf yts eye be strong,
Ande yf yts aym be true,
Bye yts stroke hope dyes forever.

—Passage MCLXXX
Wytches Book of Tyme

chapter one

Death isn't supposed to be like this.

No light. No darkness. Crying in the wilderness with no path to follow.

I fought a flash of panic. Were the Shadows coming?

But . . . what *were* Shadows, anyway? Why did I fear them? If I could grasp my name, any detail of my previous life, I might gain some understanding. I've tried and tried, but only one thought makes sense.

Before I died, I might have been a witch.

Witches spoke about Summerland, the other world people travel to after their Earth-life. Some witches even knew about Talamadden, the special Sanctuary within Summerland, for those who might have a second chance at life.

Before I died, I might have been a witch.

2

Was I supposed to have a second chance?

In my nothing space in the nothing place, I wished for an end to my nothing existence. I couldn't even see myself, not my legs or arms or clothes. For all I knew, I was only air and thought. More nothing.

Help me, Goddess. Please. If you ever knew me, help me now because I can't take much more.

If I had been a witch, maybe the Great Mother would listen. I felt sure I once believed in her, but did she still believe in me?

A faint rustling noise made me look up. It was the first sound I could remember in so, so long.

"Show yourself! Are you Shadows?" My voice sounded small and cracked and desperate. I wished I had a sword, then wondered why.

"Speak," I demanded, though I knew I had no power to compel.

"Rise, Jasmina."

The low command rang from my right side, and I jerked around to see a bird drifting gracefully out of the darkness. He was not made of the dreaded Shadows, no. A real creature with a jaunty step and bright, well-cleaned feathers.

Jasmina. He called me Jasmina.

That was right! My name. Names had power. I could feel a stirring in my belly, sense a warming in my cheeks.

Jasmina.

From some echo deep within my essence, a boy's whisper . . .

Jazz . . .

3

A heaviness overcame me, like I had gone from air and thought to something much more solid. My thoughts became more solid, too.

Squinting and blinking to clear my senses, I tried to believe what my mind perceived. The last thing I expected to find in the land of the dead was a talking peacock who knew my name. Animals were supposed to be innocents, never having to worry about spiritual struggles.

That's witch-knowing, Jasmina. I had to have been a witch. Jasmina, the witch.

Then again, that whisper. *Jazz . . .*

I couldn't imagine why a peacock would be an exception to the innocent animal idea, so the very sight of his sparkling blue body and long feather train made me nervous—not to mention the way he looked at me, like he had known me . . . *before*. His black-pearl eyes glittered like candles lit by dark magic. Only, there was no magic in Talamadden. At least not magic I could use, if indeed I had been a witch.

Staring at the bird, I stiffened my back against the leafless tree on the grassless patch of ground. Not far from the tree stood a hut I had never entered. I hadn't encountered another being since I died. Only the hut, the dusty ground, a stream, and that tree. I had come to consider it my tree, though it had no life, no leaves, no tree-heart beating beneath its spongy bark. Its scrawny branches reached toward the starless, moonless sky like dozens of hag fingers, clawing out the night's eyes.

The stream, if such black, inky depths could be called a stream, was odd. It moved in a way it shouldn't—backward, against nature. I didn't know if the water was warm or cool because I never really felt thirsty or hungry. I never lost weight or gained weight. Nothing was ever dirty, and nothing was ever clean. I felt peaceful, yet disturbed. Alone, yet surrounded by strange energies somewhere in the darkness, far beyond my limited square of existence.

Now, I was nearly nose-to-nose with a haughty-looking peacock who shouldn't be in the land of the dead at all.

"You must leave this place," the bird said flatly. "Darkness is coming, and it's hungry for you."

I swallowed hard, trying to wet my lips and tongue enough to speak again. "What are you?"

The peacock paused a few seconds to preen, flicking bits of dirt in my direction. Then he seemed to recover himself and once more fixed me with that glittering ebony gaze.

"Jasmina Corey, Queen of the Witches, please stop wasting time and get up."

Hearing that name and title jarred my senses. I shook my head, suddenly aware of the weight of my hair. It was—or had been in life—the same shade of black as the bird's unrelenting eyes. In human form, I *did* have black hair. In full magical form, I was a brilliant gold, like most witches born to the craft.

Slowly, slowly, I did know. And I became what I knew. That girl who had been. That girl who still existed. Legs, arms, hair, eyes—I was me, and I did believe the bird was right. Once, I had been Queen of the Witches. Before death, before battling an evil so great it killed me before my time, before being forced to face my destiny at sixteen years of age.

Was I still sixteen? Had I been here a day? A week? Who could say how time moved in death's haven?

"Summerland," the bird said, reading my thoughts without effort. "At least the main part. This section where you hide, it is Talamadden, yes, death's haven—but it soon will be no haven for you. On your feet."

A chill overtook me, and I shivered. That surprised me. I had felt neither hot nor cold since my death. "What *are* you?" I demanded again.

At this, the peacock gave a great sigh. "The last thing you will ever see or know if you do not stand and follow me."

I complied, moving first to my knees, then towering above the unusual blue-feathered creature.

Goddess, but standing was an effort.

"Don't you understand?" the bird asked calmly, as if he were speaking to a stubborn toddler. "It's true. Death shouldn't be like this. More importantly, the land of the dead shouldn't be like this, dark and lifeless and soul-draining. Summerland—especially Talamadden—is a place of renewal and contemplation, a place of heightened existence and choices."

"That's not what I've found." I wrapped my arms around myself and rocked, toe to heel, toe to heel.

"Because you haven't looked." Truth flowed through the notes of the bird's forceful bass. I found myself breathing in short, sharp gasps. "My name is Egidus," he added. "And you need to follow me out of this blighted nowhere."

"Egidus," I muttered as I tried to take a step. The name troubled me, as if I should recognize it. I didn't have time to focus on triviality, however. My legs felt like leaden machinery. A wracking, painful sensation crawled up my spine. My chest ached.

"This is why I stopped looking." I rubbed my ribs and neck at the same time. "If I move again, I'll have a vision. I'll be able to see, smell, taste, hear—but never touch—never be a part of what I'm seeing. If I move too much, or make too much noise, the Shadows might come to steal me—everything feels like punishment."

"Not everything in the universe is about you, Jasmina." The bird sounded so confident I wanted to kick him, and that emotion gave me new and deeper surprise. "Visions always come for a reason. Before you forgot yourself, you knew this fact."

Irked by his insult, I managed another step away from the tree and toward the peacock. In response, he edged toward the unnatural stream, on the far side of the leafless tree. I glanced toward the water, then at the impenetrable darkness masking its flow a few yards away.

If Shadows weren't a figment of my imagination, surely they lived beyond these boundaries. I would be consumed by them. Swallowed alive!

My body tensed.

At that moment, a window opened in the blackness, a long, tempting window from ground to the height of the lowest tree branches, playing life like a movie I didn't want to watch.

Jazz . . .

I remembered him then, my Bren, my champion. The companion of my heart. I could see him! Ah, gods, how my heart ached, just recognizing his familiar stride. Beside him, the giant-like Rol, who had once been my Training Master and the father I so needed when my own was murdered.

"Jasmina's passing to death's haven—it was no fault of yours." Rol placed his hand on Bren's shoulder and squeezed, drawing Bren's gaze back to his. "You must release this guilt and some of your anger, or you will be unable to meet the queen again."

Bren shivered like a ghost had just passed across his flesh. "What are you talking about?"

Rol stared at his battered boots and looked back to Bren. "I . . . thought you knew. I was impressed, even, that you had made no impulsive attempt to find what cannot be found."

Bren jerked, his fists clenching and unclenching. "Quit talking in riddles, Rol. You're making it sound like Jazz didn't die."

"She died," he said flatly. "Too young, from evil intent."

Rol! I went stiff again, fighting what I was seeing. How could he remind Bren of the way I died? How could he give Bren information that might lead Bren to believe he could come for me?

I squeezed my eyes shut, but I could still see them standing there in my mind's eye. Rol, my loyal Training Master—Bren, almost as tall as Rol, with his own set of muscles. And that hair, now golden brown and longer than I remembered. A day's dark stubble as always, and those warm oak-brown eyes. He looked the champion more than ever. The Shadowalker. The new King of the Witches.

A wave of sadness made me choke. Could I miss him any more?

But Rol had no business putting ideas in Bren's head. What if the fool tried to find me? He'd be killed, or possessed, or worse.

For a moment, the visions eased. Egidus kept quiet. The sight of Bren bruised my thoughts.

"I was Jasmina Corey, Queen of the Witches," I muttered. "I perished because of a Shadow wound I received while helping Bren defeat Nire, the most evil being ever known. Too bad Nire was Bren's mother."

"You kidnapped the boy, the one you call Bren," Egidus intoned. "You forced him to help you in your quest to save the witches. You trapped him on the Path and gave him almost no choice about becoming the Shadowalker."

"Don't remind me." I clenched my fists. My hands and arms seemed to weigh hundreds of pounds.

"But I must," the bird said coldly. "You owe him a debt that cannot be repaid so long as you submit to the dark forces conspiring to eliminate you even here, in Talamadden."

"No one knows how to leave the land of the dead," I countered, growing more animated with fear for Bren. "And if the living enter, they aren't the living for long. Worse yet, because they died by their own folly, they would move on, like my father did. No Talamadden. No second chance."

"Then we're agreed." Rol sounded more confident than he looked. "You won't attempt some foolhardy search for Talamadden?"

The vision's return ambushed me. I dug my fingers into my palms and watched, helpless.

Red crept across Bren's cheeks. "Of course not. I'm King of the Witches now. I have responsibility—and Dad and Todd and everything."

The look Bren got from Rol communicated no belief in the lie Bren had no doubt just spoken.

For his part, Rol seemed to be deciding about something, then turned rocklike and mute.

I had the sense that Bren wanted to turn Rol into a real boulder just for kicks.

"Are you awake?" Egidus asked in a smooth, taunting voice, startling me into looking at his unsettling eyes.

I glared, but I nodded.

"Pay attention," he instructed.

I blinked, but saw no more darkness. Again, the wavy, fuzzy visions of the living world filled my senses.

Sunset.

Bren looked close to frenzied. He kept rubbing the jagged scar on his right cheek as he checked on Rol, and on my mother, then slipped off to the glen behind the general store in Live Oak Springs Township. L.O.S.T., my favorite spot in the town I made. The town I never got to enjoy.

"I can talk to her." Bren's harsh, sad voice grabbed my attention. "I have to believe we meant that much to each other."

At this, I started to cry. The tears felt cold and useless on my cheeks. Something in Bren's determination unsettled me, but I kept staring, unable to turn away. Even in autumn, the glen looked beautiful, as it always did. Trees, the small pond—ah, the wind, forcing ripples across the blue surface and leaves falling in lazy spirals to land in the dry grass around Bren. We had no wind in Talamadden. It was lovely to watch and imagine.

Bren sat in the grass beside the pond. He looked deep in thought, alternately angry and helpless, then bright and full of energy. He frowned and gazed into the water, seeming to study his own reflection. His fingers absently traced the lines of his scar.

I jolted back to my own reality, heart pounding. The ends of my fingers tingled. I had touched that scar long ago. I remembered the warm, wounded feel of it, right before I told Bren I loved him. Right before I died. For one long, eerie moment, I felt like I was back in the world of the living.

I could imagine settling into the grass beside the pool and touching Bren's soft brown hair. I could almost hear him dressing me down for changing him into a donkey when I got angry.

Just then, in the vision, he turned his attention to the pond and acted like I was sitting beside him. I *felt* like I was sitting beside him, barrier or no. This no longer felt like an image, but a real, live happening. I stood shaking, leaning hard against the barrier between us.

"Mom—I mean Nire—I still can't get past that."

Bren sounded so clear and real.

"I've written down everything I know about her and given copies to the oldeFolke, so if she ever shows back up again, maybe they can keep her contained." He sighed. "Dad divorced her not long after I . . . um . . . cut her loose. What else could he do?"

My heart felt like two fists were squeezing it. How I wanted to reach through time and space and death and life to hold him. He was so lonely!

"I—I miss her, though." He picked up a flat rock and skipped it across the pond. "Not Nire. I miss the mom I loved when I was growing up, like Todd does. It's like she died, too, you know?"

My poor Bren. What did I do to you? I let out a deep sigh, and the wind in my vision blew, and the waves on the pond picked up. A few of them splashed against the grassy shore.

Bren found another stone and flung it toward the pond. "Todd and I still haven't found Alderon. It's too bad he got away before we had a chance to capture him. But we will." He scooped up yet another rock, this time flinging it to the other side of the pond and into the grove of live oaks. "Finding all of our half brothers will be a hell of a job. It's been a challenge figuring out if those we come across are loyal to Nire or actually good people, but it has to be done."

I left you with such a mess. Another sigh escaped me, and more wind blew across the pond in my vision. More waves splashed against the ground.

"Your mom's a real pain in the ass." Bren started to pull at the drawstring on his shirt, and then dropped his hand. "She's helping me a lot with this King of the Witches business, though. She and Dad argue all the time, but I'm afraid that deep down, he really likes her. Kind of like us. Opposites attracting, and all that garbage."

Without thinking, I laughed. That was beyond imagining. Bren's normal-as-normal father, and my perfectionistic, unforgiving witch of a mother, getting along.

Bren shook his head. "My dad—I never would have believed he'd take all this in stride. But he said if Todd and I belonged here, he belonged with us. And then he made that computer program to help us keep track of witches we rescue, and where we take them.

"The new Path's doing well. I've been able to attach two Sanctuaries." He smiled. "Dad's computer program helps with that, too, since he's loaded in so much history information and gives me a hand picking the best places."

He rubbed his palm over his face. "Oh, hell, Jazz. I can't do this. Rol told me about Summerland. About Talamadden—death's haven, and the fact your soul might still be hanging around somewhere."

At these words, I wanted to find a way to kill Rol. I should have beheaded him the minute he told Bren about the probability I was in Talamadden. How could he do this to me? To Bren?

"I can't believe all this time, I could have been looking for you," Bren continued. "That maybe you could have been talking to me, or sending me dreams, or something."

"That is not why you're hearing this," Egidus warned from somewhere, seemingly a million miles away. I had forgotten about him, and wished he had disappeared. "Just listen."

Bren looked beyond hurt. I could tell he was swallowing curse after curse, and I wanted to throw my arms around him. He would have felt nothing, even if I could have managed such a feat.

"Are you out there?" he yelled. "Don't leave me hanging like this, you arrogant witch from hell! I—"

His words got all choked up, but he coughed just like my mother always did and made himself finish. "I love you! I won't ever love anyone else, and I'm coming to find you no matter what, so . . . so, you might as well just talk, if you can."

Caution left me in a rush. I pounded against the barrier between us. It shimmered, like the surface of the pond, but didn't give.

"Bren!" I screamed. "I would if I could!"

On the other side of the barrier, the clearing remained as quiet as a tomb . . . then, a puff of breeze grew stronger and lifted Bren's hair from his shoulders. He looked around, sniffing.

I staggered back, then forward again, pressing my hands against the barrier.

Did I have some presence he could sense?

"Bren, please. Forgive yourself and let me go," I sobbed. "Forgive!"

Bren seemed to listen for a moment. Then he mumbled. "What Rol said . . . I know I need to get over it. But if I had been stronger! If only I had thrown that damn golem far, far away, you would have lived."

He closed his eyes.

"Forgive," I sobbed again, falling forward, pressing my whole body against the barrier.

Eyes still closed, Bren lifted his head and faced exactly in my direction. "I love you, Jazz," he said, this time gently, with all the feeling I had wanted to hear.

Face pressed against the barrier, arms outstretched, I answered with the force of my own feeling. *I love you, too, Bren.*

My heart pounded as Bren seemed to catch my desperate whisper. He turned his head to and fro, taking in a scent that pleased him.

Cinnamon and peaches. He always said I smelled like cinnamon and peaches.

Bren opened his eyes. He held up his hand, as if willing me to reach out of death and touch his fingers.

"Jazz?" he asked simply, with every emotion in the world in that single word.

"On another Path, another day, we'll be together again, Bren." I hoped—prayed—he could hear me. "Don't come looking for me in Talamadden, please. You'll only get yourself killed."

"I miss you so much." He swallowed and seemed to choke back a rush of emotion. "I want to be with you now."

"Another Path. Another day." I felt weak. My voice was failing. The barrier itself seemed to repel me, force me backward. "Don't do anything stupid. Just know I love you."

"Don't leave me." Bren jumped to his feet, but he knew I was already gone. "Come back!"

But of course, I couldn't. All I could do was sit, then fall back on the cold dark earth and watch. Bren's heart, his incredible spirit and force of will—of course he would come after me. Of course he would try to storm Talamadden, wherever it was, whatever it was—no way would he rest until he found me and brought me home—or died in the process.

"That went poorly," Egidus commented. "I expected you to have more awareness. I thought you would dissuade him from coming because he will be much needed in L.O.S.T. His absence will have . . . consequences." The bird sighed. "Moreover, now he faces even more danger. More than you, perhaps. If that is possible."

I opened my mouth to shout at him to shut up, but tears kept my voice a choked croak. Oddly, the window to the world of the living hadn't closed. And yet, it was different. It was . . . changing.

"Something else happened earlier today," Egidus said evenly. "Before your little tryst at the pond."

The vision-figure emerging was one I recognized only too well. Broad shoulders, stringy blond hair, glowing blue eyes like bruises in his hateful, sneering face—it was Bren's half brother Alderon. Oh, yes. The cur himself. Nire's wicked spawn, my false champion. I had thrown him from the Path the day I met Bren, but the bastard had tried to help his beast of a mother kill us in Old Salem.

Only this Alderon seemed much, much more powerful. He radiated a hateful, dark energy I had long associated only with Nire—but how? Nire had been defeated, hadn't she?

To look at Alderon, it was easy to doubt. The bastard had been polished and cleaned up, as if by one of my tidying spells. He wore his greasy hair in a ponytail, and he was dressed in jeans and a black tunic, like some modern-day guru. To complete the image, he was sitting on the edge of what looked like a teacher's desk, talking to what looked like a devoted pupil.

"Emotion is a luxury, a drug for the weak and simpering." Alderon's oily voice was placating and resolutely false. "Power is the only truth. Courage the only virtue."

He sighed, and his despicable eyes cast a blue glow in the dim classroom, empty but for the two of them, the dark-eyed girl and him. "Aren't you tired of being tortured by your so-called friends, Sherise?"

The dark-eyed Sherise nodded, her gaze darting toward the row of windows on the right. Outside, clearly visible through the dirty rectangular panes, a dozen or more teens milled outside. A waiting pack of jackals, and she was their prey.

"I don't want to go out there, Alderon," Sherise murmured in a soft Georgia drawl.

"This time, things will end differently. You have my word as High Priest of your Coven."

The girl smeared sweating palms across her black jeans and black sweater. Her badly-applied concealment makeup barely contained her burgeoning golden glow. Sherise was obviously just coming into her own, powerful and full of potential.

And yet, she had a shyness, a thickness of thought.

I could almost read Alderon's mind, how he believed she was the perfect choice to fool his half siblings, the lauded royal witch brothers, Bren and Todd. Alderon must have worked for months, drawing Sherise under his charms and spells. He was her undisputed leader. Her protector. He was all things to her, and she would do as he bade her to do.

"Are you sure about this Path, Alderon? About a haven for real witches and the boys who plan to destroy it?"

"Absolutely." And then a little truth from the master of lies. "I've been there before. I grew up on the Path. Like we've discussed, I'm not from your time. You believe me, don't you?"

Sherise gave the mob outside the classroom one last nervous glance, then nodded.

"Take my talisman." He handed her the small carving, careful to keep its leering face turned away. All she could see was the smiling, peaceful side. "Put it in your pocket and never, ever show it to anyone. It will keep you safe. Oh, you might suffer a few bumps and bruises—but nothing permanent. My talisman will help me find you any time, any place."

Sherise shoved the carving into her pocket without studying it. She took a slow breath, then looked her leader straight in the face. "Will I ever see you again?"

He gave his best grin and shrugged. "Of course. I'd never let my strongest witch go for long."

Sherise brightened. She straightened herself, set a stoic expression on her face, and walked out of the classroom without looking back.

In minutes, the beating began. I heard Sherise screaming, and watched as Alderon frowned from the window. Of course, the bastard made no effort to intervene. He was watching the sky. My nails dug harder into my palms, and my eyes burned.

It was a long wait, but not too long. Sherise probably thought differently, lying on the ground whimpering as she was, even though her attackers had moved on. She was still in a ball, cringing, when Bren and Todd landed two large slithers soundlessly nearby.

"Big specimens," I muttered, surprised by the wingspans, the size of the teeth, and the length of the fire plumes. "And out in daylight, no less. Someone's been running a successful breeding program."

Bren kept a spelled cloak around the healthy-looking beasts as his younger brother swaggered up to Sherise.

My keen hearing caught the entire exchange.

"Hi," Todd said, sinking down on his haunches beside her.

Sherise looked up, and I heard her gasp as she recognized the silvery witch-light shining from Todd.

He grinned. "So, what do you say, beautiful? Want to get L.O.S.T.?"

At that, Bren groaned. I did the same.

Sherise played her role to perfection, taking Todd's hand and allowing him to lead her to one of the giant two-hearted slithers.

She managed a yelp of surprise, but Todd patted her on the shoulder. "Don't sweat it. It's just our ride. Brooms aren't my style."

And just like that, the vision ended. But not before I grasped the truth. Even as I had been trying to reach Bren in the clearing, the spy was getting a tour of her new home. Alderon had an informant on the Path now, the Path Bren had so carefully rebuilt. Alderon had placed a golem in the protected Sanctuaries of the witches. Now, he could begin forging alliances with disgruntled oldeFolke, those half-human, incredibly powerful witches of ancient days. He could even determine where his mother Nire, the most powerful being ever known, was trapped.

He could free her, and then kill Bren and Todd and everyone I knew.

The loss of the people I loved—that would destroy my hope and forever seal me in death's sanctuary. No one could stand against Nire then.

This time, she would triumph.

"And now," said Egidus in his disaffected tone, "I trust you see the problem."

I staggered forward, almost stepping on the peacock, almost plunging into the repellent darkness.

"Who are you?" I demanded. "*What* are you?"

The bird ruffled his indigo feathers, fluffed in indignation, then let his plumage settle into its normal, placid state.

"I can be friend or foe." He made no attempt to temper his cryptic comment with a friendly expression. "That depends on your perspective. Now, follow me into this stream, or die forever."

chapter two

BREN

Life isn't supposed to be like this.

A big wad of anger throbbed where my heart was supposed to be, and my guts had been permanently tied into a giant knot. Half the time, food tasted like paper. Even sunlight bugged me. The Path, my life, the whole world had been wrong since Jazz died, and now that I was sure there was a way to get her back, to bring her back to the land of the living—well. Forget it. Nothing else mattered.

Life wasn't supposed to be like this, and damn it, I was getting ready to change it.

My muscles ached from sitting, and my eyes burned and watered from all the reading I had been doing. Muttering to myself, I slammed down yet another decrepit volume of death lore and necromancy, sending a cloud of dust through the repository. Dim candles flickered in sconces, casting eerie shadows over the ancient book and wooden table. If I'd had my way, I would have used magical light, but the scrollkeeper would have had a cow. More like laid an egg. There was something way too bird-like about the oldeFolke version of a librarian.

Even though I was King of the Witches, that pointy-looking bitch watched everything I touched, every second. If I touched it too much or too long, she actually clucked. I bet if I lifted her cloak, I would have found chicken wings. Even now, she was hovering a few tables away, buggy-bird eyes fixed on my hands. On the book, I guess. All she cared about was the book.

And all I cared about was finding a way to get to Jazz.

"*Find a true guide unwilling.* Like that makes any sense." I wanted to snap my quill and use the pieces to scratch rude comments on the scarred table, but I stuffed that little mental revenge dream. Instead, I made a note on the parchment I was using as a crib sheet. Most of the books I had been trying to read were written in languages I couldn't understand, even though I'd learned a couple in the five months since Jazz had died. I had translators for others—but oldeFolke. I swear. They never told me all of anything. Just my luck that everything about Talamadden was scrawled in the most ancient of runes and riddles. Past that, the parchment pages looked like somebody spit on them and erased half the lines for good measure.

Whatever. At least I had yet another piece of the friggin' puzzle.

Find a true guide unwilling.

It felt like I'd been at this hunting, reading, and note-taking forever in the week since I had heard Jazz by the pond, and books were definitely not my thing. I rubbed the tingling scar on my cheek, imagining I could smell her cinnamon and peaches scent, could still picture her black hair and golden eyes. A sense of urgency made me feel like I was going to crawl out of my skin with the need to find her. I didn't want to wait, I wanted to leave *now*. But how could I make sense out of all this crap?

Me studying like a college scholar—now, that should have been enough to upset the natural balance of the universe, but so far, things still seemed pretty normal. Well, normal for a Sanctuary full of witches, oldeFolke, mythical creatures, and my dad making mooney-eyes at an uptight witch who just happened to be my dead girlfriend's mother. Oh, and let's not forget my nutcase baby brother spending his time developing breeding and improvement programs for whatever monster made him yell, "Cool!"

Rol said I needed to spend more time with the little twit, that losing Mom—I mean Nire—had been hard on him. Rol also said I had no business in the repository hunting down information about how to find Jazz.

You have responsibilities. Your subjects need you.

It's like my dad went hippie and his old do-what-I-say dad-spirit migrated into Rol. And believe me, a giant disapproving pseudo-dad with a broadsword was something I could do without most days. The jerk followed me around like he was my conscience. Except in the repository. When I headed for the forbidden stacks of books and scrolls, the big guy made himself scarce.

At least I'd had a little peace while I went following breadcrumbs down a trail of runes and smeared ink scrawls. A sentence here. A paragraph there. Bits and pieces—like Jazz would have to command strong enough magic and have a strong enough will to draw the physical form of her body back to her. Otherwise she'd be in spirit form.

No, my girl would never put up with just being a floaty ghost. Too messy and all.

I almost smiled at the thought, then frowned again as I stared at the clues on the parchment.

The door lies in lands forgotten.

The living shall not cross.

Those who search forever wander.

Beware the Guardian.

Only the old blood may pass.

Find a true guide unwilling.

"Wonderful." I crumpled the edge of the thin brown paper. "I'll look for, what? A million years? Then I've got to be dead to enter. Seems like that defeats the purpose."

The librarian-bird-thing clucked. She was probably worried I'd fidget with the book and crumple its pages if she left it in front of me long enough.

"Yeah, yeah. I'm going." I snatched up my parchment notes and crammed them into my breeches pocket. Before the biddy could peck me or make me help her dust, I stormed out, sword smacking my leg with every step.

The weight of the blade gave me some comfort, but then I got mad about that, too. Why couldn't I just prove myself in some battle? I was good at battles. If I just had to slay a giant five-headed slither to get into Talamadden, that would be no sweat. But all this riddle-and-dire-warning crap—it was really getting on my nerves.

Light half-blinded me as I stalked outside, into the olde-Towne section of L.O.S.T., built by the oldeFolke on the outskirts of the Sanctuary after Jazz and I brought down Nire. I mean, my mother. I mean—damn. I so didn't want to go *there* on top of everything else.

As I passed a pack of hags clustered around a big outdoor cauldron (no, I did not want to see what they were boiling), some of them started chanting death threats. To me, of course, for reading the old forbidden scrolls. I was ready to kill them, hissing snaky hag-spirits and all.

If only I'd had my baseball bat, that would have done the trick. Swords were too messy with hags. All that stinky black blood.

As fast as I could, I left the dark-hooded, chanting witches behind me, and climbed the rise that separated oldeTowne from the main village. Wintry winds chilled my face. Over the western horizon, dark storm clouds brewed like the hags' cauldron, the air smelled of sulfur and oncoming rain, and leafless trees swayed in a strong gust of air. I could almost swear I heard a klatchKeeper's song on the wind.

But that was impossible. Keepers didn't sing in L.O.S.T.—Live Oak Springs Township. The treaty between all witches had kept the peace for the past six months—ever since Nire had been trapped and her Sanctuary separated from the Path.

Just as I crested the hill, I saw a massive crowd. It looked like everyone in the Sanctuary had come running to the town square. Fists were shaking, spell-sparks crackled, and angry shouts broiled up the rise.

So much for peace. I didn't *even* need to look to see who was responsible for this mess. With a groan of frustration, I marched down the hill to where my fourteen-year-old brother was trying to calm one of his biggest slithers. The giant winged reptile had rumbled out of its day-lair much earlier than it should have—probably thanks to Todd's day-vision breeding adjustments. The iridescent red monstrosity had just stomped on a pumpkin cart and knocked over at least a dozen witches and oldeFolke with its massive wings. My dad was running in circles, dodging spells and trying to pick up the fallen witches and oldeFolke. Dame Edwina Corey, Jazz's mother, was doing her best to placate a surly group of elflings who had drawn their daggers.

I was just about to send the slither back where it belonged when I saw the rest of the problem. Unicorns were eating carrots off displays. Giant toads flopped across wagon tracks. A singing ferret crooned loudly on top of a furious hag's head, a pack of poms—slothlike creatures the size of hogs—rooted for apple peels on every corner, while shims—a covey of man-eating quail—eyed the nearest group of screaming children. Shouts rang between houses as people ran away from hairy bugbears that snarled a lot, but really just seemed to want the pumpkin pieces.

Well, crap. Had Todd turned his entire menagerie loose?

I cursed and fired containments at whatever wriggled, hopped, snorted, stomped, or looked remotely not-human.

Meanwhile, the oldeFolke took it to my little brother.

"You want a piece of me?" Todd yelled to the hag closest to him as he backed away from the slither and the exploded pumpkin cart. "Bite me, you old bitch!"

The hag came at him, jaws open wide, spittle flying from her mouth, only too pleased to follow *that* order. Her hag-spirit reared high above her head, dark crown swaying, fangs bared.

Todd whipped out his sword and grasped the hilt with both hands as he waited for her attack.

At the exact same moment, a singing klatchKeeper and her entire klatchKoven flowed over the rise. Within moments the swaying, dancing women surrounded my dad, their ethereal beauty and song instantly mesmerizing him. No mere mortal could withstand the klatchKeeper's song; only the most powerful of witches could. From the corner of my eye I caught the baker stuffing cotton into his ears and several male witches clapping their hands over theirs. Thanks to Jazz, I had learned to defend myself against that tempting sound, but most guys weren't so lucky.

Todd didn't even seem to notice the singing. He took a swipe at the hag, who darted back too quickly for his sword to do any damage.

Jaws slack and eyes glazed, Dad dropped to his knees before the klatchKeeper, who appeared to most men as the most gorgeous woman ever. As King of the Witches, I saw her for exactly what she was—a hideous beast with a head that looked like a gigantic eggplant, and a mouth filled with jagged teeth.

The hag screeched and went for Todd's throat. The klatch-Keeper swooped down on my dad, razor-toothed mouth stretched wide.

I unsheathed my sword, bringing it up in a lightning-fast movement. With all the power I had, magnified through my sword, my voice bellowed throughout the village, "Stop!"

Everything ceased to move. Even wind stopped blowing and clouds paused in the sky. The blade of my sword glittered in the half-sunlight as I slowly lowered it.

Every witch, hag, elfling, child, and creature remained motionless, like wax statues in that Madame something-or-other's famous house of wax. The slither's head was thrown back, puffs of smoke frozen in the late afternoon sky.

That is, everyone was motionless except for my brother and the silver glow that surrounded him. Even as I stared in amazement, Todd's sword came within an inch of hacking off the hag's head before he pulled himself back.

Shock blasted through me that my magic hadn't fazed him this time, but more than that, what I felt was *pissed*.

"What the hell do you think you're doing?" I strode toward Todd, my voice carrying throughout the silent village. "And what are all these—these—*things* doing tearing the village apart? That hag could have killed you!"

Todd's own expression of surprise was quickly replaced by a scowl. "I don't need your help. I could have taken her by myself."

"Are you some kind of moron?" I reached him and it was all I could do not to slug the twit. "You would have violated the treaty between witches and oldeFolke, and then we'd have a freaking war on our hands."

"Screw you." Todd shoved his sword into its sheath, the sound of leather against steel loud in the quiet village. He narrowed his eyes that were eerily blue like our mother's—I mean Nire's—eyes. "I just needed to take the bugbears for a run, and the toads and horned horses came with. I didn't know they broke the latches. And I didn't mean to wake up Harold, but he likes unicorns, and—"

"Not again. Not without my permission, understand? We need to plan—"

"Man, shut up! You aren't my dad." Todd's snarl echoed off the village walls. "You think you're so hot just because you're King of the Witches."

Todd and I had been in fights lots of times, but I'd never heard him sound like that—as if he was filled with as much venom as the water serpent I had battled last summer.

One by one, I spelled his menagerie back to the keeping grounds outside of oldeTowne. With each spellblast, I forced myself to calm down even though I wanted to knock my brother upside the head. The little snot didn't even try to help, not even when I had to move Harold back to his day-lair.

At last, when the final super-toad took a ride back to where it belonged, I turned on him. Todd was standing, arms folded, still glowing a soft silvery blue.

"I *am* King of the Witches," I reminded him in the quietest voice I could manage. God, I sounded like Dad. "This place and everyone in it are my responsibility."

Todd smirked and glanced at the frozen chaos that surrounded us. "Some job you're doing."

With that, he flipped me off and stalked away.

For a moment I just stared at him, wanting to kick his ass, but at the same time I wanted to figure out how to get through to him. He was becoming a powerful witch in his own right, and if he didn't learn to control that power or his anger—not to mention all the creatures he was trying to strengthen and repopulate—he could get us all into some serious trouble.

Todd vanished behind a grove of trees, in the direction of the keeping grounds and slither training compound, and I set about cleaning up the mess in the village. With a flick of my sword, I sent the klatchKeeper and her klatchKoven back to their lair. I even cleaned up all the damage the slither had caused and repaired the pumpkin cart.

My heart paused as I remembered that time in Shallym when Jazz had saved me from the witches and oldeFolke, and then she had repaired that applecart. At the time I'd been majorly pissed at her, but right now I'd give anything to have her back and griping at me for being so messy.

The door lies in lands forgotten. The living shall not cross. Those who search forever wander. I sighed. "Beware the Guardian. Only the old blood may pass, and I need to find some kind of true but unwilling guide."

I wanted to start right that second, but I couldn't. I was so exhausted I could barely think. Using so much magic wore me out and I had to rest before I allowed everything to resume. Even if it pissed off the hags. OldeFolke really, really hated being spelled, especially by a modern witch. They acknowledged me as king, but only because my magic was stronger than theirs. A halfblood ruler of modern stock was definitely not what they wanted—and I was Nire's son, on top of everything else.

I stared around me at the frozen hags, elflings, and witches, and shook my head. What was going on in L.O.S.T.?

Since that day beside the pond, the day I sensed Jazz so clearly, everything had gone berserk—more than usual. Todd had always caused trouble, but this—this was over the edge, even for him. It was as if the whole place knew I needed to leave L.O.S.T. to find Jazz, and everyone was doing their best to keep me here.

The thought made me scowl. I'd get everything back to normal and then I'd leave, just like I'd planned to. Jazz needed me, and I was going to figure out my clues and bring her back.

I held up my sword and shouted, "Resume."

Once again wind blew and people moved. Some landed on their asses from being struck by the slither's wings right before I caused everything to freeze and sent the slither back to where it came from. Voices filled the village from those who had been in mid-conversation, and dogs barked and cats yowled. My dad stood up, blushing, brushing dirt off his jeans as Dame Corey glared at him. Everyone stopped and their gazes riveted on me and my sword. I could almost hear the witches gulp and the oldeFolke grumble beneath their collective breaths.

"Settle down or you'll have me to deal with." I made my glare as menacing as possible.

The oldeFolke glared right back before returning to their business, and the witches scurried out of my path. Even the hag Todd had almost beheaded departed without incident.

It was good to be king.

The corner of my mouth curved and I almost laughed. Some king I was.

The breeze grew colder and smelled of the oncoming storm. Soon the winter solstice would be here, and everything would be so cold. But by solstice, I intended to have Jazz here, with us, and just that thought warmed something deep inside me.

I frowned at the sky before heading to the kitchen where I was sure I'd find Acaw. Maybe he would know something about the hints I'd been able to find. Rol certainly wouldn't be any help.

The elfling was stirring a pot of something that smelled really good—like chicken dumplings—and my stomach growled. Smells of fresh baked bread and honey cakes only made me hungrier, but I figured if I took a bite, they'd taste all flat and boring like most everything had since Jazz died.

What I would give for a couple of double cheeseburgers and fries right now. I'd tried teaching Acaw and the other elfling cooks how to make 'em, but they couldn't begin to get close to Mickey D's.

Acaw's crow-brother gave a loud caw from the nearest windowsill, and its glare was nearly as bad as Acaw's.

"Too much flour," the elfling growled, and I knew he was blaming me for freezing everyone. By the limp burlap bag in his hand, and the white stuff dusting the floor and Acaw's apron, he'd apparently been pouring flour into the dumplings to thicken them. But when I'd allowed the village to resume, a good portion of the bag had dumped into the pot before he could stop it.

"Uh, sorry." I rocked onto the balls of my feet. "Listen, I need to know more about this Talamadden place. The old scrolls and the Wytches Book of Tyme are about to drive me nuts with their riddles and the weird language. But the last scroll I read—it told me how elflings are wise about death's haven. So, I've got this much." I took a deep breath, dug the parchment out of my pocket, and handed it to him. "Does any of this make sense to you?"

Acaw's shaggy eyebrows drew close as he studied the sentences I had scrawled. As he read, he absently called forth a bucket of water from beneath the pump in the corner, then poured the water into the cauldron.

"Only peril lies in the place where one is neither alive nor dead," he finally said.

I drew closer to him, and Acaw's crow-brother squawked again and ruffled his black feathers.

"Don't give me the crap about it being too dangerous." I rested my hand on my sword hilt. "I'm going after Jazz and nothing is going to stop me."

Acaw sent the now empty bucket back to the water pump and began stirring the dumplings. "Not even your responsibilities as King of the Witches?"

"Don't start with the guilt trip." The tingling started in my cheek again. I'd been feeling it more and more since that day by the pond, and I resisted the urge to rub the scar Nire had left me. "I'll make sure everything's back in order, and that everyone is safe before I leave, so I'm not neglecting my duties. Besides, I won't be gone long. Rol, Dad, Dame Corey, and Todd can keep an eye on things."

Acaw stopped stirring the dumplings and a small tin of herbs appeared in his hand. He took a pinch of the dried green leaves and seeds and tossed it into the brew before answering me. It smelled of parsley and basil. "Your timing is ill-fated," he said.

I gritted my teeth. "I'm going to find Jazz, and I want you to help me understand how to do it. What does all that stuff mean—the door in lands forgotten, and the living shall not cross. Wandering forever, the Guardian, the old blood, the guide—I don't know what any of it means!"

"Are you commanding me to assist you?" the elfling asked even more quietly than usual.

"Well—I—no." I rubbed my palm against the hilt of my sword. Anyone but Acaw—Rol even. I could have commanded Rol.

The elfling sniffed. "If I am not under bond of command, then I do not choose to aid you in this folly. One who enters Talamadden risks possession by confused and angry spirits. Beyond that, I have negative feelings about our future on this side of the barrier between life and death."

I didn't think I had ever heard him say so many words at once, and he wasn't even finished.

"You have no way of knowing if Her Majesty Jasmina has been able to summon her former physical body. It is possible you would seek her only to find a sparrow or a vulture." His eyes flicked meaningfully to his crow-brother. "Fate can be cruel."

I frowned. I couldn't and wouldn't believe Jazz would just be a ghost. "Crossing that barrier into Talamadden—it's possible, right?" I rubbed at the scar on my cheek and tried to imagine the place where Jazz was trapped.

Acaw made the tin of herbs disappear and resumed stirring the pot. "Only the strongest souls retain awareness of their individual *ba*—their spiritual energy. They leave their *ka*, the body, never to return. Not even oldeFolke, who have the ability to resist possession, would dare to enter Talamadden. Most could not find it, even under duress."

"Whatever." I eyed him square on. "Elflings have risked it, haven't they? That's what the scrolls meant about you being wise about death's haven."

To this, Acaw said nothing. His eyes sparked, and he turned his attention back to his smoking pots. Something . . . something wasn't quite right. I never could read him. He was like a closed book. No, wait. A closed book wrapped by a chain, padlocked, and tossed into a river. The things he said meant nothing—and everything.

Still, I didn't want to command him. It seemed wrong. At the same time, it seemed like the only way.

"I want you to show me the way to Talamadden's entrance," I said, doing my best to sound calm, like Acaw always did. "When we get there you can go in with me or stay, I don't care. But I'm going in."

Acaw's crow-brother squawked, an angry, haunting sound, but the elfling still said nothing at all.

Over the next several days, I worked on weaving spells to protect the Path. I needed to ensure it would be safe from any kind of invasion from an evil being like Nire—if there was such a thing now that she was out of commission. A guy couldn't be too cautious in this strange world of witches and oldeFolke.

I also worked on re-establishing peace in the Sanctuary, but it wasn't easy. It seemed like everyone and everything was out to keep me from leaving to find Jazz. Eventually we came to agreeable terms. Jazz's mom, Dame Corey, served as intermediary. She was great at the politics, but I was angry with her for telling me over and over that I shouldn't go to Talamadden, just like everyone else. I was going after *her* daughter, and if she cared anything about Jazz, she should have been encouraging me and telling me what I needed to do to rescue her from a death that didn't have to be permanent.

In the meantime I did everything I could to learn about my clues. I even bugged Rol until he threatened to turn me into a donkey like Jazz had done when I was first learning the craft, and I promised to turn him into a baseball bat and swing him at every pumpkin I could find. Maybe a rock or two. Finally he gave in when I wouldn't give up, but what he told me was basically the same as Acaw—that I was nuts, doomed to failure, and I was neglecting my responsibilities as King of the Witches.

"The doorway is hidden to all but a few," he finally allowed. "In one of the forgotten places. Even if you found it, you could not pass through to reach Jasmina—in whatever form she might present—unless you died yourself. Besides, the Guardian would kill you along the way."

"I can take the Guardian, trust me." I tapped the hilt of my sword. "You trained me well."

For a few seconds, Rol actually looked afraid. Now, that was something I had *never* seen before. "The Guardian is evil," he said through clenched teeth. "It fights you where you do not expect, when you do not expect—and once engaged, the battle is never finished."

"Until?" I shifted, thinking about drawing my sword for a little practice. "Until I rescue her, right? Or kill the Guardian."

"No." Rol actually shivered as he turned his back on me. "Until you are dead—or wish you were."

That was it. He would say no more, no matter how hard I pressed. He even drew on me and I had to fight my way out of the practice arena.

When I got back home, Dad came next, pleading with me when logic failed. "Todd doesn't need to lose you, too. Neither do I."

"I know what I'm doing, Dad. I can save her." I fisted my hands in frustration. "I've studied the scrolls, and I can use my magic to break through the barrier between the living and the dead. I'm the most powerful witch on the Path."

"Well, you're sure the cockiest."

I glared at him. "I defeated Nire, didn't I?"

He glared at me in return, and the rest went unsaid. Yes, I had defeated Nire, with Jazz's help. With the transfer of her magical power to me. And everyone had almost died.

"She's gone, Dad." I reached for his arm, and he didn't pull away. "The worst is over now. Nothing will happen if I'm gone a little while, and I'll be fine."

That earned me a brief hug, and Dad's silent exit from my house. He didn't come back that night, and neither did Todd.

Every day that passed, I grew more anxious and more obsessed with leaving and rescuing Jazz. It took the whole second week after I had sensed her to finish securing everything in L.O.S.T. so I could leave. By then, I was so desperate to get going that I could hardly stand still.

The hardest part, I figured, would be the first couple of steps. Doing two things I really, really didn't want to do. I grabbed my backpack that had been filled with food for the journey and made sure my sword was secure in its sheath. I trudged through mud and water to the slither training grounds beyond the grove of trees behind the store.

It had been raining almost continuously for two weeks straight and the sky was overcast and threatening to rain again. The air smelled fresh and clean, but I could have done without the chill that made my nose run. Acaw, who barely spoke to me unless I made him, said it was so stormy because the Sylphs, air elementals, were displeased with me for planning to leave, but I figured it was another one of his tactics to keep me from going to Talamadden.

To no surprise, I found Todd talking with Sherise at the slither training grounds. Both were perched on wooden railings encircling the field that reminded me of rodeo grounds. Any minute now I expected a slither to charge across the grounds, its dragon-like wings flapping, the earth shaking like a 3.0 on the Richter scale, and the beast racing around striped rodeo barrels.

Todd and Sherise constantly hung around each other, and had been ever since the day we rescued her. The two had their heads close and were laughing, but when I approached, Todd's smile switched to a frown.

I hitched my pack up on my shoulder. "I'm heading out now."

Todd's expression didn't change, but he climbed down from the railing. "I can see that."

The girl smiled, and I could see why Todd liked her so much. "Like I said before, you're doing the right thing, Bren." Her white teeth flashed in the morning light.

Sherise had been the only one in L.O.S.T. who hadn't told me I was a fruitcake for going to Talamadden, and I liked her even more for that. Yet whenever I was around her, I always had a peculiar feeling that I just couldn't shake. Like now.

"Yeah," I finally said as I rubbed my tingling scar. "I couldn't live with myself if I didn't try to get Jazz back."

Todd's blond hair ruffled in the breeze. "We'll take care of things around here."

Out of a habit I'd had since I was a kid, I found myself pulling at the bindings on my leather shirt. I forced myself to stop. "Take care of Dad. He needs you."

This made Todd grunt.

Sherise slipped off the railing and into the mud. She came up to me, an even brighter smile lighting her face. She held out her hand and I took the stone she offered. It hung from a thick silver chain. "Moonstone. A Goddess stone for moon magic, safe travel, and intuition. I'm offering it on loan, so be sure to keep yourself safe and return it—and you—in one piece." She smiled. "I'll light a candle for you, too. And for Jazz to be in her body instead of her spirit form."

My fingers tingled as I slipped the chain and stone over my head. "Uh, thanks."

While smoothing her black hair behind her ear, she added, "Bring Jasmina back safely."

"I will." I gave a nod to her and Todd, then turned my back and walked through the grove of trees toward the clearing where I knew Acaw had gone to pick some herbs.

Now that the goodbye scene with my brother was over, I had to face this next part. Man. I so didn't want to, but I didn't see any other way.

I found Acaw stooping over a patch of mint, arranging an unusual amount of spices, herbs, and salves in his bag. He held a long walking stick with symbols of all four elements engraved upon it—earth, air, water, and fire. Strung through a hole in the staff were a hawk feather on a yellow string, a hematite with a hole through it on a green string, a dragon's scale on a red string, and a seashell on a blue string. Charms for power, to heal, for courage, and for second sight. Including his pointed hat, he was clad in leathers of brown and green that blended with trees and ground, and his crow-brother perched on his shoulder.

All in all, he looked ready to travel.

I was stunned. "You—you knew, didn't you? That I would command you after all."

Acaw's crow-brother gave a squawk and ruffled his blue-black feathers as he glared at me. The bird's expression was only slightly kinder than Acaw's. I sighed. Maybe I should be taking Sherise instead of Acaw since she was the only one who had expressed any kind of faith in me. But Sherise had no more idea than me where to find the hidden entrance to the land of the dead. It had to be Acaw.

I faced the elfling as Rol came through the trees and strode over to us. He stopped beside Acaw and folded his powerful arms across his massive chest. As always, his ebony skin was well oiled, like a professional bodybuilder's, and he looked like he could pound telephone poles into the ground with his fist. No doubt he could.

At the moment, Rol looked like he wanted to hex me into a statue to keep me from leaving. "You are making a foolish mistake," he said in a growl, and then, "Your Highness."

I was so tired of constantly being told I was an idiot. I was ready to take Rol on barehanded, even though he was built like a brick house.

My dad came next, walking hands in pockets, wearing a serious expression on his bearded face. "I want you to reconsider, Bren."

"I've made my decision." I gritted my teeth before I spoke again. "You already know that I've reinforced the Path, and I've ensured the treaty with the oldeFolke will keep them from stirring up trouble. Dame Corey can handle them." I was really getting sick of repeating myself.

"It's clear you intend to go on this mission." Rol flexed his huge biceps. "But it is likely you will not return to us."

I clenched my fists. "Thanks for your faith in me, big guy."

My dad reached me, his brown eyes filled with a concern I'd never seen in them before. "Take care of yourself, Bren." He turned to Acaw. "Make sure he stays out of trouble."

Acaw's crow-brother squawked and if the elfling ever showed emotion, I could picture him rolling his tiny eyes.

Instead Acaw gazed up at me, obviously waiting.

"Fine." I blew out a breath, exasperated. "Acaw, I command you to lead me to the entrance to Talamadden."

Rol lowered his head.

Acaw's expression did not change. He bowed, then headed out of the clearing, his staff grinding the dirt with every step he took.

I looked from my father to Rol, then turned and followed Acaw.

chapter three

JAZZ

Pursuing a peacock against the flow of an unnatural stream was no easy task. The bird walked gracefully, tail lifted, keeping his feathers free of the freezing water. The coldness stunned me, along with the sense of motion. I made it a few steps—not even to the blinding darkness—then fell. Icy water flowed over my lower legs. My knees throbbed from what felt like bruises and cuts.

Why had I never noticed that the stream had stones, just below the surface?

"Do your legs hurt from the rocks?" Egidus asked, stopping but not turning around.

I ground my teeth. "Yes."

"Good. The pain will help you think. Perhaps you will remember more, and faster." The bird started walking again, strutting relentlessly into the darkness. His head disappeared, then his shoulders, and half of his bluer-than-blue body.

At that moment, the tree I had been sheltering beneath seemed to reach out and yank me backward. Not literally, with branch-claws or gaping knothole mouth. Instead, I felt a dark energy, subtle at first, building to a powerful rage. It gripped my shoulders and jerked at my soul. My heart—if I still had a heart—fluttered, then pounded.

Shadows! They'll kill me!

"Bird!" My shout tore at the furious, oppressive silence. "Egidus. Wait!"

I can only lead you, the peacock answered in my mind. *This passage is yours to make.*

"Great. Thanks for nothing!" Seeing my entire past instantly, powerfully reminded of my worst moments with Bren, I reached for my old magic and shouted, "Cease!"

Of course, nothing happened. I already knew Talamadden had no traditional magic, and besides, I had transferred my Earthly power to Bren before my death. The vicious pull on my insides continued. I fell on my backside and gasped at the sudden cold from the water.

"Let me go," I demanded, struggling back to my feet. My teeth started to chatter. Tremulous shaking competed with a new, hot flash in my chest. Rage of my own. A fury so complete I thought my head would catch fire.

I turned back toward the dark patch of ground, the hut, and the leafless tree. All trembling came to an abrupt halt. Squinting, I thought I could make out a huge, shadowy presence hovering just above the entire area.

A Shadow. It has to be.

My hands grew weak, and I wanted to kneel and scream. Of all the things I might have to battle, why the one thing I knew could—and would—defeat me?

"Leave me alone." My voice came out in a low, menacing growl, sounding much more courageous than I felt. "I may not have my magic, but I have my will. I know the essence of life and spellcraft. I would dare to battle you. Beyond that, I would want no credit past my own satisfaction at your destruction!"

The black entity flexed, showing its massive muscle. I thought I could make out its true shape in that instant—falcon-like, with huge retractable talons behind human-like hands, topped by a human-like face. Not a Shadow. It looked more like . . . a harpy?

Relief struck me like a bolt of fresh energy. After Nire and the horrors of the Shadowmaster's nearly successful quest, I was not impressed by a simple monster, no matter how ancient or mythic. I had never seen one before, but I knew of the beasts from my long studies with Father. He told me many strange old creatures still existed, but preferred never to be seen, even by most oldeFolke. Harpies were among those secretive clans, best left alone to their own pursuits.

With deliberate force and slow consideration, I took a long, even breath. My right hand, I fisted and curled over my heart. My left hand, I extended and pointed at the hovering creature. I might not have magic left, but any witch or human can invoke if they believe, if they know the words and ask with a true heart. I didn't know if I could tap the essence of Talamadden as I had the Earth, but I certainly had to try.

Giving up was no longer in my regimen, my recent death aside.

"Goddess, I beg you, hear my call," I chanted while I pointed toward the creature. "Bind this evil, bind it all. Keep me safe, pray heed my plea. Bless my journey. So mote it be."

The harpy-thing flexed again, turning a darker black. I whispered another invocation, asking help from the stones, the unnatural stream, even the grassless ground and the leafless tree.

A roar cleaved the suddenly roiling air, and the empty nothingness began to rumble and quake. The hut cracked at the walls and roof, then tumbled in on itself with a bone-rattling crash. I no longer felt the water's cold on my ankles, but I wasn't going numb. Either I was heating the water, or it was heating me.

The being before me took even more form now. I could see it beating its fierce wings against the darkness.

Water splashed against my thighs and knees as the stream widened. I held my stance, kept my eye contact with the creature who had been trapping me—who was determined to keep me under spell.

"Release me in the name of the Goddess," I commanded.

More roars answered me, high-pitched, ear-bursting, along with a doubling of the pull on my soul. I felt like I might separate, crack at the sides and topple like my hut and tumble in on myself, but this only made me more resolute.

Changing tactics, I tried a less complicated, more natural instruction. "Go away!"

As I spoke, I prayed the fiber of Talamadden, whatever it was, would respond to my honest invocation. I didn't expect much, but I was wrong. The words flew from my mouth like a sledgehammer, backed by a searing glow even brighter than the golden blaze usually emitted by a witch. My physical body seemed to fall away, and I became what I knew true witches to be—more light than substance. A part of the natural, no matter which world or plane we visited.

The dark beast let loose with another high-pitched wail, like a creature in infinite pain.

The pitiful sound reached inside me and twisted my heart. Tears sprang to my eyes. Inexplicably, I wanted to run to the beast and fling my arms around it like it was nothing more than a hurt human child.

Oh, had I been in the darkness too long.

With a flap of its substantial wings, the harpy lifted from the patch of ground, high above the leafless tree. Before I could give in to my absurd urges or lower my hand, it was gone.

With it went the stifling pull, and all the darkness around me. To my great surprise, I found myself standing in a pleasantly cool blue stream, so clear I could see the smooth stones lining its bed. Verdant grass rippled off both banks, and the leafless tree now boasted a thick crown of shimmering green leaves. An oak, it was. A live oak.

I turned slowly, my eyes just beginning to adjust to the bright, hot sunlight as it chased away the shadows.

Egidus stood a few yards away, tail spread in a brilliant fan of blues and greens. I could see every detail now, from his impressive crown of slender feathers to the multi-hued splendor of each plume and bit of down. The "eyes" on his decorative train were the most beautiful shade of indigo I had ever seen. His actual eyes seemed much less menacing in the daylight.

"Congratulations," he offered, lowering his tail. With a shake, he settled each feather back into place. "Other than looking like you wet yourself, you're no worse for the battle. I wasn't certain you would escape that first minor trial."

Minor trial? Minor trial?

"Was that a harpy?" I frowned, glancing at where the ruined hut lay, sprouting yellow flowers that bloomed even as I watched. "This is Talamadden, yes? What was something like that thing doing here?"

Egidus made a sound like laughter. "Do you think only good creatures die by spellcraft? Or that evil leaves its evil behind in death?"

I opened my mouth to answer, thought better of it, and closed it with a snap. Of course evil creatures died by spellcraft, before their time, just as I did. And of course they didn't leave their essence behind in the world of the living. That would unbalance the universe, since enlightened souls take their enlightenment with them when they transition to a new plane.

"When a dark-souled creature enters Talamadden, they seek or make dark places, where they are most content." Egidus now sounded temperate and thoughtful, like a teacher or parent. Once more, I was struck with a sense of familiarity. I shivered, uncertain of the meaning of my instinct.

Egidus. I should know what that word means. It sounds so *familiar.* The image of a goat intruded into my thoughts—not a menacing or Pan-like goat, but a typical billy, barely a yearling and munching a mouthful of tender spring grass.

I had no idea why a brilliant blue bird made me think of goats. Perhaps my thoughts were still a bit jumbled. After all, I had died fighting the world's greatest evil, then almost been sucked dry by some ancient demon-being for Goddess-only-knew how long. And then I got approached and challenged by a talking bird, and tapped the essence of the world of the dead.

All in all, I'd say I had been under a tad bit of mind-boggling stress.

"Yes, you have faced stress, Jasmina Corey, Queen of the Witches." Egidus took a few bird steps into the taller grass leading away from the stream and out into the seemingly endless meadow. "Unfortunately, your experiences to date are only a sample of what lies ahead."

"What are you talking about?" I hurried after the peacock, surprised that I found it difficult to keep up with him. His head bobbed forward at a maddening pace, challenging me with each thrust.

"You must find the way out of Talamadden, back to the land of the living, or all of your sacrifices will be meaningless." Bob-bob-bob-bob went his feather-crowned head. His train made a quiet shushing noise on the soft grass. "Your debt—the boy you kidnapped and forced into service—he will die, and soon, if you fail."

That got my supposedly dead heart beating hard all over again. I thought about the visions I had been shown, of Alderon and the spy. I thought about how Bren would most likely try to find me. Somehow, those two factors were destined to merge in some horrible fashion, and I had to stop it.

"Will you show me the way out?"

At this, the peacock began preening nervously, avoiding my gaze. After a few moments of pecking at dirt and whatever else might be on bird feathers, he said, "I can only lead you."

Grimacing, I finished the sentence for him. "The passage is mine to make."

"Most are not fortunate enough to have a guide." His tone was peevish, but also teasing. "You should make a count of your blessings instead of wanting more than you're given."

I shifted from foot to foot, feeling oddly chastised. Not like I did when my impossible-to-please mother dressed me down for an infraction, but more like I did when my father used to express disappointment in me.

"What are you?" I asked, returning to my initial curiosity and question. "How do you know who I am?"

"You should pay attention, Jasmina. Words are important." The bird blinked at me, and I had the oddest impression that he was smiling. "I've already told you what I am."

"You're a peacock," I muttered, searching my mind for what the handsome blue fowl had told me. "You're here to lead, not solve my problems. Most are not fortunate enough to have a—oh! You're a guide. My spirit guide!"

Egidus blinked one eye, like a roguish wink. "A bit slower than I would have liked, but impressive nonetheless."

"Thanks, I guess." I shook my head. "I can't tell if you're being nice or sarcastic."

With another settling of feathers, Egidus set off again, this time walking slowly enough that I could keep up.

"You're a thinker, Jasmina, and a consummate practitioner." He sounded resolute in his opinions. "Very few could have cast the spell to find the true Shadowalker, and fewer still could have helped their champion defeat Nire. And you managed to invoke the natural magic of Talamadden, since this area of death's haven is still attached to the world of the living."

My thoughts were already turning to Bren, to his warm eyes and soft, wild hair. Even to the stubble on his chin. My chest ached. Bren was in danger because of me—again. He needed my help, and more than anything I wanted to give it. I *had* to find my way back to the world of the living. I had to save Bren, to give him back the loyalty and courage he had freely offered me.

To see him once more, to touch his face with my fingertips, even if only for a moment . . .

"What do I have to do to get out, Egidus?"

"The way out of Talamadden is different for every traveler." The peacock had stiffened into the teacher-bird again, speaking in even, crisp tones. "That is why few discover the right path. Even if we proceed, the journey may be in vain if no one comes to meet you on the other side."

I fell silent, considering his words, since he had made a point earlier to tell me how important words were. Few discover the right path. That put me in mind of the Path that protected all witches from persecution. Bren had built it back again, at least in part. He was easily powerful enough to isolate moments in time and connect them, and to escort witches from one time to another to avoid those inevitable moments when humans rose against that which they failed to understand.

Whether or not he had learned to manage the oldeFolke, now that was a question. Bren had shown an aptitude for angering hags and failing to perceive the dangers of ancient beings like klatchKeepers. Sometimes Bren was headstrong—and he was always impulsive.

"Walk faster," I urged the peacock. "I'm afraid he'll die before we get there."

"A very good idea, my lovely queen, but not for the sake of the boy." The bird picked up his pace. His wings rustled as if he were considering flight.

Before I could ask what he meant this time, or demand that he stop speaking in riddles, I heard the sickening sound of huge, beating wings coupled with blood-freezing screams. And the sounds were coming closer.

Something like sunset overtook the beautiful meadow, and the air grew colder by the second.

"The harpy has returned." Egidus half-hopped, half-ran, tempting me to do the same. "With friends."

chapter four

I followed Acaw out of the woods and into the main village of L.O.S.T. without hesitating. A king shouldn't hesitate once he's made a choice and issued a command, right? Besides, I wanted to see where he would take me.

The door lies in lands forgotten. The living shall not cross. Those who search forever wander. "Beware the Guardian," I mumbled, going through the usual recitation. "Old blood. True guide unwilling."

My eyebrows shot up.

I had that last part, didn't I? An unwilling guide. And a true guide, too. Elflings knew about the land of the dead, and they were always loyal. I'd had to command him, but Acaw was doing what I had asked him to do.

That thought gave me a little juice, at least. A guide. Yeah. Willing or not.

As for the rest of it, I was really counting on Acaw.

It was no real surprise when he led me directly into the general store, toward the back, toward the Path. Of course Talamadden would have to be on the Path. Anyone who wasn't a witch or oldeFolke wouldn't see the magical highway through time from the outside. To a human or the unconverted, it simply looked like whatever environment it happened to be in—and in L.O.S.T., the major contact point happened to be in that general store full of herbs, spices, batwings, lizard eyes, and, well, fingers and stuff. What the oldeFolke did with fingers, I really didn't want to know.

"Come, boy." Acaw glanced back as we moved beyond the store's last aisles full of paws, hides, skeletal remains, and hanging, furry tails. "No woolgathering. If we're to do this, we should be away before the hags raise a protest."

Acaw's crow-brother gave an impatient flap of his wings as I stepped up to the back wall, drew my sword, and slid the tip down the side of the Path to make us a doorway.

"Why should the hags protest?" I sheathed my sword as a rush of cool air slipped through and caused my hair to lift from my shoulders. The chain and moonstone around my neck seemed to absorb the chill, turn it slowly aside as if it had never touched me. "This has nothing to do with them."

Acaw mumbled something in the ancient tongue of the oldeFolke, then translated, "Old legends say that the day the living journey to the land of the dead, more than *ba* and *ka* will return."

"Jazz will return," I shot back.

The elfling narrowed his eyes. "You see only what you wish to see. I fear that blindness may cost your life at the Guardian's hands."

"What's that supposed to mean?" I stood before the Path opening and glared at him. "Are you going to start on me like Rol and Dad about rushing headlong into things?"

"No. This you did not rush." He paused, then continued, "You studied, much to my surprise, but do you grasp the meaning of the words?"

I ticked off each point with the fingers of my free hand. "There's a forgotten door, the living can't cross through it, those who search wander forever, I should beware of the Guardian, only old blood can pass–and I had to find an unwilling true guide–you. Did I miss anything?"

Acaw shook his head and sighed. "Nothing. And all."

His crow-brother said a little more with that blazing go-to-the-dark-side stare as Acaw moved past me to peer inside the shimmering opening in the Path.

Unlike during the days of Nire, we didn't have to rush to close the Path behind us to keep the Shadows in and the bad guys out. Now the only beings on the Path were those that my brother Todd and I escorted from Sanctuary to Sanctuary.

"Come." Acaw pushed his way through the slit I had opened.

"Yeah. Whatever." I adjusted the moonstone chain, hitched up my backpack over my shoulders, and followed him inside. The scent of fresh earth, a spring breeze, and moonlight swept over me. Gone was the rotten stench of the Nire days. Gone were the haunted Shadows that had scrabbled and clawed at any being that had been escorted down the Path. Now the walls hummed a soft silver, reminding me of a futuristic hallway from a Star Trek movie. The walls cast enough of a glow that we didn't need my sword's magic to light the way.

After sealing the entrance to the Path, we started walking against the moving floor. At least I had learned to do that without getting sick—which was a major accomplishment, if I do say so myself. The King of the Witches shouldn't double as vomit-boy every time he heads out for a rescue.

Live Oak Springs Township, L.O.S.T., was at the very end of the Path, modern day, where time continued through the new millennium. Every other Sanctuary on the Path was somewhere back in history, yet time progressed in each Sanctuary, just as it did in our own. It took me awhile to actually get how that worked.

If Jazz was here, she could explain it with her floating gold bubbles and mystical ribbons, but that was something I'd never done.

Maybe because it reminded me too much of Jazz. And I'd thought I'd never see her again.

What an idiot I'd been to not find out the truth about Talamadden sooner.

I gritted my teeth and held onto the hilt of my sword as I trudged down the shining walkway of the Path. As always, I felt we were wasting too much time, taking too long.

"Which Sanctuary is it in?" I asked from behind Acaw. "How long will it take for us to get there?"

His crow-brother cast an irritated look over his shoulder, and I felt like a kid in the backseat of a car asking "Are we there yet?" every five seconds.

"As much time as is necessary," Acaw answered in his gravelly voice, and I glared at his back.

He was about half my height, had a weathered face, and always had an expression of being inconvenienced—which no doubt was exactly how he felt at that moment. The short guy never seemed to be in a hurry. The only time I'd ever seen him be anything other than an elfling version of a monk was when the Shadows attacked us at Jazz's old castle back in Shallym. That day, Acaw turned into some sort of Kung Fu master, and his crow-brother, too. The bird killed anything that moved, and Acaw used a kitchen fork and a short dagger better than two broadswords.

I thought about it later, that I'd rather not see him that mad ever again. OldeFolke—they were always mysterious, irritating—and you never really knew where they stood.

Neutral alliance, Jazz's mother had tried to explain. The oldeFolke had simple goals of survival and living as they had always lived. They were allied with nature and the natural, not the modern witches. I could go to hell as far as they were concerned, king or not. The only reason they remained peaceful was because it was in their best interests, and they respected the power I had. Not a great situation, but the best we could hope for given the circumstances.

Acaw had always seemed so loyal to Jazz, and I found out later that elflings lived and died by the promises they made. Once they swore an oath of service, they took it to the bitter end, if necessary. I remember the very moment Jazz released him as she was dying, and the uncharacteristic emotion in his usually stoic expression. *"It has been a pleasure to be in your service,"* he'd said. *"Most of the time."*

The humor in his last statement was bittersweet. Now, Acaw was in my service, even though lots of times he seemed like he'd rather kill me and cook me for dinner.

He probably wouldn't cook me for dinner anytime soon. I felt almost certain about that. Yeah. My command for him to lead me to Talamadden helped with that. I hoped.

The only sounds as we walked along the silvery Path were its normal hum, the quiet patter of Acaw's charms on his walking stick, and the soft thump of my boots.

We passed Sanctuary entrance after Sanctuary entrance, all familiar, all well-known to me. A couple were new, which I had created, but the rest were Sanctuaries Jazz and her father had attached to the Path a long time ago. Todd and I had been able to restore the bonds after I severed them to defeat the Shadowmaster.

We passed one Sanctuary that led into the Wild West, which was one of the cool Sanctuaries I'd attached. Another led into eighteenth-century France, and then, of course, the one to Salem—the Sanctuary where we had fought Nire—where we had learned she was my mother.

My mother.

I still missed her. Fire balled up in my chest and I had to fight back the heat. She had been an ancient being who had chosen my father to be her mate, to produce heirs in hopes she would find the one who would help bring back the rule of the purest oldeFolke. The one who would help her eradicate anyone she considered impure, unworthy of living.

My gut churned at the thought. I had been that one. The one she had expected to rule by her side.

I stopped in my tracks and pounded on the door to Salem with my fist, but my hand simply bounced off the sponge-like wall. "Damn you." I could hardly hold back my emotions. "Damn you for not being the Mom I loved, for killing Jazz."

A hand gripped my shoulder and I spun, ready to punch whoever had touched me.

"None of that if you wish to reach Jasmina in time," Acaw said, but there was an unusual glint of understanding in his ancient eyes.

He turned and started back down the Path.

I straightened and relaxed my hands. "Uh, yeah." Then what he'd said struck me. "What do you mean reach Jazz *in time?*"

Acaw gave a slight shrug of one shoulder without turning to look at me. "Jasmina needs you."

I think my jaw dropped, but I was walking too fast to be sure, trying to catch up to the little bastard. How could an elfling walk so fast? "First you try to tell me not to come, then you make me command you and tell me it's ill fate or whatever, and now you tell me to hurry because Jazz needs me?" His feet seemed to move faster and I had an even harder time keeping up. "What's happened, and how do you know?"

"She needs you." Acaw said, and his crow-brother flapped his stupid black wings.

Typical oldeFolke. Reveal only what's necessary, and then not willingly. That drove me out of my flipping mind.

I marched on through the Path, fiddling with my moonstone necklace as my concern for Jazz mounted. What was going on? I tugged at the chain. Why did she need me now more than she did when we started off?

We passed the Sanctuary that led to King Arthur's time, on back to the Sanctuary of Shallym—that was now being restored after Nire's minions had invaded and nearly destroyed it over five months ago. Five long months without Jazz.

On and on we walked, past Sanctuaries to historical times, on to pre-historical times.

When we came to the place where I had severed the Sanctuary to strand Mom—I mean Nire—I had to hold back another cry of rage and frustration. My heart actually ached in my chest for the being who'd been my mother, and the being who'd been the cause of Jazz's death. She was forever lost in those ancient days now, unable to return to the highway through time. It was the best I could do. I just couldn't kill my own mother. I couldn't.

I'd passed these places lots of times before and hadn't felt this kind of emotion in ages. But for some reason, just knowing that I was on my way to find Jazz brought everything back so painfully harsh that my head ached.

I gripped the hilt of my sword and clenched my teeth. I kept walking straight past the severed Sanctuary, following the bob of Acaw's pointy hat. Nire's forever-home was in prehistoric times, so I knew we were nearly at the end of the Path. The last Sanctuary, the only one after the one I had cut loose, had to be where we would find the land of the dead.

But Acaw turned his back on the last door even as we reached it. Before I could ask him any questions, he tapped his staff against the wall directly across from that Sanctuary and the charms at the top of it tinkled softly. He tapped again and again on a wall with no doorway—a wall along the side that shouldn't have any Sanctuaries attached to it.

Yet a door opened, as neatly as if I had cut it myself . . . only circular.

A small round door.

"What the . . ." I started, but Acaw had already vanished through the hobbit-sized doorway.

The moonstone around my neck hummed. I ducked through the hole, but still managed to bang my head on what felt like solid wood. I was about to grill the elfling on how he opened the Path when only Todd and I were supposed to be able to do it—but I saw where I was and went completely speechless.

It was like fairyland. Heck, it probably *was* fairyland. After all, I followed an elfling here, right?

The door lies in lands forgotten.

This sure looked like Forgotten Land to me. Two riddles down, four to go. Assuming, of course, I hadn't missed a ton in all the old scrolls I *couldn't* read.

Acaw closed the door behind us and gave it a single tap of his staff while I stared at my surroundings.

It was the most beautiful place I'd ever been in. Golden sunlight spilled through massive trees of vivid shades of green, and the light caressed violet, blue, red, and orange flowers. Soft grass covered a pathway with flagstones leading the way through fairyland—sort of a yellow brick road that wasn't yellow. It smelled wonderful, of roses and rich, dark earth.

Elflings of all ages and sizes tended gardens in front of small houses built right into mounds of earth—no, wait. Not elflings. They were smaller, and some were—er, hairy. Were they gnomes? Dwarves?

Tiny creatures fluttered about the flowers like dragonflies. I was sure they were fairies. Especially when one of them flittered right up to my face and I saw her shimmering blonde hair and tiny perfect female body. She winked, then was gone in a flash.

"This forgotten place, is it Summerland?" I asked as I looked in awe at the beauty around us. The stone at my neck felt warm, peaceful—right. I placed my hand on it, rubbing it back and forth.

This didn't look like such a bad place to go. There were so many different types of beings around and they all appeared to work in perfect harmony. An enormous bunny went hopping by carrying a bunch of little elfling kids on its back, and that settled it for me.

I was in freaking Wonderland.

"Is this it?" I asked Acaw again. "Is this Summerland?"

Acaw gave a snort that could have been a laugh—if he ever laughed.

"A long journey lies ahead," he said, and I didn't hold back my groan.

"Where are we, then?" While I followed him on the flagstone path, I ducked a bunch of flowers that looked like wavy pink spiders. "Why didn't I know about this place?"

I was King of the Witches. I figured I had the right to know everything.

Acaw trundled past one of the most beautiful women I'd ever seen. As we passed the woman, he lowered his voice so that only I could hear and said, "Few humans, even witches, breach the borderlands ruled by the Erlking and live. It is my hope that your halfling oldeFolke blood will protect you."

I barely heard him, my head swiveling as we walked past the redheaded beauty clothed in a gauzy kind of material that clung to all her curves. She was perfect except for the slightest glint in her eyes. A hard glint. Too aware of me, almost watchful, like she was sizing me up.

An enchantress, a voice said in my head. Another voice, which sounded annoyingly like Jazz in one of her more snitty moods, said, "Things aren't always what they appear to be, Bren."

I swiveled my head back around and focused my concentration on Acaw's back. I'd give anything to hear Jazz's voice again, snooty or not.

In a rare moment of volunteering information, Acaw said, "There are more types of oldeFolke and more ancient, forgotten Sanctuaries than you know—than any modern witch knows. Many of these places existed before the time of the Path."

"But I'm King of the Witches, and this is important. Isn't there some book I can study, or someone who can teach me?"

Acaw seemed to consider for a moment, then responded simply, "No."

I didn't believe him. "Why not?"

Acaw's crow-brother cast me another of those oh-would-you-shut-up stares as the elfling said, "It is . . . the way of things. Secrets knit the fabric of time, Your Majesty. All people have secrets, and all peoples."

This made some sense. After another few strides, the concept of being in the lands of the Erlking, the legendary and ruthless ruler of the dwarves I had read about during all my studying to be a better witch-leader, started to bug me. "Um, listen. This Erlking. He doesn't really kidnap kids from the human world and eat them, right?"

The short guy didn't glance back or slow down, and the crow-brother kept his evil looks to himself. Somehow, I thought that was bad. Maybe very bad.

"Is he the Guardian I'm supposed to beware?"

"Look straight ahead," Acaw instructed. "Keep walking and touch nothing, especially when we leave the stone path and depart the meadow. The Erlking is not known to be forgiving."

We walked for hours, then a day. Light came and went. I had to grab food out of my pack and eat it on the fly. Whenever I stopped to go to the bathroom, I ended up running after Acaw, who must have had a bladder the size of the Atlantic Ocean.

A few times I had a sense of something skulking along beside us in wooded areas—something really big and not so friendly. I kept my hand on the hilt of my sword. My shoulders ached. My feet hurt. But I listened to Acaw. Along the wide path through the eerily quiet forest, I didn't touch a thing but what my boots landed on. Not a branch, not a tree, not a bush.

Jazz, I told myself over and over like a marching rhythm. *Do it for Jazz.* So what if I needed a ledger book to count my blisters? If the elfling felt so freaked out about getting to wherever Jazz was trapped, then I felt twice as freaked out. Jazz needed me.

She needs me . . .

Just the thought of her alive, of seeing her again, talking to her, putting my arms around her, kept me moving when I wanted to drop, kept my sword hand on the hilt of my blade, at the ready, when I wanted to be lazy.

By the third night, I was staggering. My sword, the stone around my neck—everything, including my feet, seemed to weigh three hundred pounds. Every time I closed my eyes, I drifted toward sleep. Sometimes I stumbled ahead and woke myself up snoring.

Those who search wander forever . . .

Jazz. Jazz needs me . . .

I kept on the trail Acaw was following, looked straight ahead, touched nothing except my sword, which I was using like a flashlight in the darkness. Ignored the sliding and rustling sounds on either side of me. Long gone was fairyland. This was totally Forest of Doom. If the sun ever touched this place in the daytime, it would never find its way through the heavy-limbed trees. They were twisted and gnarled up like broken skeletons, and I had a sick feeling they were staring at us.

If I wasn't mistaken, Acaw was walking a little straighter. His crow-brother sat stiff on his shoulder, head twitching right, then left, right, then left. They stayed just inside the beam of light from my sword.

From somewhere, low and soft, came the sound of women's voices singing on the rising wind. It wasn't like a klatchKoven. Not irresistible, but still, I wanted to listen. The sound gave a rhythm to my stride, and I was so tired I needed something—anything—to help me out.

"Are there fairies here?" My words sounded thick and soft. How long had it been since I took a swig of water? Acaw probably didn't hear me. "Jeez, the wind is icy. This place feels like the edge of the world."

"Yes." Acaw was suddenly beside me as if he had disappeared and reappeared at my side. I must have been sleepwalking again. I didn't know what he meant—that there were fairies, or that we really were walking on the edge of the world. I could have believed either.

A low-hanging branch seemed to reach out of the night to slap me. I shoved it out of my face, but it scraped my right cheek anyway. Everything seemed to irritate the scar now and it was pissing me off.

It took me two more steps to realize Acaw had stopped walking. When I turned around, the elfling was standing still as an elf-post . . . with both daggers drawn. His crow-brother was in the air, circling, buffeting on the strong wind.

"What?" I rubbed my eyes. My teeth chattered. "I don't hear anything but that fairy-singing. I wish I had a coat."

"You touched the branch," Acaw said quietly. "Raise your sword."

The singing got so loud it filled up my brain. I wanted to sleep so, so badly, but the wind—I'd freeze to death. "This is stupid. Are you going to fight me? Punish me or something?"

"No." Acaw's maddening tone never changed. He didn't move, not even when the arrow sailed out of the trees. I saw it coming, like it was flying in slow motion, but there was no way I could move in time.

It was a straight shot, a single red arrow, and it struck me dead on, right at the heart. I expected pain, blood—but there was nothing but a thump-crack. The arrow broke and dropped to the ground, useless.

Eyes wide, I raised my free hand to the spot where I had been hit, and I felt the hard, unyielding lump of the moonstone Sherise had loaned me. The point of the arrow had snapped on that tiny little rock.

"I'm not dead," I muttered, still not believing it.

A loud, furious roar answered me.

It was bellowing, really. Blasting over the wind and the singing, it was so loud, gravelly, and intense. I'd never heard a giant bear make noise, but I figured I was hearing one. When I turned around, I saw one, too.

A bear. The size of an elephant.

About three football fields away, but glowing an eerie red in the night. Waaaay too close.

Only this bear had hands and feet instead of paws. Hands and feet with great big claws attached. It had a huge head, long fangs, and a pelt like Bigfoot—and did it ever stink. The wind blew its stench straight up my nose.

I choked on the disgusting smell as it plowed down the path, heading straight at me. The thing was on all fours, but I had a feeling when it stood up to kill me, it would be bigger than a slither.

"Stop," I commanded over the deafening wind and singing, feeling half drunk.

The air around me shimmered, but the singing only got louder and the bear-thing kept coming and that frigid wind blew and blew. Two hundred yards and closing. One-fifty. One hundred. My fingers burned in the cold as I gripped my sword tighter and tighter.

"Fine, if that's how it is." My eyes were open now. Fatigue left me in a rush as my heart slammed and jammed. I hoisted my sword and readied it in baseball stance. Its light made an umbrella, silvering Acaw, the crow-brother, and me.

The bear-thing seemed to try to slow up a little, but too late. As it slammed toward me, I swung hard. My blade connected with a wet thump just before impact ripped the weapon out of my hands.

Tons of bear-monster plowed me into the ground. Pain blazed in my chest, my gut, and my back. My arms went numb as I fell hard, face-first into frozen pine needles. Dirt. Rocks. It felt like the whole forest got stuffed in my mouth. I sat up fast, spitting out grit. My lips chapped and cracked in the cold. When I tried to yell, I couldn't. Something was yelling, though. Really loud. And the singers were shrieking, like it was from the center of my brain.

Crawling, pulling myself and pushing with my knees, I scrabbled through the night toward the distant light of my blade. Had I hurt the bear-thing? How could I damage something that big? Were my arms still on my body? I didn't dare turn around. I didn't want to see what the thing had done to Acaw or the crow-brother. I didn't want to see it head back to finish me off. The sword—I just needed to get to it.

My frozen, aching fingers found the hilt and I jerked it out of the soft ground. The metal was so cold my hand actually stuck to it. Whatever. At least I'd die swinging.

When I wheeled around, I saw Acaw still standing with daggers drawn, but his ice-coated crow-brother had settled back on his shoulder. In front of him were six women—and all of them looked nearly identical to the redhead from town, the one with the curves and the gauze gown, except some were blonde and some had dark hair. They were all on their knees, cradling and petting a hairy dude even shorter than Acaw. The cold didn't seem to bother any of them at all.

As I watched, white sparks trickled out of their fingers, disappearing into the little dude's hair. In the odd light, I could tell his hair—fur?—was matted with blood. Probably from the blow I struck. I didn't know whether to be elated or humiliated. This was no giant bear. It was a scruffy man no bigger than a five year old. Maybe I'd been asleep again.

I'd fallen asleep and nearly cut some hairy forest kid in half, and now these enchantress babes would probably try to eat me. Great. My ribs grated like they were all broken, but I lifted my sword, letting the silver light cut the darkness.

"Lower your blade," Acaw instructed as the women covered their eyes and started to shriek.

Without questioning, I did what he said. My teeth chattered so loudly I thought they might break against each other as the sword's glow eased back to just me. I could still see the gauze babes and the hairy kid because they—well, they glowed. Just a little. Still red. It was enough for me to see the shadows of the huge forest trees all around us. I wondered if I was dreaming again.

"*Wer reitet so spät durch Nacht und Wind?*" Acaw asked calmly, keeping his own blades up. He was speaking German, I was sure of it. I remembered that line from a poem in school, by Goethe or somebody like that. I had heard it in German and the teacher translated it.

Who rides so late through the night and the wind?

From the ground, the hairy kid said, "*Erlkönig*!"

"*Erlkönig*!" the enchantress babes echoed.

I didn't need any translation for that word. I'd definitely heard it before.

Erlking.

From nowhere and everywhere, Jazz's memory whispered, *Not everything is as it seems, Bren . . .*

The hairy kid wasn't dead, and he wasn't a kid. In fact, he was standing up now, growing taller and larger. The pelt became wild red curls and a beard. The dude's eyebrows were long enough to comb and braid. When he finished his shifting, he was wearing hammered, dented armor crusted with black stuff I didn't want to identify, and he had a helmet that looked like a skull with horns. Only his mouth and beard that reached his chest showed out from under the edges. In his hands was a double-bladed axe easily as long as my body.

He stared at me, or I think he did, for a few long seconds as I stood there shaking, teeth chattering, and hurting like hell—probably bleeding in lots of places. Instinctively, I lifted my sword an inch or two, letting the light creep back toward the Erlking and his . . . minions, or whatever they were.

Daughters, my mind told me, remembering bits and pieces of that Goethe poem again, as if the teacher were right there in my head.

Meine Töchter sollen dich warten schön; My daughters shall attend to you so nicely.

Meine Töchter führen den nächtlichen Reihn; My daughters do their nightly dance.

Und wiegen und tanzen und singen dich ein; And they'll rock you and dance you and sing you to sleep.

No, thank you very much. More like they'll baste you and cook you and eat you for supper. They might look like one-eyed rotted squids under that gauze. They probably did. The cold stabbed at me harder and harder, and the light from my sword grew. I was getting desperate. The sword could tell and it responded with increased power.

As silver beams spilled over the Erlking's toes, he growled and turned on Acaw. "What did you shepherd to my forest, you treacherous, lying elf?"

I flinched because the man—the thing—the Erlking's voice was so loud.

Acaw didn't flinch. Neither did his crow-brother. "The halfblood," he said in that calm, quiet way that usually made me want to dropkick him. "My ruler who commanded me. I had no choice. You may not touch me."

"A halfblood." The Erlking snorted. "You would have me believe a halfblood wields power enough to turn my charge? What madness possessed me, to question a bloody elf?" To his daughters, he said, "Kill him."

"No!" I raised my sword above my head and light flashed from everywhere. I felt the magic drawing on energy I didn't have, but no way was I letting those squids at Acaw.

Once more, the women cried out when the light washed over them. The Erlking grunted and stepped into the shadows.

"He cannot touch me, Your Majesty, and he well knows it." Acaw's voice was so unbelievably calm. "I am here at the command of my ruler, and so violate no oaths or bonds to the secrets my people cherish and protect." To the Erlking, he pointed out, "I did not say *a* halfblood. I said *the* halfblood. And while we speak of blood, the boy drew yours first. By all the old rites, Guardian, you must let him pass."

Sensing the danger had lessened, I lowered my sword enough for the women-things to quit moaning and fussing. The Erlking came closer to me, studying me through that eyeless horned helmet. I couldn't see his blazing red gaze, and yet I could. This childkiller. This shapeshifting babyeater. I had half a mind to skewer him just on principle.

Easy. Easy. I blew out a breath and wondered if the mist from my mouth would freeze solid. *Not everything is as it seems. In this freaky world, boogeymen can be heroes and moms can be boogeymen. Don't forget that.*

"Aaaaaahhhh," the Erlking murmured. "You are the whelp of the Shadowmaster. The boy who slew his own kin."

"I didn't—" I started to say, but Acaw cut me off.

"He is the King of the Witches." The elfling lifted his blades. They glinted in the reflection of my sword, causing the Erlking's daughters to hide their eyes. "He defeated the Shadowmaster. He is well possessed of the old blood and he rules in all of our lands, even this place where you have been consigned. Would you challenge him again, dwarf lord?"

The Erlking turned his weird horn-head back to Acaw. "That was hardly a challenge."

"Yet the king drew first blood." Acaw's tone took on a relentless quality, colder than the cold that was killing me where I stood. "Give him his due. The old rules, the old rites. If you dishonor them, you will face more than entrapment in these vast lands."

"Be silent," the Erlking roared.

Acaw's crow-brother flapped, but not in fear. The bird's eyes blazed so brightly I could see them in the dark. Black, glinting rage. The dwarf-whatever-it-was better be glad it had on a helmet, or his—its—eyes might have been clawed out.

For a while, we all stood in silence, except for the clattering of my teeth. I was turning into a carved ice statue of myself, I was sure of it.

When the Erlking finally turned back toward me, I was ready to start yelling and charging just to get my blood flowing again. He didn't attack me, though. Instead, he waved one metal-gloved hand and barked a word I didn't understand.

"Be still," Acaw ordered as the Erlking's daughters rose and began to swirl around me.

I didn't want to be still. I wanted to put some distance between me and the red-bearded dwarf freak and his nutty offspring, but I did what Acaw told me to do.

A pressure formed in my head, like somebody poking at my thoughts. Similar to what I had felt so long ago, when Jazz had to break into my brain to find out about the golem that had stolen my will.

"Stop it," I ordered. They were hammering against my defenses, looking too far inside my essence. I hated it. So cold. So sharp.

The pressure doubled. The women got even closer.

Are you worthy? they seemed to ask, over and over as I got dizzier and dizzier.

White sparks dripped from sixty fingertips, whirling in a circle with the daughters. Around and around they went, and the sparks, the sparks bouncing and spinning, making a wind-devil, a tornado swallowing me, covering me, falling in on me—damn, it was getting warm. Hot. I was sweating. My sword hilt burned into my palm and I wanted to drop it so bad.

No. No. No! Clamping my teeth together, I held on tight. All my aches and pains faded to the back of my mind as the daughters charged into the front of my thoughts. I had to keep my sword raised. No way was I putting it down with all of this crap going on.

My consciousness started slipping and dancing with all the sparks. I was pouring sweat.

Images flooded me. Nire-Mom, and Jazz, and Dad, and Todd, and Sherise, and L.O.S.T., back to Todd, and everything I ever knew, everyone I ever knew, every place I had been. The Erlking was soiling everything, scratching claws across my little brother's face, thumbing through my memories like book pages, laughing, blood dripping from his finger tips . . .

Did you think it would be so easy, boy? His voice felt like a mallet, beating me into nothing. *What fools, to bring me a half-blood. Even one like you!*

That's when the singing started again. The singing. That beautiful singing . . .

chapter five

Egidus ran so fast his blue head moved like a piston in a modern engine. My legs pumped just as hard. Onrushing harpies blocked out the sun, turning the meadow a dangerous gray.

How did so many harpies get to the land of the dead? This was insane. But it was happening.

"We must make the barrier!" the peacock cried. He took off and flapped for a distance, then touched down, running even harder.

I wished for a live oak branch. I wished for any sort of magic beyond the simple spells even the unconverted could perform. An invocation might help with one harpy, but a sky full of the creatures? For certain, not. I could almost feel the claws tearing into my hair, my head, my skin.

Like the Shadows. Those cold, evil, foul Shadows. My heart squeezed like it might explode just from the thought of them. Pain stabbed my side like a sword and I couldn't breathe. How could I battle Shadows again? They would kill me. I would die all over again, and go back to the dark place with the hag-tree. I would lose my sanity.

"Jasmina!" Wings beat at my head, and not harpy wings by the feel of them. Bird feet drummed against my skull. Egidus was flogging me!

"Stop it!" I swept my arms upward to push him away and he dropped down to run beside me. When I glanced at him, his beak was open and I could actually see his tongue as he panted. Still, the look he managed to give me said one thing clearly.

Concentrate.

Concentrate. Yes. "These are harpies, not Shadows."

My wits came back to me. I did my best to double my pace. We were approaching the edge of the meadow. Trees loomed beautiful and tall before us. If we could just make it beneath their canopy, we might be saved.

At least the leaves and branches would slow down our onrushing attackers.

Overhead, the harpies bawled. They sounded like panicked sheep mixed with terrified hags.

Have I ever seen a terrified hag? Do hags actually feel terror?

Witches did.

The trees were close. So close. I lunged forward.

Claws raked my back, my neck. Fire. Goddess, did the beast tear me open? For a second, then two, I was off the ground, legs running in air as the harpy grasped me. My arms felt like they were tearing out of their sockets.

A call like the furious screech of a woman echoed against the bleating of the harpies. I saw a flash of blue, then feathers raining, both black and brilliant indigo.

The pressure on my arms turned loose.

Like a stone I dropped, hitting the ground with a tumbling roll. My skin sizzled where the harpy's claws had sliced me. Grabbing at grass, at sticks, at earth, I blundered forward until I slammed into the rough base of a giant pine.

All my wind left me, and I could do nothing but sit and gasp. I felt like my body had broken into three pieces. I had no feeling in my arms, my legs half-dead and tingling, and was something standing on my chest?

No, no.

Clenching my jaw, I forced myself to crawl forward, farther into the trees. I had to take cover.

Where was the peacock? Did he—no! No. I had to move. Just keep moving. If I could die again, I was about to do so, but I couldn't. I had to get to Bren, warn him about what I'd seen. I couldn't let him, let all the people I loved, fall to Alderon's new treachery.

"Goddess, help me," I pleaded as I crawled. Sharp pains, dull pains, I couldn't count them. My head would barely lift from the ground, but I thought I was making progress. A little, then a little more.

Something landed beside me, breathing hard. Wings. Feathers. Egidus was limping badly. One of his wings dragged the ground between us. "Go," he was saying over and over. "Go, go, go."

And I crawled and crawled and crawled. Rocks, stones, grass, moss, sticks—it didn't matter. I crawled.

A harpy's gurgling scream blocked out all sound, all hope. Light faded—and then there was nothing.

Bren. He was with me! Right beside me. Close enough to reach for his muscled sword arm. I couldn't wait to touch him, to know he was real. He grinned at me, his bright eyes taking me in as if I were the only girl in the world.

I touched his shoulder, his soft brown hair swept behind his ear. My heart swelled with warmth, brimmed with joy—but I found his hair coarse. Too long.

And red?

Where was I?

I stepped away from Bren.

Only, it wasn't Bren at all. It was a horrible little man with mounds of red hair and beard. Gore-coated armor formed over his huge, heavy muscles, topped finally by a horned helm that masked his cold black eyes.

"I wondered, I did." His voice was rougher than slither hide, meaner than a hag-spirit in full viper form. "Now I understand. And we will meet again, pretty. Take that for a vow."

I shivered from the sound of him, wanted to wretch. Goddess, he—it—was reaching for me. As I fell on my backside, trying to get away from him, he laughed . . . and that was the worst sound of all.

"Jasmina." My father's voice dispersed the horrid man like he was nothing more than dust. He chanted quiet spells, and the music of his words covered me like a soft blanket, soothing my wounds. His hands hovered above my broken body.

I wanted to sit up, to hug him and feel him hug me, but I couldn't move. "Father. Help me."

"No, child. Be still."

His hands hovered above my shoulders, then my chest, then my belly, hips, and knees. White-golden light blazed between his palms and my torn clothing. Deep inside my body, bone moved. Blood flow stopped and started. I felt like I could hear my heart being coaxed back to normal rhythm.

Above us, a golden light shimmered. A shield. It covered us, protected us from the dark shapes outside.

Shadows!

I opened my mouth and screamed, but no sound issued forth.

"Father!" I was finally able to get out. "The Shadows are coming!"

But he was gone as quickly as he came, fading to nothing along with the beauty of that sparkling light.

I woke, lying on my belly, covered in blood and mud and pine needles. I raised my head. There was no golden light above me, only a cold, gray slab of rock dripping with moisture. An icy splatter of water landed on my hair. I was in a cave, the faintest of misty light coming from the entrance.

Every inch of me throbbed or burned, but I found I could move enough to turn over. A fire crackled beside me, and on the other side of the fire, Egidus lay preening his feathers.

"Birds can light fires?"

The peacock paused in his grooming long enough to offer me a haughty glance. "I have many talents beyond style and grace, Jasmina."

"And humility," I muttered. As I sat up, I realized the skin on my back and neck felt better. It moved as if it were whole, as if harpy claws hadn't flayed it open on the edge of the meadow.

"How did we get here to this—wherever it is?"

"It's a cave," Egidus supplied. "We are at the foot of the Wal Mountains, and as soon as you can walk, we must risk the harpies again. The boy will die if we delay."

"How did we get here?" I repeated. His words had started me to massaging my arms and legs to see how quickly I could be on the move. "I doubt you carried me."

If peacocks could smile, Egidus offered something like a mysterious grin. "As I said, I have many talents. Though this world is connected to the physical plane, we are not truly a part of it yet. Some hard, fast laws of physics can be . . . modified. Less and less so as we proceed."

He twisted his head back and dug into his feathers again, shaking out a small cloud of dander. When he looked up again, he added, "Besides, I did not leave my magic behind when I came here."

Squeezing my eyes shut, I forced myself to my feet, sure I would find something broken. I did not. However, every muscle in my body seemed to be sore or stretched in some impossible direction.

"I dreamed I saw my father." I stretched up my arms. My fingertips brushed the cave's cool, damp ceiling. "I dreamed he healed me."

"Perhaps he did," the bird said before going into another frenzy of dander expulsion. "In death, as in life, all things are possible."

My stomach rumbled, and I gave thought to cooking the peacock if he offered one more erudite riddle.

By the good Goddess. Bren would suggest something like roasting my peacock guide. When I gave him my magic, did I take some of his personality in return?

"I have no food to offer you, and I assure you, I would not provide much in terms of nutrition." Egidus fanned his tail and shook the feathers, filling the cave's still air with a loud buzzing. "It takes a certain combination to make this journey successful—a wise guide of a certain sort, a willing traveler pure of motive—well, at any rate, if you eat me, you'll likely never find your way to the gate alone. The harpies have taken themselves elsewhere for now. Shall we go?"

After stretching another few seconds, I nodded. "But where?"

"Up, my witch. Up, up, up!" The bird managed another smile of sorts. "By the time we finish the climb to the Glorieuse, you will wish for wings as splendid as mine."

Days later, in the early evening, I not only wanted to cook the peacock, but I wished to leave his guts for the harpies to find. He hardly spoke to me at all, barely let us sleep a few hours at a time, stayed a few paces ahead, and kept that ridiculous blue head bobbing, bobbing, bobbing. His train spread along behind him, and he held it a mere inch from the dirt and rocks of the trail. If you could call the hellish twist of dirt a trail. It was more like a narrow road made to punish anyone attempting the climb.

It wound ever upward, reaching toward a darkening sky hidden in mists. We had climbed past every other peak I could see, and I was beginning to believe the accursed mountain had no top. Or if it did, I would find it only months after I died alongside the dusty, hard path.

Could one die again in the land of the dead?

Mushrooms, berries, and a raw fish courtesy of the bird—my stomach was full and empty all at once. I had water in an oilskin pouch the beastly fowl had brought back from the Goddess only knew where, and that ran thin over and over until we found another stream or puddle to fill it.

Bren. Poor Bren. Would I ever find a way to reach him? How could I possibly be in time? On the third or fourth day—I had completely lost count—I thought of nothing but Bren and my dry throat. I literally ached for a drink as I climbed a rock face, hand over foot and foot over hand, pulling myself upward with all my strength. At least the climb had loosened my sore muscles and stretched out my tight, freshly-healed skin.

Did I really see my father in a fever-dream? Did he truly heal me? That blessed bird speaks only in sayings and riddles—and who in the name of the Goddess was that red-haired man?

"What was he?" I wondered aloud as I managed to pitch forward onto a ledge instead of falling miles to my doom. It was getting dark enough to gray the scene around me.

"Very good, Jasmina," Egidus offered as he flew up to the spot I had struggled so hard to achieve. He landed without so much as a labored breath, used his beak to pull the oilskin from where it hung around my neck, then flew off.

I sat, huffing and seething, until he returned a few minutes later with the oilskin full of cool, perfect water. Unable to help myself, I drank it in a few gulps.

Egidus clucked like a chicken and shook his elegant head. "You must take more care with what the mountain gives us if you wish to reach the Glorieuse."

I shouted in frustration, just to hear the dull echo of my voice bounce back upward in the crystal cold air, seeming more and more chilly as night fell. "Are you going to tell me about the Glorieuse, or must I guess about that, too?"

Egidus considered this. "There isn't much to tell, really. It's the pinnacle of the Wals, and our destination. When we reach it, I have confidence you will know what to do."

"How can you have that confidence?" I yelled again, more from exhaustion than a wish to hear my echo. "I have failed at most everything I've tried. I—"

"Self-pity does not become you." Egidus ruffled his feathers, then let them fall into place. "That is a form of pride. Bemoaning your many failures as if you were born to succeed at all you attempt—arrogance, pure and simple. Did you know that?"

Thoughts of large blue bird roasting slowly on a spit filled my mind. "How can you speak to me of pride and arrogance? You do nothing but preen and strut, then speak high-handed nonsense."

"And what do you do, Jasmina Corey, Queen of the Witches? Did you handle your Shadowalker any differently? Your people?" Egidus studied me with black-pearl eyes. They glittered in the misty mountain light.

Rage heated me from aching head to cramping toe. The only person who could infuriate me as much as this overblown pigeon was Brenden himself.

"I did my best!" I shouted, then rubbed my already-parched throat. Using what little strength I could find, I got to my feet.

The damnable blue peacock studied me again. I could swear his eyes danced, that he wanted to smile. "So you did." He dipped his fine-feathered head. "Best you should remember that and avoid your dramatic claims of terrible failure."

I kicked at the bird, who hopped neatly aside, saying, "We should be on the move, and quickly. Our good fortune will not hold forever."

"What do you mean?" I started off after Egidus. We were thankfully back on an actual trail, for however long it lasted. Our good fortune would not hold—what did he mean?

The cold grew suddenly colder as I considered options.

The first thing I came up with was of course the worst. "Shadows? Do you think there are Shadows here?" I wanted to lunge at the peacock, grab his tail and make him answer.

This once, I didn't have to. Egidus stopped, turned, and gave me a firm, rage-cooling stare. "If you fear a thing enough, Jasmina, you will draw it to you."

My teeth slammed together of their own accord. How could the horrible bird play off my terror like that?

Something in the peacock's manner reminded me of my mother at that moment. That made me hang my head.

In silence, we began walking again, following the path, always following the path.

"Thinking of your endless failures again, O arrogant one?" Egidus kept pace beside me, strutting in that uniquely peacock manner. "Why is it that you cannot take counsel without feeling like you must have been wrong? What if, this once, I happen to know more than you because of my experience?"

His head bobbed once as I looked up.

"You were queen too young, I fear," he said in a softer tone than I remembered him using before. "You have forgotten how to learn with joy. How to grow with the fresh grace of a child."

"No witch is a finished flower," I whispered as my feet kept marching, marching onward. My father said that often enough when he worked with me at my lessons. "There is no shame in new blooms."

Egidus blessed me with a bob-nod—and the sky above us went darker than dark.

The hammer and pound of huge wings filled my ears.

"Flee!" Egidus shouted. "The harpies have found us!"

Almost at the same moment, the waning light finally surrendered into night.

Blindly, we charged up the path side-by-side, falling, hopping, lunging. The bird leaped and fluttered, keeping pace, then leading, then dropping behind me to shout instructions.

"Left. Left, girl! Right! Duck under that branch!"

I obeyed him without question, running under an inky cloud of harpies. Air stirred terrifyingly close to my neck.

"No!" I waved my arms over my head like that would do any good. At the same moment, I felt a stirring of something in my belly. Something missed, something familiar. An energy, a charge.

I felt power—*my* power, the magic I had given Bren—as if I were somehow drawing closer to its source, finding its origins once more and claiming it as my own.

The sound of something huge diving through the air made me shriek with frustration. "Cease!" I yelled. "In the name of the Goddess, cease!"

To my great surprise, all sounds halted—all motion but my own and that of Egidus. I kept stumbling forward, wanting to look up to see if the harpies were hanging in the misty air, but I dared not waste that time. Already, I could feel my control slipping. The spell wouldn't last as long as I needed it to. Whatever touch of my power I had regained, it wasn't strong.

I rounded a curve and came faceup on a shallow recess in the mountain, more a ceremonial-looking grotto than a true shelter. A silvery light bathed the scene—the moon, I realized, shining full and bright down on what had to be an altar. As I got closer, I could see it was true. A carved altar bearing candles, dried sage, a silver chalice, a silver chain with a crescent pendant, and a green circlet of what might have been laurel mingled with olive leaves. Everything I needed for a proper ritual—but what ritual, and why?

"Egidus!" I cried, but the bird had positioned himself back on the path between me and harpies—who were even now beginning to bleat and twitch. The wind was starting to blow. My ceasing spell was failing, and I didn't think I had the strength or power to cast another.

Weakness . . .

Failure . . .

With a growl, I slapped my hands against the side of my head to knock out the old thoughts. They wouldn't save me now. They wouldn't save Egidus, or help me get to Bren.

The moment I thought his name, I felt a pull in my heart. Another touch of my own power flowing back. Was he somewhere near? Farther up the path?

But no. After the grotto, the mountain seemed to end. Simply end. As if the mist and sky and night swallowed it.

Calming myself thanks to years of my father's training and my mother's drilling, I made myself focus and think. The altar. The altar.

Oh.

Behind the altar stood a wall of polished black stone. It was marble or obsidian or something else, I couldn't tell in the moonlight. It stretched into the mountain on my right, and blocked the path on my left. A small overhang of rock covered me from above, double my height but narrow indeed. Even if I stood on the altar it would offer me little protection.

The sickening drum of harpy wings began to take over the night. I shoved the sounds from my mind.

I had a little power—so what could I do? The items on the altar.

"Cast a circle. Perhaps I can make it strong enough for protection."

With that thought, I hurried forward, picked up the candles, and placed them at the four points, to the best of my discernment, starting with the yellow candle, which was supposed to go to the east. Then the southernmost candle, the red one. I rested it against the wall, instinctively avoiding any contact with the glassy surface of that frightening stone. I then placed the blue one to the west and the green one to the north.

Using a spark of magic, I set the incense to burning, anointed myself with oil I found in the silver chalice, and began the words to make a protective circle.

Egidus landed hard inside the circle before I closed it. "It will not hold for long against such negative assault," he gasped.

Indeed, the harpies were already pounding away at the energy field between us. I felt the blows on my magic as if they were striking my head and shoulders—not hard, but hard enough.

"Hurry," Egidus rasped, limping toward me. "Invoke the Goddess. It is the only way. Not midnight, not optimal, times are out of sync since it is daylight on the other side—but do it. You must open the Glorieuse. Perhaps there is yet one miracle left for the Corey family."

My gaze darted to the black stone, and I understood—more like remembered. The Glorieuse was a name from old tales. The unbreakable sword of hero knights, made of magical steel or magical stone.

The black wall was spelled somehow. Be it metal, be it rock, it must be a barrier—*the* barrier, between the land of the dead and the world of the living.

I had found my path out of Talamadden, and I had walked it.

Somehow, coming so close gave me confidence enough to shrug off the noise and pain of the harpies' attack. My thoughts sharpened.

"Invoke the Goddess," I whispered as I grasped the chain and pendant and the circlet of leaves. I no longer felt tired or sore or even thirsty. I knew what I had to do, and I knew the rest was in the hands of the gods. If they turned away from me now, I was lost.

As I put on my gifts and felt an even greater surge of power, I glanced into the dark sky, toward the shimmering silver circle of the Goddess above me.

It was time to draw down the moon.

chapter six

BREN

We had been running since I woke up at the foot of the mountains. Straight up. Forever. Yet I wasn't that tired. I still felt strong despite the fact we were climbing a mountain that had no end.

Acaw had explained that the Guardian of the land of the dead, the Erlking who had been spelled within its boundaries for eons, had been duty-bound to heal me since I had bested him in single combat. The shapeshifting bastard had let his daughters work the spell—and apparently one of them thought I was cute. So, the blonde had given me a little extra. Strength. Renewal. A burst of energy that wasn't permanent, but sure was great while it lasted. The only bad thing was an itch behind my left ear, but it was manageable.

"Maybe I got fleas from the Erlking while he was all hairy and stuff." I scratched the spot behind my ear. "That would be my luck."

"He is a proud creature," the elfling said as his legs churned beside me. "I doubt we have seen the last of him."

"Sore loser, huh?" I was a little out of breath, unlike Acaw.

"Indeed. I suspect he will try to surprise you next time."

"As long as there *is* a next time, I'm cool with that." I scratched my ear one more time, then shifted my pack on my shoulders. "Let the asshole take another swing at me, and we'll see who wins."

It sounded good, but something tugged at the back of my mind. A bad dream about book pages and blood and the sound of the Erlking laughing. Was that all part of the ritual? Was he just getting in a last blow, trying to catch me off guard? Probably, because I was alive, and running, and I felt good. If the murdering shit chose to show back up, I'd hold my own.

"When will we get there?" It was probably the millionth time I had asked. The energy from the Erlking's daughters was fading, and I tried to keep the huff out of my voice as my boots crushed wet leaves and twigs. "Give me a clue?"

The elfling didn't pause as his small legs carried him forward, around and around the winding trail up the mountain. Unlike me, he didn't make a sound as he traveled through the forest. "In due time," came his standard answer, and despite my good humor I wanted to fling a fireball at his butt.

A couple of strides later we reached the snowline. We seemed to be covering miles in just minutes, but I didn't know how fast we were running. I didn't even want to know.

And I really didn't want to fool with snow, either. I grew up a desert rat, and had never cared for the white stuff. I was already drenched and freezing my ass off and getting tired on top of everything. All I needed was snow. I scratched behind my ear and managed not to groan.

Something seemed to tug at the energy way down inside me, as if my magic had been tapped. I shook my head. That was dumb. Who would be draining off my powers way up here? Besides, it wasn't that much. Just a little. But, still . . .

The trees opened up around us and suddenly it was bright and sunny and for a moment I had to blink away the brilliance. I hadn't seen sunshine for what seemed like forever. It felt warm on my face, chasing away some of the chill, even with the snow-covered ground.

Acaw's crow-brother took flight, slowly circling us as he gave several short caws.

We rounded another bend in the path and jogged onto a flat, snowy mountaintop. But what caught my attention at once was the large, flat black stone wall right before us, directly in the middle of the clearing at the peak of the mountain. There was nothing on either side of the stone. It was just standing there, attached to nothing at all. Very weird.

Snow crunched beneath my boots as I slowed to a walk and circled the wall. As wide as a pair of double doors, as tall as a good-sized slither, but only as thick as my thigh.

"What is this?" I asked as I stopped and raised my palm to touch the pure black surface.

My hand was snatched away so fast I didn't even realize Acaw had moved up beside me. "Do not touch the sacred stone," he said in a low growl. His voice held the most emotion I'd ever heard from him and I couldn't help giving him a surprised look.

"What'd you do that for?" I jerked my hand from his grip.

"You are not prepared." He bent down beside his pack where he'd already taken out several items. I hadn't been paying attention to him at all while I'd been walking my circle around the stone, and I was surprised to see a cluster of candles, an incense burner, a jar of water, a bowl of salt, and a pair of stag horns at his feet.

"What's that stuff?" I started to touch the antlers, but Acaw slapped my hand away.

"You are not prepared," he said again, then handed me a bottle. "You must anoint yourself."

I raised one eyebrow. "Do what?"

He waved at the jar impatiently. "The oil. At your forehead, neck, and wrists."

I frowned as I opened the jar and brought it to my nose. "Roses? No way." I shook my head. "I'm not going to smell like a girl."

He was busy putting candles around the big black doorthing. A yellow candle to the east, red to the south, blue to the west, and green to the north. Each candle he lit with magic, by simply blowing on it.

"If you wish to save Her Highness, you will follow my directions exactly." He glanced up at the sun. "Almost midday. Hurry."

That tug happened again, the one down inside me, in my gut. A touch on my magic. A drawing-off of power, but larger this time.

The contact was familiar somehow.

I rubbed my stomach and closed my eyes—and in that second, I knew.

Jazz.

She was close somehow. And she was in serious trouble.

Urgency washed over me like a wave. I could feel Jazz's need for me, taste it, smell it—like she was right there in front of me and screaming.

"What do I do?" I shouted, shielding my eyes against the sun, spinning around like I might see her pop out of the woods at any second.

"Need . . . more." A voice as light as the breeze whispered past my ear. *"Help . . . open . . . break . . . through . . ."*

Then, even quieter but more insistent, *"Draw . . . down . . . sun."*

I no longer questioned anything Acaw had me do. A ritual. I preferred the sword to chanting and rhyming—but for Jazz, anything.

Magic rituals and I weren't the best of friends—too complicated, too boring. I usually just followed everyone else's lead, even though I could do them myself if I had to. This time, though, I didn't want to screw up any part. My unwilling guide had led me to the door in forgotten lands, I had wandered forever, and beaten the Guardian. I knew I had the old blood. This had to be the place, the time. I was ready.

And once I got through the door and to the other side, I was going after my girl.

Breathing hard, trying to focus, I snatched up the rose-scented stuff and smeared it everywhere Acaw told me to. I didn't even balk when he told me to put the antlers on. In the meantime, he poured water on a small flat stone, sprinkled salt on the rock next to it, and lit a white candle and incense that smelled like pine.

"Now," the voice whispered, more urgently. *"Now!"*

"Do you hear her?" My gaze cut to Acaw's. "Something's really wrong."

"Aye," he said as he handed me his staff. "Hear me. The living may not cross into the land of the dead and return. Do you understand?"

I clenched his staff in my fist. "I get it. If I cross over, I'm dead."

Acaw nodded. "Only the old blood may pass."

"What?" I cut him a look. "I thought my old blood let me defeat the Guardian. What does it have to do with this?"

For a second there, I thought I saw a look of concern or worry—but then he turned into the blank-faced monk again, and nothing more. Charms tinkled softly from the top of the wooden staff he had given me. He backed up to the treeline and his crow-brother flew down to land on his shoulder.

"What now?" I demanded as Jazz's voice became more urgent in my mind.

"Draw a circle around you and the door," Acaw said as he drew his own circle in the air.

In a big hurry, I dragged the point of the staff in the snow until it connected to where I'd started.

"Stand before the stone," Acaw instructed. This time his voice was quiet. Firm. Serious. "And draw down the sun. I can help you no more. The journey is yours from here."

I shot my gaze to where he'd been standing. But Acaw was gone. Freaking *gone.*

"Bren!" came Jazz's voice so loud it surrounded me.

"Damn." My body tensed. I kept hold of the staff, but shook out my arms, limbered up, and almost dislodged the stupid antlers from the top of my head.

Concentrate. Focus. Respond, don't react.

I clenched my fist and doubled my grip on the staff. Then I glanced up at the sky to see the sun directly overhead. Something made me reach my arms out, like I was embracing the warmth. It seeped into me. I could feel the sun as if it was drawn to me, as if it filled my entire body with heat and power—so much so that I shook with it.

My eyes opened and I lowered my gaze and looked directly at the black stone. The sun seemed to sink into it, too, and the surface shimmered, wavered . . . and I saw a reflection.

Oh.

Oh, jeez.

It wasn't mine. The reflection wasn't mine.

It was Jazz!

A real human form.

She stood just like I did, arms outstretched, but caressed in silvery moonlight instead of golden sunlight.

"Jazz," I whispered, and that ache of missing her welled up inside of me. "I'm here, baby. I've come to get you."

She moved her arms from her sides. The staff I had been holding dropped forward, against the black stone as I mimicked Jazz's motions, bringing my palms directly in front of me, to lay them flat against the stone.

Thunder rolled across the mountaintop.

My hands slipped into the rock as if it was air.

Flesh met flesh. Jazz's hands. I was touching her real, live hands!

Our fingers twined together within the dark stone and I felt her warmth, caught her scent of cinnamon and peaches.

In that instant, something sizzled through us, like when she'd given me her magic. I could see the silver and gold mesh and meld, moving between us, around us.

I saw Acaw's staff fall through the black wall and tumble onto dark ground on the other side.

I didn't stop to think about it. I started to pull Jazz to me.

A new smell clogged up my nose. This one rotten, like bad eggs or way dead animals on the side of the road. I tensed. Jazz leaned toward me, tried to fling herself into my arms. I wanted her to. I wanted to save her so badly, to make her alive again and hold her and tell her how much I needed to see her. The field inside the stone was so strong, though. It fought back each time I tried to tear her free.

From somewhere, seemingly a million miles away, women started singing. Acaw started chanting—almost like swearing. Did elflings swear? My mind felt fuzzy, like something was touching it.

From behind.

A laugh started, low, foul, and awful. The image of dripping blood filled my thoughts. On the other side of the stone, a bird shrieked, followed by a hideous, ear-pounding bawling.

"What the—" I tried to shut the images out of my mind. Clenching my jaw, I yanked twice as hard to pull Jazz out of the shimmering black stone.

Something jerked her head back.

She yelled and stumbled, still gripping my hands. At the same time, something shoved me from behind.

I heard another unearthly cry just as I tumbled forward. Fire seared every inch of my body, muscle to muscle, bone to bone. Melting. Frying. I was in the black wall. Something in my chest weighted me, tried to shove me backward—but then I was through. Shouting, clawing, fighting with all the strength I had left, I plunged into the land of the dead.

chapter seven

JAZZ

"No!" I screamed as Bren came hurtling through the doorway between the living world and the land of the dead. "You can't be here. You can't cross over!"

"Like I had a choice," he snarled as he leaped to his feet and the stag horns tumbled off his head. Only, as his image rose from the ground, it changed . . . into a large brown raptor. Some sort of hawk or eagle. His sword was clasped in his talons, but I could still see the outline of his human body. It shimmered around his winged form, anchored at his chest as if by a tether.

"Shit. I'm a bird." That was all he said, and all it took for my spirits to swell.

Goddess, Bren was here, no matter what form he took. I had been touching him, close to resting in his arms. Now he was in Talamadden in mortal peril. And he was a bird.

Harpy claws scored my cheek and neck. I ducked, swearing at the sudden pain. Egidus was doing battle with unearthly trills and screeches. All around us, the stench of decay, the horrid pounding of wings, and that sheep bleat of the deranged flying monsters drowned out all other sensations.

Bren's deep brown hawk eyes were sharp and focused as he assessed the situation. The sword in his talons lit the path and the grotto easily, as well as the air above us.

Quick as always in a battle, Bren lunged forward and used his beak to snatch up the staff that had fallen through the doorway. With a snap of his head, he tossed it to me. I could tell by the charms and carvings on the tip that it was of elfling construction, very old, very powerful. A wash of energy let me know who carved it. Who had threaded the magical charms through it. Acaw. My loyal, brave Acaw.

As I wielded the weapon to strike a harpy across the talons, Bren flapped upward, wheeling about like an expert flyer. He swiped at the closest beast with his sword, nicking off a wicked claw.

The creature reeled out of sight, bawling like a wounded baby.

Instantly, the rest of the flock swirled through the light of Bren's sword, moving upward just as fast, blatting in an eerily concerned fashion.

For a moment, the sickening calls sounded like words.

I held tight to the staff.

Wait a minute.

Those sounds *were* words. A name, cried over and over. Pleas for help and comfort from the injured harpy. And wailing, like the sobbing of a child. At that moment, the human-like faces of the beasts were quite disconcerting.

It was the staff. Acaw's staff must be giving me some of the elfling gift of translation! Well, crow-brothers were the translators, but an elfling's magic was intertwined with the energy of their familiars.

"They're—" I started, but didn't know how to finish. "I don't think we should hurt them anymore. They're pitiful."

"You *are* kidding, right?" Bren sounded incredulous and more than a little sarcastic. He finished the question with a hawk's shrill keening.

Before I could give him a proper comeback, Egidus reeled in for a landing. His black eyes glinted with horror when he saw Bren. "No. No. *You* were to go to *him*, girl!"

"I know that," I snapped. "A harpy jerked me back and I fell. Bren fell with me."

"Somebody pushed me," Bren grumbled, circling back, sword at the ready. "And who is that thing?"

As many times as I had dreamed of beheading the peacock and cooking him for a scant meal, I sighed. "This is Egidus, my spirit guide. Please don't behead him unless I ask you to."

Bren cut his hawk eyes toward the moonlit sky. Ominous harpy shadows circled high above, blotting out stars and calling to each other in that awful, pitiful way. "Fine. Can we get out of here now?"

"That would be advisable," Egidus agreed.

"What kind of name is Egidus, anyway?" Bren kept his eyes skyward as he flapped toward the stone. His shimmering human outline still waited there, tethered to him by a silver cord at the heart.

"It's Greek, thank you," said the blue bird. He sounded offended. "It means young goat, I believe."

Bren gave an eagle's screech. "That's stupid. You're a peacock."

Egidus blinked. Then he turned slowly to gaze at me. "You crossed the land of the dead to return to this?"

I shrugged, feeling a pleasant and unpleasant pounding in my chest. The shining outline of Bren on the other side of the obsidian rock looked as handsome and rugged as ever with his long hair—I knew it would be brown. And his skin would be tanned, and I thought I saw that stubble of a beard he always seemed to sport. His tunic and breeches fit better than ever, showing off the muscles he had added since I last saw him.

"He's more than he seems to be," I said quietly. "Usually kind. Loyal—well, unless he's enchanted by a golem; caring, unless he gets too angry; and—"

"Seems like a boor to me, but your choices are your own." The bird's tone was decidedly cool. "Hawks are bloodthirsty, you know. All brawn, low on brains."

"Hello?" Bren had reached the altar. "I want to go back where I'm not a bird. Jazz, you coming?"

Above us, a harpy screeched something about eating, and human, and hunger, and dinner. No time to waste.

I ran to Bren. He managed to keep himself aloft and clench his sword in one talon, but pointed it tip down as I took his other talon in my hand. Only, it felt like fingers. The sensation doubled the drumming of my heart. He was here beside me. Bren had come for me, to save me like some princess trapped in a tower—only he had risked the land of the dead—his own death, and the Goddess only knew what else.

Impulsive. Irresponsible.

When I knew him before I died, I might have said those words aloud. After Talamadden, the old words seemed just as wrong for him as they were for me. So, I thumped Acaw's staff and kept them to myself. I thought instead about the bravery. The brashness. The warmth of his bird form hovering and flapping next to me.

Together we faced the stone.

I was struck by a sense of wrongness, and realized the peacock hadn't joined us. "Egidus?" I leaned on the staff and looked back over my shoulder. "Are you coming?"

He ruffled his feathers and straightened his long blue neck. "This is not my path. It is your exit, your destiny. I regret that I cannot borrow it."

"What?" Bren hooked his talons around my hand and flapped his big wings, urging me forward. "Was that supposed to mean something?"

"He talks in riddles." I felt like I was defending the bird. *That* I couldn't believe, after all we had been through. I also couldn't believe how wrong it felt to just cross over and leave Egidus behind.

Bren's tugging on my hand grew stronger, as did the strong pumping of his wings. "Jazz . . ."

The harpy shadows dropped lower, filling the air with their rotten stench.

"Wait one moment." Egidus hurried forward to stand beside me. With a quick motion of his beak, he plucked one of his lovely iridescent feathers. I took it from him carefully when he offered it and gripped it against Acaw's staff. "Do me a kindness and give this to your mother. Tell her who sent it. And tell her—tell her love is never wrong."

"Love is never wrong," I repeated underneath the thump and thunder of harpy wings.

"Go now," the bird urged.

"We're going," Bren said. This time he tugged my hand so hard I fell forward with him into the stone. Into the blackness.

—ShadowsdearGoddessnoShadowspleasenoShadows—

Even as my fears rushed through my mind, I smelled them. Shadows. Fetid. Real. Pulling. Clawing. Trying to tear Bren away from me. I couldn't see him. Couldn't feel fingers or talons or feathers. Only nothing. Coldness.

I shouted, but made no sound. My grasping fingers felt something, a chain—a metal chain with a stone at the end. I closed my hand tight around the stone and pulled with every fiber of my being.

Let the peacock be right. Let there be one miracle left for the Corey family.

For Bren was my family. I would not lose him to the Shadows! Hauling on that precious stone, I yanked Bren to me and held on to him. He felt fully human now, pressed against me, hugging me back. I gripped his shoulders, gripped the bird feather and Acaw's staff with all my strength. I couldn't breathe. Couldn't think of what to do. Why didn't Bren raise his sword and slay the Shadows? Were we flying or sliding? I couldn't tell in the rancid darkness.

Out. I needed air. I needed land. Shadows everywhere, flailing me. Sapping me. Trying to steal what I couldn't stand to lose a second time.

Death, the wicked creatures chanted. *He belongs to us now. He belongs in the land of the dead.*

No! I made some noise this time, if only in my head. *You can't have him. You won't rip us apart a second time!*

Bren's arms locked tighter around me. I buried my face against him, letting his scent, his strength, his energy push the Shadows away.

Slimy, horrid fingers on my ankle and foot. Grabbing at my legs.

No!

We tumbled out of night into noon sun so fast the light blinded me. I coughed and choked as we struck hard, rocky earth. The staff and the peacock feather flew out of my hand as I rolled away from the still-shimmering Glorieuse.

Bren. Where was Bren?

I tried to stand up and fell. Fresh, sharp pain flared in my hip and elbow. The pains I knew in Talamadden were real enough, but this—ah. No muting. Completely real and so very, very alive.

"Easy," said a familiar elfling voice. "Give yourself a moment to regain balance, both within and without."

"Acaw?" I couldn't believe my own ears. This was too good to be true.

The tip of his staff met my throbbing hip and I felt a flash of magical warmth. The pain eased immediately. Next came my elbow, healed in the briefest of moments, and then the gashes on my cheek and neck.

"Could you give me a little of that, short guy?" Bren's voice came from behind me.

I rolled over, got to my knees, then stood slowly as Acaw ministered to Bren's bumps and bruises. Bren was human again, with no trace of the hawk except in those bright brown eyes. I could see them shining toward me as Acaw worked. The elfling had my peacock feather tucked into his waistband, and it was nearly taller than he was.

To see them both in front of me—it felt like a dream. Wonderful and fascinating. I noticed details, like the cut of Bren's tunic, the deep lines etched into Acaw's weathered face, the way the sun bounced off the crow-brother's blacker-than-black feathers.

We were on a mountaintop beneath a clear blue sky, some time after noon.

In the world of the living.

Acaw looked as stunned as I felt, but the look passed quickly.

"I'm—I'm alive." I shook my head. "I'm really alive!"

Bren got to his feet a few paces away and slowly sheathed his sword. "Me, too, and I shouldn't be. I crossed over. Though I think I had a little help."

"Only the old blood may pass." Acaw shrugged. "Your physical body remained in the stone, but your essence moved through. None but a halfblood with such ancient strength would have survived that journey."

"Was the Erlking here?" Bren's voice was deadly serious as he spoke to the elfling. In that one question, I heard the force of months as a ruler.

Acaw gave a stiff nod. "Aye. Him and his. I did what I could to drive him back, but I feared it was too late to save you."

"The Erlking." I shivered. "I had hoped never to meet him in all my days. You had to best him to get this far, did you not?"

Bren nodded as he rubbed his fingers behind his ear. His expression was a mixture of rage and determination, but as he gazed at me, my champion's sharp brown eyes went soft.

Acaw, wise as ever, stepped out of the way.

Bren approached me carefully, and I loved the way the sun gave his hair a rich, sparkling sheen. He had been a splendid hawk, but I rather liked him as a boy again. Well . . . to truth, more man than boy. That thought made me shiver again, but this time not from fear.

Was Bren going to hug me? Kiss me? I didn't know. I wanted both. Didn't care which. I just wanted to touch him.

My heart gave a leap as Bren swept me into his embrace. He pressed his stubbled cheek to mine, and for a long few moments, we simply stood together on the mountaintop and held one another tight.

"You can't know how much I've missed you," he said, his voice low in my ear. "I can't believe you're here. I can't believe you're real."

Warm shivers gripped me, then turned me loose. "I missed you, too."

My throat tightened, and tears gathered in my eyes. Where were all my wonderful words? All those things I longed to tell him? I had gone mute that fast after lamely echoing what he said to me. What kind of a greeting was that?

Bren was quiet, too. Unusually so, for him. When he pulled back to gaze into my eyes, I saw the same weight of emotion I was feeling, the same loss of words. At least I wasn't alone in my wordless state.

As if following a silent command, we moved our heads at the same moment, pressing our lips together. The awkwardness I had felt so long ago was gone. This was blissful. This was right. His kiss was so soft, but firm at the same time. He smelled like leather and rose oil, and underneath that—

I broke the kiss and pushed him back, mouth agape. "A woman's magic?"

"What?" Bren looked genuinely confused.

"Who touched you? When?" My belly twisted into knots. How could he? Where was she, anyway? Hidden down the trail in some cave or tree? "Her mark runs through you like a river!"

"I'm not following you." Bren was such an excellent actor. He sounded oh-so-convincing, but I couldn't deny what I had sensed. The unmistakable magical signature of another woman, deep in his essence. And he smelled of roses! The thought of any female other than me getting that close to him, literally under his skin—inside his very energy—I would kill him. I honestly thought I might.

"Who . . . is . . . she?" I asked through clenched teeth.

Acaw seemed to materialize from the forest floor, the tip of my peacock feather hovering over his head like a small blue halo. The elfling hurried forward and tapped Bren's elbow with his staff.

Bren leaned down, and Acaw whispered something in his ear. That fast, the elfling was gone again, back to wherever it was elflings disappeared to.

Smiling, Bren straightened back up. "You've got it wrong, Jazz. It was nothing. I mean, not what you think."

I glared at his sword and wondered if I could spell it to me before he stopped my magic.

He grabbed the hilt like he read my mind. "It was just the Erlking's daughter. One of the enchantresses we had to get past on our way up here. She—"

"An enchantress?" Now my blood reached boiling point. I pointed my fingers at the nearest rock and sent my will crackling outward. Goddess, it felt good to cast a proper spell again.

Except nothing happened.

"An enchantress!" This time I fired as I shouted.

More nothing happened.

"Is—um, something wrong with your magic, Your Highness?"

The laughter in Bren's tone made me want to slap him until his eyes crossed. "No! I mean, yes. I don't know. I had none in Talamadden because I had given it to you. I thought when I escaped, it would . . . er, come back to me?"

The fact that it hadn't bothered me to no end, especially because I couldn't turn the faithless bastard into a mouse-sized version of a reeking, squalling harpy.

Bren pointed at the nearest rock. "Allow me."

Again, nothing happened. Rock-boy looked at his fingers like they might be broken and tried again.

"Is something wrong with *your* magic, Your Highness?" I quipped. Couldn't help it. Bren still had the ability to make me angrier than any living creature.

His look was one of genuine distress. When he wheeled on me, his teeth were clenched. "Look, you ungrateful witch. You have no idea what I went through to find you. I've been walking—no, running—for days. And I fought the Erlking and beat him—that girl you think I cheated with, I don't even know which of the six it was who healed me, but she had to because I won, okay? I wasn't even conscious."

He turned away again, aimed his fingers at a small rock, and grunted. Nothing. Not even a crackle.

A slow river of guilt trickled from my brain to my heart. Bren's story made sense. I had never dealt with the Erlking or his famed wicked daughters, but I knew what the legends said. The Erlking was of the older oldeFolke. Wily, powerful, deceptive—and rumored to be a ruthless, vengeful fighter.

As I opened my mouth to apologize, he whirled back toward me and shouted, "What did you do to me?"

This caught me by surprise. "Pardon?"

"My magic was fine before you yanked me through that stupid black wall. And it was fine when I was fighting those smelly things you didn't want to hurt. Then you get mad, and poof, all my magic's gone. What did you do?"

"Nothing!"

"I swear, Jazz—"

He took a step toward me and instinct took over. I slapped him hard across the cheek, wishing I could blow up every rock on the mountaintop just to rain pebbles on his donkey-thick skull.

The second my fingers touched his flesh, the mountain seemed to shake. Tiny explosions went off in every direction, joining to make one chest-punching thunderclap.

Every rock on the mountaintop had blown up after all.

Bren and I stood there blinking at each other as tiny pebbles and rock dust tumbled over every inch of us.

"Were you—ah—thinking about the rocks, Jazz?" Bren sneezed and wiped his nose on his shirt sleeve.

"Yes," I admitted.

"Yeah, well." He sneezed again. "So was I."

"Oh." I looked down at my hand, which was still stinging from where I slapped him. "Oooooh. Bren." A desperate misery overcame me then. "I'm afraid we have a major problem."

chapter eight

BREN

By the look on Jazz's face, I knew something had to be wrong. Very wrong. And it had nothing to do with enchantresses or the Erlking.

"What?" I said, not sure I wanted to hear the answer.

Jazz cleared her throat. "I believe—I believe that somehow our powers are bound together . . . since I'm out of Talamadden now, back in the land of the living, we can't perform magic without one another."

I just stood there and looked at her, trying to digest what she said. My words came out slow. Measured. "I have no magic without you. And you have no magic without me."

Jazz nodded, looking apologetic and angry at the same time. "I'm afraid we're going to have to work together to perform any kind of magic. At least for now, until we figure out a way to get our own powers back."

Frustration boiled up inside me and I wanted to pound something, anything. "Well, that's just freaking great." I kicked at one of the larger stones that had rained down around us. Then a thought occurred to me. "Maybe you're wrong."

I turned away from Jazz and focused hard on a spot in the snow, trying to conjure up a slither. Not a real one, but one that would look real enough to scare the crap out of someone. I focused . . . focused . . .

Nothing.

I narrowed my eyes and concentrated so hard my head ached.

Nothing, dammit! Nothing happened!

I cut my gaze back to Jazz. "Try it with me. This time think about the image of a slither."

She took my hand and we both stared at the same spot. Within seconds the air shimmered. Silver and gold flowed between Jazz and me.

A huge red slither appeared and flapped its massive wings. Snow spun and swirled in the gust it caused, and I felt the heat of its breath.

Jazz and I looked at each other.

The slither image vanished.

"No." I shook my head. "I still don't believe it."

I pulled my hand away from Jazz's. I drew my sword and held it high. "Stop!" I shouted, ordering all noise, all motion to come to a complete halt.

Just like before, nothing happened.

I clenched my fists and looked at Jazz. "You try."

Jazz raised her chin and said in her loudest, most queenliest voice, "Cease!"

Birds still chirped and trees swayed in the breeze. Acaw was studying us with his impassive features, the charms on his staff making a soft tinkling sound when he moved his arm. The silly peacock feather lightly bobbed above his head. Acaw's crow-brother gave us an irritated blink.

Jazz and I looked at each other. We grabbed hands and at the same time I shouted "Stop!" and Jazz called out "Cease!"

Everything, absolutely everything stopped moving, but Jazz and me. The softness of her breathing was the only sound I heard, and her glance around us the only movement. I lifted my face and saw the clouds had halted against the blue-green sky. When I turned my gaze to Acaw, he looked like a garden statue, and his crow-brother was frozen in mid feather-ruffle.

"Oh, shit." I dropped her hand and rubbed my face, the stubble scraping my palm. "We're in deep." Anger snapped through me and I glared at Jazz. "What did you do to us?"

She returned my glare. "Obviously something happened when we crossed over together. Maybe when your *ba* essence was still pulled apart from your *ka.* If you hadn't come into Talamadden, I'm certain this wouldn't have happened."

"So you're saying it's my fault." My anger swelled higher. "You ungrateful . . ." I started to continue when I noticed Jazz rubbing her arm where the Shadows had dug into her, and eventually killed her and sent her to Talamadden. A long, thick, pink scar was there, almost matching the one on my cheek.

The memory of her dying, of her being taken away from me, ripped through my gut, opening my heart, draining my anger. How could I be mad about anything right now? I had Jazz back. I really had her back.

She stopped rubbing her arm and gazed at me. The lines of her face relaxed. "I'm sorry," she whispered. "I was wrong to speak so sharply. You did an amazing thing, opening the gateway from the living side, sending an aspect of your spirit through to defend me like that. You risked so much, just to save me."

Jazz? Apologizing? Admitting she was wrong?

Amazing.

She seemed so real and vulnerable, so much . . . *softer.*

I stepped close to her and she looked like she wasn't even breathing. I cupped her face in my hands and looked down at her beautiful features. Her golden eyes, her long black hair. She felt warm in my hands and I brushed one thumb across her cheek as I brought my face closer to hers. "I missed you," was all I could think to say, but she smiled.

"I missed you, too." Her words were just a whisper, but I could feel the warmth of her breath.

I kissed her then, hard. Still not believing she was real, not believing she was truly there. I slid my hands down her shoulders to her waist and brought her closer to me as we kissed. She *felt* real. Warm. Solid. *Real.*

I realized then that our magic was melding, moving between us and around us. Silver twined with gold, and so strong I felt as if I could hold my hand out and grasp it.

When I raised my head, and we pulled away from one another, our magic continued to flow between us in a silvery gold ball of light. I reached out to touch it, but it faded away, seeping into each of us. Connecting us.

I couldn't help giving her a crooked smile. "At least we make good magic together."

She smiled back. "That's one way to think about it."

I took her hand in mine and gripped it tight. "Come on. It's time to go home."

After we undid our ceasing spell, Acaw led us back down the endless mountain. The peacock feather bobbed above his head like a piece of seaweed on the ocean. Kind of a silly way to carry a peacock feather, if you ask me, but whatever worked for him. The elfling seemed nervous as we entered the main section of the Erlking's realm and started back toward the Path.

I was none too happy about that, either. The sound of the Erlking's laughter, the feel of his gnarled hand on my back as he shoved me into the land of the dead, the way blood dripped from his nasty fingertips as he pawed through my memories . . . If the son of a bitch dared show his ugly shapeshifting face around me again, I'd probably cut off his head.

Somehow I sensed I would have my chance.

"He frightens you," Jazz said quietly. She took my hand in hers, and I gave her fingers a squeeze as I nodded.

The old me would have yelled about being scared of nothing, but the Erlking made my skin crawl. I remembered how Rol had reacted, and now I understood.

From somewhere in the back of my mind, the bastard chuckled.

I grimaced. "Feels like he's living in my head now. Some piece of him at least."

Jazz's hand felt so warm in mine. "My father said something like that once. He had to come here a long time ago, when I was little. The Erlking sent word to him, a protest, because Nire's Shadows had invaded his realm. Father described his laugh—" She broke off, shuddering.

My sword had never felt so good against my leg. "If he shows up, I'll handle him. Trust me."

Jazz's golden eyes lit up as she looked at me. "I do."

The walk didn't seem as long or as difficult now that Jazz was with us. I couldn't believe she was really next to me, and that she was alive again.

"This place seems . . . questionable," she murmured as we passed through a particularly dark, thick stretch of woods several days into the trek.

"Yeah. No kidding." On this wide section of path, I walked shoulder to shoulder with her, not wanting her too open to sudden attack from the trees. We hadn't seen that bastard of an Erlking, but I swear, I felt his nastiness skulking around—or I imagined I did. I glanced at Jazz. "Nothing here is what it seems. Even the beautiful stuff—well, you know. You have to be careful."

Jazz gave me a quirky, surprised sort of smile. I couldn't tell, but she looked—I don't know. Proud, maybe.

Later, I kept her between me and Acaw as we walked single file down the narrow, tree-crowded path. I took up the rear, sword in hand, because I was going to make sure that nothing hurt her again. To my surprise, Jazz didn't argue with this. She didn't even make smart remarks or try to joke about my decision. Instead, she flexed her hands as if to keep herself ready.

She's letting me take the lead. She's letting me protect her.

The feeling was enough to swell my head.

At night, when we made camp, Jazz and I experimented with joining our magic, practicing strategies until we could do simple spells without touching, so long as we were near each other to draw the energy we needed. Major spells were a lot harder, and lots of times, we had to have physical contact to make them work. That was just fine with me. I made a point to keep Jazz close, especially when she slept. Acaw's crow-brother was on constant lookout, too, and I wondered if he even slept. He stayed close by, as if concerned about Jazz's welfare. Maybe even mine. We were a jumpy little group—but we were making progress.

The next morning, I woke with that itch behind my ear again. Maybe I really did have fleas. When I got back to L.O.S.T., I planned to take a very long, very hot bath, and if I had to, I'd see the oldeFolke about some sort of powder to remove forgotten-lands-cooties. There had to be something.

As I finished scratching, my attention turned to where Jazz had bedded down for the night. She was there in the clearing, sitting on her knees, gazing at pine needles and grass, absently running her fingers across the drops of dew glistening in the early morning sun.

She was so beautiful like that, all distracted, her long hair flowing down her back and her golden eyes distant and misty. I got up quietly, so as not to disturb Acaw, who was actually snoring for a second. Even his crow-brother had his crow eyes closed for once.

It only took me a few steps to reach the miracle that was Jazz on her knees in a clearing in the land of the living, breathing, smiling—real. Right there, beside me again.

I knelt next to her. "Good morning."

She looked at me and smiled, holding up her damp fingers. When she touched them to the scar along my cheek, they were cool.

"It feels so good to be cold." She giggled. I mean really—Jasmina Corey actually giggled. "To touch soft, wet forest grass, tough pine needles." Another smile, this one bigger as she stroked my morning stubble. "Even your rough beard."

"Almost beard." I grinned and took her hand.

Her face—she looked so thrilled just to be alive. I think she was appreciating life in a way she never had before. Man, if I had died, I would probably feel the same way, especially after what she told me about Talamadden and the harpies and stuff. Just the thought of what she'd gone through made my flesh crawl. My five minutes with separate body and soul—that was nothing.

We got underway not long afterwards, the three of us walking and talking, getting a little more relaxed as we went. I toyed with the moonstone around my neck, appreciating it for stopping that arrow—and I think it helped hold me together when I passed in and out of Talamadden. Sherise was due a major thank-you from me once we got home.

The Path and L.O.S.T were drawing closer and closer, and the day seemed brighter than ever. The only hitch was having to use our magic together. That was frustrating every time I tried to do something I was used to doing alone and had to ask her to help me. Still, I tried not to get pissed off about it. Jazz said we'd figure something out. I hoped she was right.

As the morning passed slowly around us, I caught up to Jazz on a narrow section of trail and held her hand. "I can't wait to get you home. Your mom and Rol—are they ever going to be glad to see you. And you—just wait until you see how much L.O.S.T. has grown. It's unreal."

Jazz smiled, but the radiance faded fast. She looked distant for a second or two. Her fingers even went slack in my hand.

"What is it?" I glanced left and right, but I didn't see anything out of the ordinary.

At first, Jazz only shrugged. Then she opened her mouth and closed it. Finally, she said, "It's nothing. I'm just—nervous. About seeing everyone and everything."

This sounded reasonable enough, but my gut twisted in a bad way. I studied her face for a few paces, then let go of her hand and dropped back. She didn't try to stop me.

If I wasn't imagining things, she seemed more tense now, like the old, uptight Jazz. Was the pressure of being queen already getting to her again before we even made it to the Path? I didn't get that. I mean, I would be there to help her, and my dad, her mom, Rol—lots of witches. And Nire was gone, so . . . Once more, I stared at the tight, hurried way she was walking.

Was she hiding something?

No way. Why would she do that? Yet that same twist in my gut relaxed a little as if to say, yeah, king-boy. That's the ticket. She's up to her old tricks, keeping something major to herself.

Before she died, I would have confronted her, demanded that she spill it right now or else. Now, I didn't know. People who had been to the land of the dead and made it out—maybe they should be allowed a few secrets. At least for a while.

So, for the time being, I brushed those thoughts aside and concentrated on how happy Rol and Dame Corey would be to see Jazz. Man, was everyone going to be shocked to see her alive again. They had doubted me, but I'd proved them wrong.

About an hour after we stopped for lunch, we finally reached fairyland, and I was able to walk side-by-side with Jazz and hold her hand in that place without worrying. It was so bright, so peaceful—and I had a sense it was truly safe. I could concentrate on other things, like how much I really liked Jazz's small fingers in mine. It made me feel good. Made me feel like a king.

Oh, yeah. I was a king. But now a king without his magic—sort of. But a king with his queen.

That thought made me smile, then frown. We loved each other, but we were too young to get married. I didn't *even* want to think about that.

In fairyland, Jazz stared in amazement at the sun-filled place overflowing with brightly colored flowers and exotic vegetation. Stuff I'd never seen before our first trip through here. Not to mention the dwarves and the playful, tiny fairies.

"Where are we?" Jazz asked, her golden eyes wide. For a witch who always seemed to know everything before she had gone to Talamadden, I was amazed she didn't know about this place, too.

"The Sacred Lands, Your Majesty," Acaw said before I could answer.

Jazz nodded, as if with understanding. "The mythic home of the small folk."

I scratched my probably-fleas and glared at Acaw's back for giving Jazz information he hadn't given to me. Just like the twerp to play favorites.

When we reached the round door, Jazz stopped and stared at it. "This is an entrance to the Path?"

"Yeah." I tugged her hand. "Come on."

She remained stock still, her face growing whiter by the second. "Shadows," she whispered. "The Shadows—I can't."

It dawned on me that she was afraid of the things that had killed her. I put my arm around her shoulders and gave her a light squeeze. "It's all right. They're gone. Todd and me, we cleaned this puppy out."

I felt her release of breath, and some of the color returned to her cheeks. She straightened her shoulders. "Of course you would have."

Acaw reached for the door, but Jazz held up her hand to halt him. "Wait." She turned to me. "There's something I have to tell you."

By the sound of her voice, I could tell it was serious. "Okay. Shoot."

She visibly took a deep breath. "You brought a new witch into L.O.S.T. not long ago. Her name is Sherise, and she's a spy sent by Alderon."

"Sherise?" I shook my head as my hand automatically reached for the moonstone tucked beneath my tunic. "No way. I can't believe—"

"Believe it," Jazz snapped, her golden eyes lit with that fire that usually either pissed me off, or made me want to kiss her just to shut her up. "In Talamadden, Egidus showed me a vision of her and Alderon. And of Alderon giving her a golem."

I let go of the stone in a hurry. The mere thought of a golem in L.O.S.T. made my blood run cold. My scalp prickled and a wave of cold heat washed through me. "All this time there's been a golem in L.O.S.T. and you're just now telling me?"

"I didn't want to worry you until we got close enough to do something about it." She glanced at Acaw and then me. "We couldn't have reached L.O.S.T. any faster if you did know."

"You had no right holding back information from me." I whirled and pounded on the round door with my fist. The damn thing didn't open. "I'm as much king as you are queen."

Even though I still couldn't get the friggin' door to open.

"Allow me, Your Majesty." Acaw eased in front of me and tapped on the door with his staff. The wooden door swung wide and silver light spilled out of the opening. Those fresh smells enveloped us, and I realized they matched the scents of the Sacred Lands. I felt a surge of elation, an urge to jump through the opening and run down the Path. Freedom. At last. I was getting out of this place!

But at the same time, my chest was tight with anger. Was there really a golem in L.O.S.T.?

Beside us, Jazz had her arms folded across her chest like she was cold—and still afraid.

My anger and my weird elation died as fast as it came. I was such an idiot. I unclenched my fists and took her hand. "Sorry," I mumbled, and squeezed her fingers. "Let's get home and make sure nothing's happened. We can clear up this whole thing about Sherise once we get back."

Jazz nodded and followed me onto the Path. She jumped when the little door slammed shut behind us. The door disappeared again, like it had never been there at all. Once more, I felt that rush of over-the-top joy. A big part of me hoped I would never, ever see that place again.

I put Jazz in front of me so that I was following her down the narrow Path, but she kept a tight grip on my hand—so tight it almost hurt.

"You did it." She stumbled a little, like she wasn't used to the moving floor, and I helped steady her. "You restored the Path to its former glory."

Her face didn't seem so pale in the silvery light, and I felt a little swell of pride. "Yeah, me and Todd really worked to clean it up."

"Impressive," she said, and I smiled.

"Come," Acaw's voice was urgent, and I realized he was a ways ahead of us now.

Both Jazz and I practically ran down the Path after him now. The realization of what could be happening in L.O.S.T.

balled in my gut like a fist. I couldn't and wouldn't regret going after Jazz. All I could do now was make right whatever could be wrong, if anything. As for Sherise, her moonstone had saved my life once, maybe twice. No way would I believe she brought a golem into L.O.S.T. unless I saw it with my own eyes.

When we reached the door to L.O.S.T., I tried to open a slit with the point of my sword, but nothing happened. It was like the very first time I'd tried to open a doorway onto the Path, and my sword had just slid down the rubbery skin and hadn't worked.

Jazz looked at me, then tried her hand at it, literally, by running her finger down the doorway. It stayed closed.

"We'll have to do it together," Jazz said in an irritated tone.

"How?" The frustration in my voice matched hers.

"Work in harmony." Acaw waved impatiently with his staff, then glanced over his shoulder. If I wasn't mistaken, he was actually sniffing the air of the Path behind us. "You must hurry."

Jazz and I looked at one another. It was never a good thing when an elfling told anyone to hurry. That much I'd figured out, for sure.

Was it getting darker? But, no. That couldn't be. Still, it seemed like the silver of the Path walls was slowly turning a pale gray.

Both frowning, Jazz and I grasped hands. We turned our gazes to the doorway. I put my sword point to the wall, and she pressed her finger into the spongy material next to it. I was careful to not get my blade too close to her hand as we slowly slid an opening into the dimming silver.

Immediately, familiar odors filled my nose. The smell of modern-day pollution, the incense and herbs sold in the store we were about to enter. But then there was a stench that didn't belong. A stench of filth and dead things.

The doorway fully opened and we both went completely still.

The store was a disaster. Bolts of cloth were unrolled down the pathways, herbs and broken potion bottles scattered across the floor. Baskets of dead spiders and dried newts were upside down.

But what was worse was the screaming and shouts we heard coming from outside the wrecked store.

Jazz and I bolted through the opening of the Path and then came up short, like our minds were one. We turned in tandem, grabbed hands, and sealed the Path behind Acaw. For a second, my head ached, like a spike punched into my left eye. I let out a shout, let go of Jazz, and pressed my hand to the spot. Then quick as it came, the pain was gone.

"Bren?" Jazz sounded way past urgent.

"Yeah. Coming." I grabbed her hand again and we stumbled through the mess of a store to the chaos outside.

Giant harpy things—way bigger than the ones I'd seen in Talamadden—were swooping down on the oldeFolke and witches. Huge talons popped out of their hairy arms right above their human-looking hands, and their twisted, filthy human faces were so ugly they hurt my eyes. The beasts' unearthly screeches made me want to clamp my hands over my ears and caused chills to run down my spine.

I dropped Jazz's hand and shouted "Stop!" as I charged into the melee, waving my sword.

The only thing that happened was that I caught the attention of the biggest harpy of all. It swooped down at me, its ugly face twisted with fury. I braced myself and readied my sword. A touch of silver glinted from the blade, but my power felt drained. For the first time in a long time, fear climbed my spine.

The harpy dove at me, screeching. I ducked, but its talons scraped the scar on my face, drawing blood. Pain and fury drove me to swing my sword at the beast, but I missed as it swept back up into the sky.

I glanced over my shoulder, looking for Jazz to grab her hand and cast our ceasing spell together. She wasn't there.

Not too far away I saw Rol shooting golden arrows from his head. They flew all around the harpies, but few made contact. The hits didn't seem to do much damage, either. Acaw fought with his dagger and big fork. Where did he get a fork? Did I want to know?

I didn't see Todd anywhere, though. And Jazz—

She was holding Acaw's staff and shouting something in a strange language as she dodged one of the harpies. The thing screeched back at her, like it was talking to her.

At that second, Todd came charging into view, waving the sword Rol made for him. I felt a flash of panic—he'd been getting the hang of using the weapon, but I didn't think he was ready for a battle like this.

"Get back!" I shouted, but nobody could hear over all that madness.

Dad and Sherise were right behind him, along with what looked like dozens of slithers. My little brother was bringing an army of creatures to fight. I was about to give a whoop of triumph when a harpy virtually fell out of the sky and raked a massive claw right across Todd's chest. The cut seemed to tear him in half.

I heard Todd shout just as his sword flew out of his hand.

He went down hard.

Dad lunged forward and threw himself over Todd, shielding him as best he could. The slithers trumpeted furiously and bore down on the attacking harpy. Sherise actually snatched up Todd's sword and swung it at the beast, trying to drive it back.

Anguish tore through me like a hot knife. No way could Todd have survived that attack. I ran forward just as a skin-stripping shriek sounded behind me. I whirled around to see the huge harpy again, this time diving straight for me, fast as any rocket.

I raised my sword, but too late. The harpy tore my weapon from my grip, almost taking my hand with it. Pain screamed through me and blood spurted. My hand was covered in red. It poured down my arm until I lowered it, and then started dripping on the ground. The burning throb was so great I almost dropped to my knees.

Someone grabbed my right hand as I cradled my sword arm against my chest. I whipped my head around and saw it was Jazz.

"Together!" she shouted. "Now!"

My teeth chattered from the sudden cold that slid through my body. I squeezed her hand and at the same time I yelled "Stop!" and she shouted "Cease!"

The spell worked in a big way.

Acaw froze in mid-movement, and his crow-brother in flight. Witches, hags, elflings, and other oldeFolke looked like stone statues, either running away or fighting. Rol had a bolt of yellow light hanging over his head, and I saw sparks at the end of Dame Corey's fingertips. My dad and Todd—I didn't see them anywhere. Or Sherise.

OldeTowne was a complete mess. Cauldrons had been spilled and cook fires doused, leaving frozen spirals of smoke in the air. Caved-in roofs marked at least a third of the huts. Walls had been torn apart. Wounded witches and oldeFolke lay everywhere.

Not dead, I prayed. *Don't let Todd be dead. Don't let anyone be dead.*

Even those ugly harpy things dangled in the air as if suspended from invisible ropes attached to the sky. They were more hideous when I was able to take a good look at them. The one holding my sword was so close, gripping my weapon. The bastard had been about to run me through with my own blade.

This time I did fall to my knees in exhaustion and pain. My hand. My sword hand hurt so badly. Pain—pain like I'd never felt before. I smelled blood, my own blood, mingled with harpy stink, smoke, and other odors from all the destruction.

Jazz knelt beside me, sounding out of breath. She was holding Acaw's staff in one hand, and her other still gripped mine.

"The harpies," she said, her eyes lit with some kind of knowledge, like a light bulb had appeared over her head. "I tried to talk to them. I think we could try to communicate—"

Her gaze dropped to where I held my arm to my chest. "Oh, Goddess, you're bleeding."

"No kidding." I ground my teeth. My fingers. My fingers hurt so badly.

"Let me see." She released my other hand and moved in front of me.

I didn't want to move. My fingers, my hand, my whole arm—on fire. My gut heaved from the pressure of the air on my skin, but I held my hand out. Dark spots flashed in front of my eyes. It couldn't be. No way. I could feel them. The pain—I felt it in all my fingers, all the way up my arm.

But they weren't there.

All I saw on my left hand, my sword hand, was my pinky, my index finger, and my thumb.

And two bloody stumps in between.

chapter nine

JAZZ

Blood seemed to be everywhere all at once. My heart hammered. "Bren. Look at me. Think with me. We have to slow the blood flow."

Pale, with teeth clenched—he was shaking violently. Could he hear me? He swore once, twice, then met my eyes. The misery I saw in his face tore at my heart. I placed Acaw's staff on the ground by his side, hoping the ancient elfling-crafted wood might lend him some strength.

Together, we murmured a spell of basic healing. Gold and silver energy flowed between us, then over Bren's maimed hand. He grunted, then swore more as the light sizzled and crackled over the stumps where his missing fingers should have been. The bleeding slowed to a trickle, then gradually stopped. The magic was no more than a bandage. He needed true healing, deep healing, time, safety—none of which I could grant him at the moment.

The strain of the ceasing spell began to pull at both of us, and Bren sagged backward in my arms. I couldn't hold him up, so I eased him down on the blood-soaked grass. Even his face was covered in blood where his scar had been re-opened. His eyes fluttered and closed.

The spell—the battle—what could I do? Would the magic fail when I stepped away from him, even though we'd practiced doing some magic apart? Bren would be a helpless target . . .

Slowly, carefully, I broke contact with Bren enough to stand. I couldn't seem to take my eyes off his chest, watching it move up and down, up and down. He was wounded, but not dead.

Not dead. Not dead. Not dead.

The devastation around me was unimaginable. I had no idea who had been slain, who was alive, or who could be saved. Tears washed down my face as I bent down, grabbed Acaw's staff, and risked moving a few steps away from Bren. I still felt his magic, his power, mingling with mine.

The spell held. Thank the Goddess. I had to think. What—how—there had to be—

Gripping the staff, I drew from its innate power and stared at the ribbons of energy connecting Bren to me, and an idea formed. Biting my lip, letting the pain focus my will, I teased a little of my gold from his silver. The gold didn't want to cooperate, but I narrowed my eyes and forced it into compliance. Bit by bit, I moved the strand out, out, toward the solid form of Rol.

My knees started to give. The effort of so many spells when I had been so long without magic, without practice or training . . .

Grinding my teeth, I refused any negative thoughts. The gold light wavered, then snaked toward Rol, wrapping around his feet.

The moment it touched him, he roused from his motionless state. The arrow he had been firing flew and struck its mark. A small hole opened in the head of one of the smaller harpies. I winced, wanted to shout—but it was too late to take back my actions.

Rol whirled and stared at me. Awe filled his handsome ebony face. He seemed caught between the urge to run to me smiling and the reality of our grave situation.

Without comment, I flicked Acaw's staff and moved the gold rope of energy away from Rol and snaked it toward the woman beside him. My mother. I needed help, and she was the strongest witch I knew outside of Rol and Bren.

Mother woke much as Rol did. Her gaze flew from the energy to me. "Goddess," she whispered. "Goddess be praised! Jasmina, I—"

Her gaze cut from Bren to Rol, and finally to the scene around her. I saw her tamp down her amazement at my return, and I felt grateful. For now, we had no time for emotional reunions.

"Kill the beasts," Mother said to Rol. "Make sure they—"

"No!" My shout stabbed through the unnatural silence like one of Bren's sword strikes. "Do not hurt them. Bind them so that I can release the spell, but harm none."

"Jasmina—" my mother began.

"Do as I say," I said firmly but as gently as I could, given the circumstance. My confidence didn't waver for a moment even though it was my mother at the challenge. "I haven't the energy to hold these spells and explain myself to you."

With a look of absolute surprise, my mother closed her mouth. Rol responded by stalking over to the harpy that had attacked Bren and ripping the sword from the beast's sharp claws. He cleaned the blade on his breeches, then carried it to Bren's side, where he placed it on the ground with care.

When Rol looked up at me, his eyes were bright with worry and other emotions I couldn't identify. Yet he was Rol. My wonderful Rol. I wanted to throw my arms around his neck, but there simply wasn't time. Of course, Rol understood this. He gave me a short but deep, respectful bow. Then, wordless, he returned to my mother and they proceeded with the tedious process of wrapping the harpies in bindings of magic that would hold indefinitely. They were careful to loop their feet and pull them to the ground so they wouldn't simply fall out of the sky.

It took so long, seemingly forever. Goddess. I sagged against Acaw's staff, praying for the strength to stay upright. I didn't think I could hold on much longer. The ceasing spell was draining me and I was afraid it would be released too soon. And Bren—his hand was already bleeding again. The wound looked angrier and angrier, red spreading slowly up his arm like a wicked burn.

At last, when Mother and Rol had secured all of the attacking harpies, and after they had positioned a group of olde-Folke and witches in a giant circle to enforce a containment spell, I gripped Bren's good hand and spoke the word I dreaded.

"Resume."

Everything happened at once. The harpy shot by Rol's arrow collapsed to the ground. The other harpies set up a shrieking and fought against their bonds. The witches in the circle faltered, panicked, regained themselves at Mother's command, and managed to cast a containment for extra safety. Bit by bit, the noise of the beasts died away as the magic tamped it down.

"To the storage barn!" someone shouted. "We can ward them in!"

A chorus of voices spoke spells of lifting and movement, and I knew the harpies were on their way to a temporary prison. As they departed, moans lifted through the heavy, smoky air. The odor of blood, of fire, of torn earth, and scorched flesh assailed me, as did a sense of Bren's horrid pain. I dropped Acaw's staff and pushed at my eyes, my ears, trying to block it out, but I couldn't. Everything seemed to fall on me at once.

And so one of my first official acts as the returned Queen of the Witches was to sink to my knees and scream.

As if in response, a boy came charging through the flames, one hand pressed against his chest.

For a moment, I blinked hard, denying what I saw. It was Bren—but not Bren. Lighter hair, and as he approached, I could see the bright blue eyes and the torn halves of his shirt.

Todd. Yes. It had to be Bren's brother. I had known that the moment I saw the harpy attack him. *Kill* him. Yet here he came, very much alive. His shirt was ripped shoulder to waist—not even a superficial wound or a speck of blood. Did he have some sort of healing magic? Did Nire's blood protect him from harm? But that couldn't be right, or Bren would be protected, too.

Stop borrowing trouble. There's enough to be had all around, wherever you look. Deal with this later.

Behind Todd came a virtual army of slithers, some in the air, young ones thundering across the ground. Slithers—in the daytime. Heavens, but someone was doing very, very well with breeding modifications.

The boy pulled up short at the sight of me. Then his eyes fell on Bren.

"Damn!" he shouted. He barked a command to the slithers, but they ignored him. He had to yell two or three times to make them listen, but at last, they settled to the ground and fell still.

Todd hurried to his brother and dropped down beside him. He touched Bren's wounded hand, and Bren moaned and thrashed at him, like Todd was causing him pain.

"Don't," I said, forcing myself to get up long enough to go to Todd and kneel down beside him. "I think the wound is magical, at least a little. He needs true healing."

"Then do it!" The boy glared at me with those unearthly blue eyes. Silver energy rippled across his skin, causing me to rock backward.

"I—I can't. My magic—as soon as we have the situation in hand, healers will tend to him."

Todd's expression twisted into something like disdain mixed with an emotion I couldn't identify. Surprise? Triumph? His look startled me, bothered me at some deep level I couldn't grasp. Before I could name my discomfort, he snorted and turned back to Bren, dismissing me as if I were useless. Every time he placed a hand on Bren, Bren writhed beneath his touch. Silver sparks fired from his skin, flailing at Todd, pushing him back. I even felt a pull on our combined energy, but I couldn't risk a major healing spell. What if our connection failed in the middle of my effort? I could do more harm than good.

Something sank inside me. In many ways, I was as useless as Todd thought—but, no. I couldn't think like that. I had to get up, go help where I could and how I could. Yet, if I left Bren's side, I wouldn't even be able to do small magic.

Todd reached for Bren again, only to be smacked back by a rush of silver energy. The boy took out his frustration with a murderous glare in my direction.

A man hurried over, followed by my mother and a black-haired girl I recognized with sudden dread. Sherise. The little witch who had come to L.O.S.T. carrying Alderon's golem. Now she was carrying a sword. It was well-crafted, powerful, but not Bren's. Likely the blade had been made for Todd, and I remembered now that this traitor had snatched it up when he was wounded by a harpy.

Every muscle in my body tensed.

Where was the hateful golem? In her pocket? Perhaps she had it on a chain about her neck. No matter. She had to be disarmed, immediately.

As soon as she approached, pains shot through the scar on my arm—the wound the Shadows had made—the one that sent me to Talamadden.

"Stop!" I stood, then almost fell as I backed away from her. I needed to delve into her mind and force the knowledge out, but the sick feeling in my scar—I couldn't. I'd have to use other means. I didn't want to get too close to this girl, or her evil talisman from Alderon. "Drop your weapon and stay where you are, traitor!"

Sherise stumbled like I had struck her. In fact, I had, a little. A bit of blended silver-gold magical energy fell to the ground as she righted herself. In a big hurry, she dropped the blade she was carrying. It fell point-down into the earth and stuck there, rocking back and forth.

As if sensing my distress, Rol and Acaw came running toward me. I wanted to order them to stop, to turn immediately and fetch healers for Bren, but I knew I had to place duty over personal feelings until the danger was truly quelled.

"Jasmina," my mother said. "Why are you attacking the child? This madness isn't her doing."

Bren's father knelt beside his wounded son, even as Todd whirled on me. He hesitated for a second, as if fishing for the right words, then shot off a fine volley. "Don't talk to Sherise like that. And don't you dare touch her again."

"She is in league with evil," I said as steadily as I could manage, forcing my gaze away from Bren and meeting Todd's furious glare. "She has a golem, one of Alderon's. He sent her here with the hateful thing, no doubt to make an attack like this all the easier."

"I—I don't know what you're talking about." Sherise folded her arms. Her voice was small and weak against the chaos around us. "I wouldn't hurt anyone here. Not now."

"She wouldn't," confirmed Bren's father. "She's been a great help in Bren's absence, and she and Todd are close—when the harpy attacked him, she drove it back. Oh. I'm sorry. We've never really been introduced, have we?"

He was about to continue when Rol and Acaw reached us. "Search her." I nodded to Sherise. "She has a golem. I saw it in a vision."

Todd let out a shout of anger and made as if to block their path to the girl. Acaw retrieved his staff from the ground and slipped around the boy in typical elfling fashion. Rol, in typical Rol fashion, simply moved the boy out of his way, prompting my mother to take Todd by both arms from behind. He struggled in her grip, but I could tell it was halfhearted. He knew he was bested, and he didn't much like it. Only a few yards away, his slithers stamped and snorted, no doubt feeling his distress.

"Send them back to their day-lairs," Mother told him.

"Go to hell!" Todd shot back, and didn't even hang his head when his father gave him a stern look.

To my tremendous surprise, my mother did not slap the boy for his impudence. She didn't even chastise him. Instead, she turned loose one of his hands and waited patiently, keeping a tight hold on his other wrist.

As Rol and Acaw took hold of Sherise—who, to her credit, did not struggle—Todd made a gesture to the slithers and called out a few amplified words in the speech of the olde-Folke. The slithers hesitated, but then, to a one, they departed by wing or by foot, disappearing into the swirling smoke.

Witches and hags and other oldeFolke came slowly toward us, limping and grimacing, cradling damaged limbs. They saw me, reacted with muttered prayers, some curses—combinations of shock and disbelief at my return. Many were burned, cut, or bitten. Their clothes were in tatters. Blood smeared so many faces. I stopped looking. I couldn't deal with it, not yet, not with Bren so desperately hurt himself and the girl and the golem . . . oh. I closed my eyes. Too, too much.

When I opened them again, Acaw was passing his staff over Sherise inch by inch while Rol kept his massive hands on her shoulders. She looked scared and miserable, not at all angry and sullen as I had expected. I wanted to order the elfling to hurry, but I held my tongue. Actually, I bit it. All I wanted at that moment was to fall to the ground and cradle Bren, but that wouldn't make him any safer. Not until the golem was destroyed. Who knew what other monsters might follow its beacon-call to evil? We could be beset by more harpies, by anything. Even Shadows.

I shivered. *There are no Shadows. Nire is gone. Stop panicking over nothing!*

By the time Acaw reached Sherise's left leg, it seemed like the entire population of L.O.S.T. was crowded around. Gazes directed at me were full of shock and wonder, except for the hags, who glared as they always did. Many onlookers stared at Bren and clasped and unclasped their hands, clearly concerned. Still others gaped at the inspection of Sherise until Acaw spoke.

"It is here, Your Majesty." He gestured toward the girl's left shoe.

My mother stiffened. Todd's glare reached inferno proportions.

Sherise hung her head, then shook it slowly back and forth. "I wouldn't hurt anyone here," she repeated. "I wouldn't, honest. You have to believe me."

"Be silent," I snapped, hugging myself. "Acaw, remove it." To Mother, in the best concession I could make to Todd, I said, "Will you help her through the death of the monstrosity? I don't want her to die, though that would be a fitting punishment."

And I don't want to be the one to go into her mind. A wave of shivers claimed me for a second as I remembered having to delve into Bren's consciousness—and the ancient magic he inherited from Nire. That had been a nasty surprise, indeed.

My mother hesitated briefly, but at last, she nodded.

"My mother will assist you in breaking free of its hold, if you cooperate." I couldn't help the strength of my glare, directed fully at Sherise. "Otherwise, you'll die as it dies. Do you understand?"

Rol lifted Sherise a few inches from the ground, and the elfling used his staff to pull off the girl's shoe. It fell to the grass—and out tumbled a writhing, leering horror formed of mud, thatch, and vile blood-magic.

As one, the crowd drew back. Hags and hag-spirits hissed, crow-brothers squawked, and witches muttered wards and protections. My mother, always coolheaded in any crisis, handed Todd to his father and quickly bound the wriggling horror with the appropriate spells. Then she turned her attention to Sherise. I saw Mother draw deep within herself as she connected with the girl, pushing back the golem's influence, severing the connection Alderon had established.

Mother's eyes went wide.

Sherise shook from head to toe, but she didn't cry out or fall down.

By the look of it, Sherise was not fighting my mother's aid. Bit by bit, their shared looks of distress receded, until they both sagged at the shoulders, releasing their connection. I could tell they were successful, because the golem quickly grew weak, and Sherise's life energy did not diminish.

When the golem at last grew still, Acaw removed a cloth bag from his pocket, wrapped the creature into the folds, and tied it securely with a charmed string. This bundle he returned to his pocket, and I knew he would see to its destruction.

Then all eyes turned to Sherise, who hung limply in Rol's grasp. She was sobbing now, murmuring "I'm sorry" over and over.

My mother stepped forward to say something, then glanced at me and thought better of it. Instead, she returned to Bren's father and Todd, and awaited my judgment.

The three of them looked equally miserable, and I could tell by the cold hatred in Todd's eyes that I had made an enemy of Bren's brother even though I had been right. Perhaps *because* I had been right. I couldn't help a sigh.

It was time to be a queen again. I found I didn't relish the job any more than I did the first time I was alive.

"Put her in the store's anteroom under a containment spell. Have two witches on guard at all times. We haven't the time to determine how much of this slaughter lies at her feet. Yet."

Rol nodded, and he and Acaw departed with the traitorous witch.

At the same time, several healers pushed through the crowd and took over the care of Bren. A third took me by the arm, and I didn't fight as she led me toward a healing hut. My mother fell into step beside me as I craned my neck to see where they were taking Bren. I had to know, to get to him as soon as possible. We were stronger together than apart. He needed me, or maybe I needed him. At that moment, I didn't care.

"He will be fine, daughter," my mother said gently. "As will Todd. The boy's temper—well, he is much like his brother used to be. Bren has grown into his responsibilities."

"I know." I felt my mother's arm drape around my shoulders, and the sensation startled me. When had she become one to show affection? And in front of people, no less?

As we entered the healing hut, I cast one more look over my shoulder. L.O.S.T. smoldered sadly in the background.

"Later," my mother said, helping the healer steer me to a bed. "We will have time to count our losses and bind our wounds. An accounting, surely, and we must determine what to do with those harpies. For now, though, you need rest and nourishment."

The healer forced me to lie down, and when she turned her back to gather her supplies, my mother actually pulled the sheet up to cover me, as if I were still a small girl. Shock mingled with fatigue, but my eyes grew too heavy too fast to say anything to her.

"Well done, my beautiful young woman," she whispered softly, lifting one of my hands to her lips. "You can't imagine how proud I am, or how happy I am to see you. Welcome home, Jasmina."

Then, through my sleepy haze, I thought I saw my mother crying.

chapter ten

My sight wavered. Fuzzy. Dim. I couldn't concentrate. Couldn't focus on what was going on around me. Dreams. Memories. Two people half dragging me, half carrying me to a healing hut. Rol? My dad? I couldn't tell.

Images flashed through my mind. Jazz at Shadowbridge, dying from the wound in her arm. Alderon at the gates of Nire's lair in Old Salem. My mother—Nire—laughing, laughing. But no, wait. Not her. Someone else. Todd. A little man too shadowy to see. A hairy giant made out of fleas. A flea-giant with huge square teeth. Everything whirled together. The laughing had to stop, or I'd lose my mind. The flea-giant bent down and bit off my arm.

I shouted from the agony, and the giant vanished.

A bed. I was in a bed and something was wrong. Bad wrong.

Pain. God, the pain. Creeping up my arm to my shoulder. Memories came back to me in small bursts. The harpy. My sword. My fingers.

No. It wasn't real. I'd only imagined I'd lost my fingers. I could feel them.

Ghost pains, some distant memory spoke to me, and I remembered hearing how people who lost legs and arms still felt as if they were really there.

"No," I mumbled. My words came out slurred as I tried to speak. "They *are* there."

"Shush, lad." The healer was suddenly standing over me, but I could barely make out her wrinkled face.

"Todd. My brother . . ."

"Your brother has no injuries. Spend no worry on his account."

No worry? But the harpy cut him down!

"I saw—" my voice choked. I felt so weak I couldn't lift my head.

"Do not doubt me, boy," came the harsh command. "Todd is in fine shape. Would that I could say the same for you."

She began chanting in the olde language. I cried out as a burning sensation rushed up my arm. My head was going to explode! What was she doing to me? What was happening?

I tried to jerk my arm away. Tried to get up, but I was pinned by the shoulders. Rol, I thought. The big walking rock was holding me down.

One of the oldeFolke mumbled a healing spell as she pressed a cool cloth to my forehead. Scents of passionflower and poppy seed overwhelmed my senses . . . then everything went black.

My head ached so badly I didn't want to open my eyes. I heard whispers in the background, but I kept my lids shut as I tried to piece together where I was. What had happened.

Jazz. I'd gotten her back. The thought made my head ache a little less and I almost smiled.

But then the memory of the harpy attack came rushing back to me. My eyes shot open and I bolted upright on the bed. My head spun so badly I almost threw up.

The first thing I saw was Jazz. She was safe! But then my gaze cut to my left hand and I saw the bandages wrapped between my fingers—my whole fingers—and over the two stumps in between.

I did vomit then. I leaned over the side of the bed and everything came up in an acidic rush. My eyes watered and my chest heaved.

"Bren!" Jazz's cry echoed in the healing hut, but I couldn't look at her. I wiped my mouth with the bedsheet and tried not to throw up again from the smell of the puke.

Someone threw cloths and herbs over the puddle and the next thing I knew Jazz was on the bed, her arms wrapped around my neck and her face pressed against my chest. I smelled her cinnamon and peaches scent and once again I couldn't believe that she was really there. I felt our magical strength combine again, just by being there together.

"You're all right," she said, my shirt muffling her words. "You're alive and you're okay." She hiccuped and I could tell she was crying. I patted her on the back with my good hand, feeling so much emotion and pain I couldn't sort one thing out from another. Love for her, anger at the harpies, fury at the bastard who had sent the golem into our Sanctuary.

And a keen sense of uselessness. My hand—I'd never be able to hold a sword in it again. I was as good as worthless. Maybe that's why Jazz was crying.

I drew away from her, and our magic shimmered between us for a moment. She sat on the bed beside me, her golden eyes shining with tears. "I was so worried. The harpy—the dark magic it put into your wound. But the healers did an outstanding job. I think you'll be okay."

I looked at my hand then, *really* looked at it. My wrist was an angry red above the green healers' wrappings. I could feel the poultice beneath the bandages, smell the yarrow, mugwort, marigold, and green tea that the witches had used to help speed the healing and knitting of my skin.

"Talk about useless," I mumbled as I stared at the horror. "What good is a King of the Witches without his sword hand?"

Jazz took my good hand in hers and I looked up at her. "Don't say that." An angry spark lit her eyes. "You're a good king. I've seen what you've accomplished since I've been gone, and I have no doubt that's not going to change."

"Yeah, right." I jerked away from her and pushed myself off the bed, cradling my injured hand to my chest. For a moment, black spots floated behind my eyes again, and I had to steady myself.

When I gained my bearings, I stalked across the hut, Jazz following me. I threw open the door and stared at the destruction outside. "What a king. I couldn't even defend my own people." I whirled on Jazz and she jumped back. "I couldn't even protect you."

She looked like she felt sorry for me, and like she didn't know what to say. "Bren—"

"Listen," I snapped at her. "I don't need your pity, or you trying to make me feel like I'm whole now. 'Cause I'm not. We both know I'm not."

Great. She looked like she was going to cry again, and I couldn't handle it. Not at all.

Without another word, I stormed out of the hut, ignored how tired I felt, and marched all the way to Rol, who was talking with my dad near the store. By the time I got there, I was covered in sweat, but I didn't care. It felt good to move. At least my damned legs were whole.

As I glanced around, I could tell witches and oldeFolke had been performing spellwork to clean up the mess so that everything didn't look so bad. A lot had been accomplished. Without me, of course.

"Your Majesties." Rol inclined his head to me and then to Jazz, who joined us without comment. The big guy's eyes held a special light when he looked at her, and then back at me, like he was proud and pleased with us both. When his gaze landed on my useless hand, though, that light in his eyes dimmed. "May I be of assistance to you?"

"I'm not helpless," I snarled, and both my dad and Rol stepped back.

"Of course not, son," Dad said. "I'm glad to see you up. Todd will be thrilled. He's asked after you every day."

I ignored all three of them and stared out at the Sanctuary. The landscape was busy with witches restoring everything back to the way it had been before the harpy attack.

"Where are the harpies?" I asked Rol. "Were they all destroyed?"

"They're in the storage barns," Jazz said and I jerked my attention to her.

"Why are they still alive?" I growled. "The friggin' things attacked my people." *And took my fingers*, I wanted to shout.

Jazz raised her chin. "The harpies—they were trying to tell us something. I'm certain they didn't attack by happenchance, and we need to discover their purpose, not to mention who sent them."

Curses ran through my thoughts, one after the other. "Right. Now you listen—"

Before I could say anything else, my dad gripped my shoulder and my attention cut back to him. "I'm proud of you, son. You brought Jasmina back and helped stop the harpy attack."

"Indeed." Rol gave a deep bow. "You have proven to be a fine King of the Witches."

"Listen. You can cut the crap." I shook off my father's hold. "What good am I without my sword hand?"

Rol frowned. Dad had an expression of pity on his face, which pissed me off.

Jazz actually looked mad. "Stop feeling sorry for yourself, Brenden. As you would so aptly put it, 'get over yourself and get on with it.' We have work to do."

We just stood and glared at one another for a long moment. Dad and Rol slipped away and it was only the two of us standing in front of the store, virtually at the head of the village.

"You don't know what you're talking about," I said through gritted teeth. "This isn't something you just get over."

She balled her fists and raised up on her toes as if to match my height. "I was dead. *Dead,* Bren."

The thought took me back for a moment and I couldn't think of anything to say while she continued, "I had to fight to get to the gate to the real world, just as you had to fight to get to the gate of Talamadden. But it was you who saved me, you who brought me back."

"I had my sword hand then." My face was growing hotter by the second. "If I didn't, I wouldn't have bested the Erl-king, or reached you."

"Fine." Jazz threw her hands up in the air. "Poor you with missing fingers. You can't swing a sword like you used to, so you're just going to give up?"

"Never," I growled, not knowing where that came from.

Before Jazz could say anything else, I pushed by her and headed away from the store, in the general direction of olde-Towne, Todd's zoo, and the storage barns. The Queen of the Witches decided not to follow me.

Good. That was fine, too. Except it felt lousy at the same time.

As I got closer to the barns, the smell of dust and harpy filth deadened my nose. Oh, they were in there, for sure. Thoughts of setting fire to the whole compound went to war with fantasies of rushing in and slitting lots of harpy throats.

As it was, I just stomped into the paddock, and then into the first of the three big barns. Something clenched deep in my gut to see all of those ugly creatures bound with magical ties and forced to lie on their sides. They still managed to look proud and furious, despite the fact they were helpless.

One of the harpies, the biggest one, growled in what sounded like some kind of language. I jerked my gaze toward the beast and began shaking with anger. "Bastard," I said. "You're the one who took my fingers."

Again he spoke. I mean, it sounded to me like he was speaking. Not screeching in that unearthly way that they did when they were fighting. But like he was trying to have a conversation with me.

See? I imagined Jazz saying in that I'm-always-right tone she could get. *They're trying to communicate.*

"Bullshit." I turned, my heel grinding in the dirt of the barn's floor. Stupid monsters would probably give me fleas again if I didn't watch out. Grumbling, I walked away from the things that had attacked my people and maimed me. One way or another, I'd deal with them. I just needed some time to think.

This time, I headed back toward the main village. I didn't know exactly where I was going, but I had to do something, anything. As I walked, I glanced down and looked at my bandaged hand. An absurd thought came to me—all I had to do was hold my thumb in and I would be giving the Vulcan greeting. Permanently. The image made me sick. I shook my head and focused on my anger. Anger felt good right now. I was walking so fast that the moonstone around my neck bounced up and down on my chest.

Moonstone. Sherise! Shit.

My hand and head throbbed, and I started to sweat more as I picked up speed. How could I have forgotten about Sherise? If Jazz hadn't expelled her, she'd be in the general store anteroom where we locked the occasional drunk elfling overnight. Intoxicated oldeFolke could do some real damage, so we kept the barred room cleaned out and ready, just in case. Sometimes we used it for a witch or one of the olde-Folke who needed to cool off before they blasted somebody and ended up in real trouble. But those times were few and far between, and never lasted very long. I didn't believe in making my own people prisoners. Ours was a society of compromise and treaty. Those who didn't wish to follow our simple rules were escorted on the Path to other Sanctuaries that better suited their needs.

Jazz was still standing at the store when I got there. I didn't speak to her as I yanked open the door and stormed inside. Still, I heard Jazz's footsteps behind me, so I knew she was following.

When I reached the back, I turned left and walked straight to the anteroom. When I looked through the bars on the door, I saw Sherise. She was huddled on a wooden bench, her arms wrapped around her legs, staring into the space in front of her. She looked completely miserable, and her face was streaked with dirt and tears.

I whirled on Jazz. "Why are you keeping her in here? I told you, she's no traitor."

"She was carrying a golem that Alderon gave her. She brought the harpies to L.O.S.T." Jazz looked angry and defiant as she spoke. "She *is* a traitor, and she's dangerous."

"She saved my life. More than once." I pulled out the moonstone on the silver chain. "She loaned me this before I left to find you. It stopped an arrow, and I think it kept my soul tied to my body in Talamadden so I wouldn't die."

Jazz's eyes widened at the sight of the stone. She reached for it, and I let her touch it. A memory passed between us then. Jazz, gripping the stone, using its strength to pull me away from snarling Shadows . . .

"But the vision," she whispered, letting the stone fall back to my chest. "I saw her with Alderon, saw her agree to help him destroy you and Todd."

"Maybe it was a mistake," I said through clenched teeth. "Maybe he hid it or fooled her like he did me."

Jazz shook her head. "She accepted it willingly."

"Then Alderon tricked her some other way!" I turned my back on Jazz and tried to move the simple wooden bar from its hold with my good hand. It wouldn't budge. It was spelled solid. I brought my right hand up for a spell, but it barely fizzled out, too weak to matter.

Man, did it piss me off to no end to know that I had to turn and ask Jazz for her help.

She just stood there with her arms folded across her chest.

"Help me." I ground my teeth. "I want her out."

Jazz shook her head. "I'm not about to turn her loose to hurt my people again. Something will have to be done with her."

"They're my people too, and you will help me let her go." I approached Jazz with slow, even steps, growing angrier by the minute. My bad hand screamed with pain when I instinctively clenched my hands. Black spots danced before my eyes, but I ignored them.

When I reached Jazz, she tilted her head to look up at me, her arms still tightly crossing her chest. "Help me release her," I commanded again.

Our magic crackled between us, silver and gold snapping with tension.

"No." Jazz waved one hand to the anteroom cell. "Sherise is a danger to everyone. We'll have to decide what to do with her, but we won't just set her free to hurt us again."

Taking a deep breath, I counted to ten, very slowly. Winter sunlight peeked through the clouds, shining through store windows. My injured hand ached like crazy, but I still managed to focus on the problems on hand. First problem, harpies. Second problem, Sherise.

I hadn't been using my head. I was reacting instead of responding. I was trying to use intimidation and anger instead of figuring out a way to make everything work.

I exhaled and said, "I'll make you a deal. We let Sherise out of the holding cell and we let her stay in L.O.S.T." Jazz started to shake her head, when I held up my good hand to stop her. "You do your best to work with Sherise and figure out what's really going on with her, and I won't behead the harpies."

That was surly and I knew it. Damn. "I mean, I'll try to talk to those filthy bastards and figure out why they attacked. Negotiate. That's what you want, right?"

Jazz paused a moment, like she was shocked. Then she looked like she was thinking it through. "Negotiation," she murmured, as if she didn't really believe me. "A compromise."

"Compromise. Nice word." I reached out my good hand. "And we start by letting Sherise out now."

Jazz paused again, then raised her own and gripped mine tight.

We both turned to look at the bar on the anteroom holding cell. Silver and gold crackled between us, and the bar easily slid out of its brackets, then fell to the ground.

I let go of Jazz, went to the cell door, and opened it. Sherise glanced up at me, but when she saw Jazz at my side, she turned away again.

My boots clunked on the wooden floor of the cell that smelled of herbs and cedar. The anteroom wasn't uncomfortable, not like a jail or dungeon. There was a nice soft bed, a bench beneath the window on the other side, and a sink and toilet. There was even a small fridge that was filled with snacks for witches. I won't even go there as far as what it held for the oldeFolke.

Anyway, the anteroom was only meant to be temporary. We never left anyone in there longer than a night.

"Hey, you." I lifted the moonstone necklace over my head and gently lowered it over hers. "I think this is yours. It's in one piece, and thanks to it, so am I."

This got me a tiny smile. It lasted about two seconds. Sherise reached up and gripped the moonstone like it might give her a little warmth in a cold, cold place.

"Come on." I held my good hand out to the scared kid and gave her a smile. "Everything's okay now."

Sherise avoided looking at Jazz, but took my hand. I felt her trembling as she got to her feet. She was so scared. The sight of her fear made me clench my jaw.

I glared at Jazz. "Stop looking at her like that. You're making it worse—and we have a deal."

Jazz turned away, and we followed her out of the anteroom, then out of the general store.

It was at that moment that Todd came storming out of nowhere, a herd of his biggest slithers following him. Some caused the ground to shake with every step they made and others swooped overhead. The flying slithers slowly circled us then landed with a reverberating thump.

"Good thing you let her out," Todd said, his fiery glower fixed on Jazz. "We were just about to effect a rescue."

My jaw dropped. *Effect a rescue? Who is this guy? Sheesh. Too many old animal-care scrolls must have bent his brain.*

Jazz looked like she wanted to say something, but she didn't.

"She's okay, little brother." I dropped Sherise's hand, and she ran up to Todd and threw her arms around his neck.

He flinched. For a second I thought he was going to push her away, but then his face grew softer as he rubbed her back. "It's okay. You're okay."

"Let's hope," Jazz grumbled under her breath.

I cut her a glare, then looked back at my brother. The sight of him with his girl in his arms made me happy. In fact, seeing Todd healthy and well—that was cool all by itself. During the battle, I was pretty sure that harpy had killed him. But no. Todd was a tough kid. Of course he was. He was my little brother, right?

After some arguing, Todd reluctantly agreed to the four of us having dinner at L.O.S.T.'s one and only restaurant. It was run by the best elfling chefs, and it had been ages since I'd eaten a good, full meal that didn't taste like paper. I figured we needed to talk, but we also needed some good chow before we all snapped one another's heads off.

We took a private room at the restaurant where we wouldn't be disturbed. Jazz seated herself next to me, while Todd and Sherise sat down together. No one talked much, and I did my best not to show my frustration at having to use my right hand to pick up my glass of iced herb tea while we waited for dinner. My other hand ached and I could feel my missing fingers like they were still there.

Dinner was worse. I'd never used my right hand to eat before, and I kept dropping pieces of elfling-style lasagna off my fork when I tried to eat it. It really pissed me off, but I managed to maintain my cool. The whole time we ate, Todd kept glaring at Jazz, while Sherise wouldn't even look at her.

When the table was cleared, the elfling waiter wisely vanished, leaving us free to talk.

Of course at first, no one did. It was up to me to get the ball rolling. "Sherise, will you tell us about the golem? Did Alderon give it to you?"

Fear, real fear, crossed her pretty features. She pushed a lock of wavy black hair behind her ear and kept her dark eyes downcast. "I can't—I'm not supposed to say anything about it."

"He can't harm you here," Todd said. "Don't be afraid of him. I could defeat him—" He cut me a look, coughed, then changed course. "Bren and I could kick his ass."

Jazz went stiff beside me, but she kept her mouth shut. Probably because I was using my boot to crush her toes. Just a little.

"After my mom died, my dad got married really fast. Then he and my stepmother threw me out when I wouldn't stop practicing the craft like Mom had. I didn't have anywhere to go, just the streets." Sherise's story tumbled out in a rush. "I couldn't go to school that much because of the other kids. They knew I was different. They always cornered me, beat on me—I didn't know what to do. My magic was real. Stuff kept happening, and I was freaking out."

"Alderon offered you safety?" Jazz asked in a measured tone. "He took you into his Coven?"

Pleasantly surprised, I took my heel off her toes.

"Y-Yes." Sherise wouldn't meet Jazz's eyes. "Most of them were guys, but there were a few girls like me. They gave me a place to stay, and Alderon told me about the Path, about Sanctuaries. They all did. Everyone kept saying how wonderful my life could be. But Alderon insisted Bren and Todd were evil, that they were corrupting everything and planned to destroy our chances to be safe and happy on the Path."

"I see." Jazz folded her hands in front of her, and for a second, I hated her for being able to lace her fingers together so easily.

"He said it was a talisman." Sherise's Georgia drawl became more obvious as she slowed down. "It felt all wrong, that thing. And I sort of knew better, but I didn't want to think that Alderon would lie to me. After I got here and met you guys, it was like I just forgot the golem. Any time I thought about it—"

"Yeah. That part I know." I smiled at her. "Been there, done that."

"Did Jasmina put *you* in the anteroom?" Todd grumbled.

"The Shadows attacked," I snapped back. "And call her Jazz. You've definitely been hanging out with the oldeFolke too much. You're even starting to sound like one."

Jazz put her hand over mine. "Sherise, you have much potential, but you need training, especially in protecting yourself against bastards like Alderon. If we allow you to stay—"

"If?" Todd cut in loudly. He looked like he was about to stand up, so I kicked him. He kicked me right back. The flare in his eyes was nothing short of violent, and for a second, I felt a little dizzy. Was I looking at Todd? At Mom?

Nire . . .

Way, way back in my head, the Erlking's laughter made my blood turn to ice.

I clamped my teeth together and shoved the image of that nasty shapeshifter as far from my thoughts as I could get him.

Meanwhile, Jazz was finishing her question to Sherise. "Would you allow me to train you, to be certain you're cleansed of Alderon's treachery?"

"That won't happen." Todd stood up so fast I didn't have time to kick him this time. "She's afraid of you." His glare turned on me. His lips tightened, then he blew out a breath and added, "You're a bitch, Jazz, and you've treated Sherise like shit!"

"Just a minute." I got up, wincing as I pushed on the table with my bandaged hand. "Keep it calm, Todd. Jazz—"

"Don't tell me what to do." Todd was seething. I could see that unbelievable hatred in his eyes, anger so strong it almost flared red behind all that icy blue.

"I'll do it." Sherise's agreement cut through the rising anger and frustration. "Jazz is right. I need help, and . . . and she's strong. Strong enough to fight Alderon."

"We're strong enough," Todd and I said at the same time. Then we both looked down like we always did when we felt stupid.

When Todd and I straightened up again, Sherise was in the middle of rolling her eyes, and Jazz had covered her mouth to hide a smile.

chapter eleven

JAZZ

They came to me by ones and twos, by threes and fours, slithering, flying, crawling, stumbling. I hurtled left. Right. I ran. I threw myself into the night, but I couldn't escape them. The scar on my arm burst open and bled. My own warm blood flowed over my hands, leaking my life out across the frozen ground.

I ran until I had no breath, no more heart for the flight. Bleeding so badly. My body failed in a spectacular skidding fall. Face down in the icy dirt, I waited for death.

Sick chittering filled the air, and it was the sound of sand crabs worrying a fish. The sound of scavengers at a carcass. Throaty hums. Teeth champing. I rolled over, but they came in darkness so complete I could see nothing at all, not even the hands I raised to spell them to oblivion. My body shook from cold, from despair. Shadows. Shadows everywhere! They covered L.O.S.T. like an evil, smothering blanket.

In seconds they would overtake me, consume me, send me back to the land of the dead, this time to stay forever.

The force of my magic swelled within me, and I fired the largest blast I could manage. It barely served to light a small circle around me. Shadows! So many they were legion, like a sea of evil, waves that would never stop. Around them swirled a horrid laughter, a sound I'd never heard, but thought I should recognize.

So falls Jasmina Corey and all she sought to rule.

The words were as much in my head as in the air. The voice was my mother's, my father's. It was Bren's and Todd's. It was Sherise and Rol and everyone I had known much or cared to remember. They laughed at me again, but the Shadows did not laugh.

The Shadows moved in for the kill.

"Your Majesty?"

I woke with a shout, grabbing a fistful of someone else's hair and pulling out the dagger I kept beneath my pillow. Sherise shrieked as I pressed the blade to her throat. Only the chain of her moonstone necklace stopped the tip from drawing blood.

"Jasmina." My mother's voice cut into the flare of my panic. "Put the knife down."

Hand shaking, I eased the dagger away from Sherise's vulnerable flesh and let go of her dark curls. She reeled away, collapsing into the arms of my mother.

"I have done my best not to gainsay you since your return," Mother said calmly. "But perhaps that was extreme?"

"My apologies," I croaked. My throat was so dry the words hurt. "I was having a nightmare."

Mother patted Sherise's head and helped her stand upright. "Obviously."

There are potions to prevent that. Draughts even a first-year student can conjure. That much Mother left unsaid, a small blessing at least, but I could see it in her eyes.

Morning light spilled through the modest bedroom in the modern house my mother had agreed to share with me. Yellow walls, hardwood floors, brass bed. It was hard to believe my mother lived so comfortably without the trappings of Old Salem, where I had grown up until Nire attacked that Sanctuary and killed my father. At the same time, Nire kidnapped my mother and most of the witches I knew. In truth, then, I had never gotten to know Mother in another time. I had never really gotten to know her at all. She was strange to me now, like most things.

As for Sherise, I had brought her home with me the night before, to begin more adequate training—and to keep an eye on her. She had taken the small spare cot in my room without protest. And I, in my infinite brilliance, had almost cut her throat before the day began. Mother led her away. The sight of the girl's shaking made me hang my head.

With a sigh, I threw back the covers and headed to the very modern bathroom with its very modern shower. Undressing, setting the water—it was all a blur as my mind strove to list the many mistakes I had made since leaving Talamadden. It wasn't until the warm water struck me, washing away the shards of the dream, that I realized what I was doing. The voice of that blue bird Egidus rang in my mind, talking of different kinds of arrogance, of the many subtle ways in which I thought myself better than others.

To expect success. To demand perfection and bemoan the fates when I could not achieve it. Bren, Sherise—even my mother. Did I expect perfection from them as well?

Little by little, I let the gentle water wear down the sharp edges of my worry. By the time I dressed and joined Mother and Sherise for breakfast, I felt more centered, and I offered the girl more apologies.

Sherise accepted them quietly. Most of the time she kept her head down, but when she chanced a look up, I caught a spark in her dark eyes.

Was it anger?

Fear?

". . . ways to separate your magic," Mother was saying as she helped herself to more toast, baked sprouts, and oat porridge. "I've only had a day, but the old scrolls seem silent on the subject. Even the hags have never known it to happen, two witches sharing the same magical source. Then again, they have no record of any witch successfully returning from Talamadden."

"So, there's no known way to restore our powers." I poked at my porridge. It looked good enough, and I knew I needed to eat, but . . . "Will the people expect us to step down, then?"

Mother met this question with a confused stare.

"How can the Queen of the Witches have no magic? Or the King of the Witches, for that matter."

"But my dear, you have plenty of magic, as does Bren." Mother smiled. I found that jarring, having few memories of such an expression on her stern face. "Your powers are simply joined. Together, the two of you wield a strength none can stand against—not even Nire, if you'll remember."

Memories, both real and dreamed, crept through my mind and sent chills down the back of my neck. "I'd rather not, thanks."

"Yes. I—well." Mother actually looked distressed. "In any case, I doubt there will be a cry for you to abdicate. Most are too thrilled to have you back amongst us."

I studied Sherise's lowered head and wondered if Mother might be delusional. The witches had never seemed overly fond of me. Respectful and fearful, yes, but fond—no.

You gave them few reasons to love you past your title and duties, my brain informed me in a voice that sounded overly much like that infernal peacock. *But people rally about a leader willing to die to save them.*

Nire, leader, dying . . . I rubbed my eyes for a moment, then brought my thoughts to rivers, to trees swaying in breezes, to soft rains and bright sunshine. Holding to these more comforting images, I made myself eat my mother's porridge.

That afternoon, Sherise and I sat cross-legged in a quiet forest clearing. It was a chilly autumn afternoon, but just being alive chased away any cold that might have taken hold of me. Anything and everything felt good these days. Emotions, smells, tastes, pain . . . it all reminded me that I was alive. And it was so very good to be alive again.

Sherise had worked well with her meditations and small spells, and she spoke more freely of her troubled past. It was easy to be in her company, which distanced her some from Alderon in my regard. He was always a perfect bastard, and being in his presence had been unsettling. Even the hags stayed away from him.

Pushing visions of Alderon's hateful blue eyes aside, I used what residual power I possessed to help Sherise learn wards and protections, to understand the abstractions behind such spells, and the mindset and energy necessary to cast them. We were wending through mental images of personal shielding when her eyes came open.

"You love Bren, don't you?" she asked in that soft, disarming drawl.

"Yes." My answer left my lips before I considered it, but I didn't regret my openness. My feelings for Bren could hardly be a secret to the people of L.O.S.T. Every witch in every Sanctuary might know by now.

Sherise shifted on the ground, using a trick I had taught her to increase bloodflow in her legs. "Why aren't you with him today? He's got to be having a hard time with his fingers and all. Besides, you've only been alive—back, I mean, for a little while. I know you've got a lot of catching up to do."

"Sometimes Bren needs his own thoughts." This answer came as automatically as the first, and I wondered at it. Why I said it—and how I knew it was true. "I pushed him yesterday, and he has a difficult task ahead. When he wants my help, he'll come to me. Besides, I have a duty to you."

"Alderon spoke a lot about duty." Sherise wrapped her arms around herself. "And I listened."

"You needed what he had to offer. That's a powerful inducement."

The girl's frown deepened. "I need what you have to offer, too. You and Bren and Todd and L.O.S.T. So how can I be sure this is different? What if I'm wandering down that same path again, turning myself over to people with more power, more strength. What if you use me, too?"

The question surprised me more than angered me, and this time, my answer took some time to form. I listened to the softest of breezes shift through the clearing as I organized my words, then finally gave it a try. "The main difference I see is that we will not ask you to turn yourself over to us. Your soul, your beliefs, your choices—they must be your own. We will teach you and in return ask your loyalty, but whether or not you give it is up to you."

"If I never want to fight again, or deal with Alderon—could I go to some faraway Sanctuary in some other time?" Her face brightened at this dream, and it was a dream I knew all too well. "Could I live a peaceful life and leave the protections and wars and big magic to other witches?"

"If that is your choice." I said this, sensing even as I did that such would not be Sherise's destiny. "Know this. Any leader might ask you to do something against your own comfort or desires, something outside what you believe to be your strengths or abilities—but the final choice lies in your hands. A true leader never robs you of free choice by using fear, intimidation, humiliation, pain, threats, or lies."

"I think I understand." Sherise's head dropped, but then she lifted it once more. Her dark eyes sparked again, and I realized it was neither anger nor fear I saw in the soft light of that forest clearing. It was strength. It was the clearing of shame, the righting of purpose as she shed Alderon's bitter influence.

Bren had been right about this one. What a tragedy it would have been to cast her aside. Now that my own trust had increased, I eyed her silver chain and its stone, then broached the one question yet remaining in my mind. "Before Bren left to retrieve me from Talamadden, you loaned him your moonstone. If I'm not much mistaken, it's a family treasure? Something that would have passed hand to hand through the female witches of your line over many centuries. What moved you to part with it?"

"My grandmother—my Mom's mom—gave it to me after my thirteenth birthday. Last year, when my mother got killed." Sherise's sadness laced through each word. "Guess she figured I needed something since my Dad lost his mind and started dating right away, leaving me alone all the time. Anyway, Grandmother told me to cherish it, to keep it close, but never be afraid to send it on a journey. One way or another, she said, that stone would always find its way back to the hand of the Ash. That's our family name. Ash."

Somehow, I kept my smile from faltering.

Why had I never asked the girl's surname before?

Ash. The oldest of the known clans. Any Coven with a true Ash as a member was formidable indeed. And her grandmother's words were quite telling. The stone would always find its way back to the hand of *the* Ash. The true heir to that powerful legacy. No wonder Alderon had selected this girl amongst the many he might have pursued.

"We should work more with your moonstone, I think." I gazed at the treasure, admiring the depth of its warm glimmer. "Heirlooms like this often have tremendous power. It might even magnify your gift."

Sherise's eyebrows shot up in surprise. She picked up the stone and rubbed it between her thumb and forefinger. "So, what would I do? Meditate on it or something?"

"It's like that, yes. I'll try to teach you to concentrate through the stone, to use it to expand the force behind your spells—but not today. We're both too tired."

Obediently, Sherise let the stone drop back to her chest.

"One more question before we stop for the day, just to let me know a little more about you." I made my tone casual, conversational, even as I steeled myself for the answer to what I didn't want to ask. "How did your mother die?"

Sherise's expression reflected pain and unhappiness the minute the words left my mouth, but she didn't hesitate. "Mom was coming back from the Magic Journey store when some asshole in a purple truck ran her down. They never caught him. Never even found that truck—and you'd think that would have been easy, at least."

"I'm sorry." I covered Sherise's smaller hand with mine. Inside, I was seething, wishing I could find Alderon and do unspeakable things to him on Sherise's behalf. And on behalf of her murdered mother. "Perhaps her killer will find justice someday."

At my hand, or at Bren's, by the Goddess.

Sherise's only answer was a wistful smile.

We made ready to stand up, but the wind chose that moment to pick up. Then something blocked the sun above us.

A red slither slammed down into the clearing, shaking the earth. Its wings snapped tree branches as Todd leaped down and jogged toward us.

"I need your help," he said to Sherise without even glancing in my direction. "One of the poms got into some Oleander seeds, and she's really ill. It's Karina, and you know how she is. I can't get her to calm down enough for a healing."

Sherise stood and dusted off her hands. "Thanks for today, Jazz. Will we start back tomorrow?"

I nodded.

"Sherise!" Todd was already back to his slither. He climbed on the beast's long neck, and then he did look at me.

The expression was less than friendly.

Nevertheless, it melted back to concern and worry as Sherise joined him. The two of them flew off, bruising pine and oak alike before they reached sufficient altitude. The slither circled once, seemed to pause and vibrate, then was gone, flapping away toward oldeTowne.

At the same instant, a large load of slither dung splattered into the clearing, coating me with the foulest of hot green goo, from head to toe.

I leaped to my feet, shouting curses.

The snot! Of all the–twit! Ooooh, for enough power to blast that little ass right off the back of his winged lizard. Into a cart full of ox droppings!

Todd did that on purpose. I just knew he did!

I didn't even have the strength of magic to perform a cleansing spell without Bren, and that made me even angrier.

Growling worse than a wounded hag-spirit, I stormed out of the clearing, dripping a nasty trail as I went.

chapter twelve

BREN

"Again." Rol raised his blade. It gleamed in the afternoon sunlight.

Cold winter winds ruffled my hair as I lifted my sword clumsily, holding it as tightly as I could in my right hand. My stance was good. I even rotated to give myself a little advantage.

"Ready." I nodded.

Rol nodded back. Then he disarmed me with a single swing.

"Damn it!" I kicked at the packed dirt of the training arena. We had been at this for hours. All day, in fact. We had stopped for lunch and gone straight back at it, but I still couldn't handle a blade any better than a four-year-old child.

Rol retrieved my sword from the dirt and extended it toward me, hilt first.

"Put it down," I snarled. "This is useless."

"Training is never useless," he countered. I could have said that before he did. I'd heard it enough times. "Besides, you are not yet well from your wounds. The healers did not wish for you to begin as yet—"

"Don't talk to me about healers."

"Jasmina—"

"And don't talk to me about her!" I stalked over to the small training forge and threw myself down on one of the benches, flat on my back. The fires felt warm on my cold skin, and they eased the ache in my bloody bandaged hand. Nothing eased the ache in my chest, though. Okay, so it had only been a couple of days since I lost my fingers, but I wanted to feel better faster. I *needed* to feel better. Jazz was back. I wanted to be my old self, go grab her, spend time with her.

But right now, I just couldn't. Everything was getting on my nerves. Those harpies—I had to go talk to them. Acaw even said he would help, but facing them longer than a few seconds without being able to hold a sword—no way. I didn't care how many magical bonds kept them still. Shit, if Jazz wasn't right beside me, I couldn't even use magic if I had to.

Rol entered the forge and sat down nearby. It always amazed me that such a huge guy could move without making a sound. That sure wasn't a skill I'd picked up. He didn't say a word, just went about cleaning, sharpening, and polishing the blades we had used. The scrape of oilstone on steel was so familiar, so right, yet so wrong all at the same time. I knew the feel of my blade better than I knew my own name, but when I touched it now, it felt alien. Like I'd never lifted it or used it to fight. My right hand just wasn't up to the job. It got tired every few minutes, and I couldn't coordinate it with my thoughts. I knew what I wanted the hand to do, but I just couldn't make it behave.

"Sorry," I grumbled to Rol.

He grunted and scraped and polished.

I lifted my mangled hand. Man, did the filthy, bloody bandages ever need to be changed. But I couldn't bear to see those stumps. Just the thought made me want to puke again. "I'm not mad at Jazz or anything. I just don't want to take this out on her."

Another grunt from Rol.

"Besides, she's training Sherise, making sure the kid's okay."

"Sherise is a special witch," Rol said. The sentence was so quiet I almost didn't hear it. Besides, I was expecting a grunt.

"You think so, too?"

Rol leaned his sword against his bench and started on mine. "Impulsive. Brash. Foolish at times, but very loyal. I think I could train her to a sword as well."

My turn to grunt. "Kinda like—kinda like me when I first got here?"

"Yes. Unfortunately for her. But I have hope."

"She's good for Todd."

This brought silence. Then, "I am not certain Todd is good for her."

"Hey." I pushed myself up on my elbows, wincing as my wounded hand banged the wooden bench. "Todd needs somebody on his side."

Rol snorted. “Todd needs frequent beatings with a rawhide strap.”

“That’s harsh.” I sat up and stared at the big guy. Even though it was nearly freezing outside, Rol still didn’t wear a shirt. His dark skin rippled as he worked my blade, bringing it to a razor edge and a bright shine. “Todd’s just young and impulsive like Sherise—like me.”

“Except for physical appearance, Todd is nothing like you.” Rol stopped his work on my sword. “I should think you could see this by now. While you were away, the whelp became practically unmanageable—as if he thought he might be king in your absence. I had hoped Dame Corey would force him to heel, but since you’ve returned, he barely respects even her. In the old days, she would have consigned him to life as a newt three times over.”

“But—”

“Son?” My dad came hurrying into the training arena lugging a big wooden box. There were pieces of folded parchment inside. Some of them were hopping up and down. “We’ve got some serious trouble here. I need you to listen to some of these Shadowhispers.”

I could already hear them, and he wasn’t even halfway across the yard. Hag voices. Keepers singing their displeasure. Chirpy tones from whatever those librarians were. Modern witches, snarling away.

“. . . keeping those foul creatures in *our* barns . . .”

“. . . poor things. It’s so undignified . . .”

“. . . eating up our winter stores!”

“What kind of king leaves such a mess . . .”

“Spare the harpies!”

"Slay the harpies!"

". . . that girl with the golem?"

"The oldeFolke are really the most upset," Dad shouted over the racket as he reached the forge and set the box at my feet. "Winnie's doing her best, but the Keepers are gathering the klatchKovens for a sit-down, and the hags won't speak to anybody."

"Winnie?" It was all I could say. I mean, I knew this was a serious situation, but . . . "Winnie?"

"Edwina. Jazz's mother." Dad blinked at me like I was a little nuts. "She's down at oldeTowne now."

"She is not." Rol used my sword to point to the training arena entrance. A crowd was surging inside despite Dame Corey's best efforts to hold them back without magical means. She shouted and pleaded, arms spread wide, but still they came, hags first, followed by klatch witches, moderns, elflings—it looked like half the town.

I looked at Dad one more time. "Winnie?"

He gave me a mighty frown, but his cheeks turned red.

At least I won that round. Doubtful I'd win this next one.

Doing my best to rein my temper, I straightened my shoulders and strolled out of the meager cover offered by the small forge.

At the sight of me, the crowd stopped moving, but kept up their shouting.

"The harpies should leave, leave, leave," sang a klatch-Keeper as male witches plugged their ears. I hoped Rol and Dad were doing the same, because this one was one majorly ugly eggplant with way too many teeth.

“Send them back to their own lands,” an elfling shouted as his crow-brother squawked. He looked a lot like Acaw, but then a lot of elflings looked like Acaw. Even some of the girls. “They are but beasts used by a witch with ill intent, and we should not harm them.”

“Justice!” A hag raised her fist, and her hag-spirit rose above her to hiss its approval. “We suffered more losses than any—a full dozen of our sisters slain. We have the right to blood-debt under all of the old laws!”

My hand throbbed. I felt sweat break across my forehead even though it was way past cold outside. What could I do? I agreed with the hag, but I had made my deal with Jazz—and she was right a lot of the time. Anything I said would piss off half the group, and I had no magic to stop them, not without Jazz beside me. Dame Corey and Rol would do what they could, but the hags were strong—and really, really mad.

“I hear you,” I shouted over the dull roar. Behind me, I heard the snap of Rol spelling the box of Shadowhispers into silence. “Each of you makes a valid point.”

This brought the noise level down, but not much. I ground my teeth to handle the pain of moving and walked closer to the crowd.

“As you all know, our queen was recently restored to us. Jazz—uh—Jasmina Corey believes the harpies have valuable information about the bastard who sent them to attack us. I plan to question them this evening.”

Rol and Dad came to stand beside me as the hags muttered angrily amongst themselves. Dame Corey stepped back to join us, and Dad reached for her hand.

"They are beasts," said an elfling. "They can tell us nothing, and you torture them by keeping them prisoners."

"They have language, of a sort. I've heard it." I held up my bandaged hand. "I don't like the harpies any more than most of you do, though fingers can't be compared to lives."

"Indeed not," hissed the closest hag. Her serpentine hag-spirit slithered down her side and stretched its angular head toward me, its shadowy tongue flicking in and out.

"I will question them," I repeated, "and then the queen and I will decide what's to be done with them."

"Kill them!" the hags demanded at the same time.

"Or give them to us," snarled the hag in front. Dame Corey had to give her hag-spirit a little magical slap to keep it away from my feet.

Where was Jazz? My face heated up. I looked like an idiot, not being able to do stuff like that for myself.

"Kill them!" the hags demanded again. "Kill them now! Kill them now!"

The klatchKeepers picked up the chant, forcing Dad and Rol to cover their ears, along with the other men in the crowd. The elflings started shouting at the hags and the Keepers, and the moderns started shouting at each other.

The crowd suddenly parted, and something green and stinky stormed toward me screaming louder than anyone else. It looked human, the way it walked—but that stench! I grabbed my nose with my good hand.

"What the—"

"Your brother!" the green stinky thing shrieked as it shook its fist. "Your pain-in-the-ass little brother!"

Magic surged between us, gold to silver and silver to gold, swelling. Rage mingled with my nervousness. I felt a power surge, then a force like a sudden hurricane, blowing in every direction.

A huge *pop* nearly burst my eardrums.

The crowd became an assortment of ferns, flowers, and large pieces of fungus. Only, they seemed . . . bigger than they should have been. Huge, actually. And divided into lots of pieces. My eyes swiveled in a complete circle, taking in the scene. Well, at least two of my eyes. The other three looked straight ahead as I raised my spiky front legs high and touched them together in front of me. When I tried to move, two legs on either side supported my elongated neck and torso.

Next to me I saw a hissing spiky hedgehog with a beard a lot like my father's, a black frog with stoic eyes not even bothering to croak, and a skunk with tail raised. It was stomping its back feet and turning slowly to aim its butt right at the now massively gigantic stinky green thing.

"I'm a praying mantis," I grumbled to that gargantuan green thing, which obviously had to be Jazz. "And you turned your mother into a skunk."

My voice sounded like something out of a cartoon, but Jazz seemed to hear it. She lowered her fist and seemed to come back to reality. "Oh. Sorry."

"Take care of the crowd first," the hedgehog suggested.

Blushing like crazy, Jazz leaned down and let me crawl onto her goo-coated palm. Whatever the stuff was, it was thick and nasty and hard to walk through, even with four thin legs.

I held back any smart remarks, not wanting to make her any madder. A praying mantis was bad enough, but I'd been a donkey before, and who knew what else her brain might fire out if I said the wrong thing?

Together we faced the crowd. Using our combined magic, Jazz aimed and fired, restoring hag, elfling, modern, and klatch witch alike. They all looked down at their bodies, then back up at Jazz. As if somebody shot a gun to start a race, they turned around and ran like hell.

Couldn't say I blamed them.

The Queen of the Witches was definitely home. *Yeah, baby.*

Next, we restored my dad, followed by Rol and Dame Corey. I was last, and by then I was swimming in whatever it was Jazz had all over her.

Jazz put me down, pointed at me, and in a single tingle-blaze-pop, I was myself again. Only I stunk really, really bad.

"What is this stuff?" I wiped my eyes, which were only two now, and none of them on stalks, thank the universe.

"Slither dung," Rol said in his oh-so-toneless tone.

"Explain yourself," Dad said to Jazz, still looking lots like a hedgehog with his hair sticking in every direction.

"What on earth made you do that?" Dame Corey sputtered, straightening her white blouse.

Jazz's color rose again, and I felt the snap of magic as she yelled, "Todd!"

Behind us, the forge fire exploded, raining bits of ash all over the training yard.

Rol sighed. "Ah. I understand completely. Too bad the whelp wasn't present." The big guy flexed his fingers, then left to go clean up the forge mess.

My dad and Dame Corey nodded, their anger draining immediately away. Jazz's mother spelled us both clean, then said, "Bren, your father and I will find the boy and deal with this latest . . . problem."

Winnie, Winnie, Winnie, I thought, holding back a roar of nutso laughter. I was way too tired. My control over my ADHD was slipping, and my thoughts were starting to ping. Any second now, I'd start unraveling my clothes, if I even could with just one hand.

Dad nodded. He reached for good old Winnie's hand, but she shook him off and stalked away. With a perplexed look, my father trotted after her.

"I think you need to sit down, Bren. Where it's warm."

"No argument." I let Jazz take my arm and steer me toward the part of the forge Rol had already restored.

"I'm—uh—I didn't mean to change you into a bug," she said as she helped me past the box of spelled Shadowhispers.

"No sweat." I sat down on the bench, and man, did that ever feel good. "A praying mantis isn't that bad, as far as bugs go."

"It wasn't a donkey," she said in an embarrassed voice. It almost sounded like she was laughing at herself. "I don't know where the hedgehog came from."

"Hey, on a better day, I might have paid you to pull that one off."

She sat down beside me, and for the first time that day, I felt better. Her golden eyes were deep and wide, and her dark hair hung around her face in long, soft wisps. Without thinking, I raised my wrapped left hand to touch her cheek.

Both of us flinched.

At least Dame Corey's spell had cleaned off the bandages. The good feeling left me in a hurry, but Jazz quickly grabbed my right hand and picked it up. Before I could pull away from her, she kissed my fingers, one at a time.

"When the others are better, I'll kiss them, too. You still have three, right?"

Frowning, I nodded.

"Then that's three kisses I owe you."

The musical sound of her voice made me laugh in spite of everything. "Can I have one now if I ask nicely?"

Jazz smiled, lighting up the forge. She leaned forward. I wrapped both arms around her and pressed my lips against hers. She always tasted so clean and sweet, and she felt so, so soft. Why had I stayed away from her all day? For the life of me, I couldn't remember. I'd gone to hell and back to bring home this wonderful feeling, and I didn't need to cut myself off from her again, for any reason.

"Want me to show you my place?" I said, noticing how low and rough my voice sounded, even though I didn't feel low or rough at all. "Rol let me have his weapons shed. I've even got a couch—"

At that second, the big guy walked through the forge carrying our swords. As he placed mine on the bench beside us and walked away, he cleared his throat.

"Sounded like he said 'harpies,'" Jazz murmured.

"He did say harpies. Damn it." I pulled back from her and rubbed my eyes. "This long as hell day isn't over yet, is it?"

"I guess not." She stood and offered me her hand. "Let's find Acaw and finish this."

"Yeah, yeah." I let her pull me to my feet. As we started out of the forge, my foot bumped the edge of the box of Shadowhispers.

As if from a million miles away, I heard a soft, nasty chuckle that sounded way too much like the Erlking.

"Whoa." I stopped. Looked back at the box. "Did you hear that, Jazz?"

She shook her head. "I didn't hear anything."

Holding on to her, I focused a bolt of our energy at the box and blew it to smithereens.

"Feel better?" Jazz asked as we walked away amidst the raining sparkles.

"Yep," I said. But I didn't. Not really.

chapter thirteen

JAZZ

I filled Bren in on the events of the afternoon, and the terrible truths I had learned from Sherise. The news of Alderon's cruelty and murder turned Bren's face and mood dark, which I understood. To learn your half-brother's treachery rivaled that of your exiled mother's—well, it wasn't pleasant. I knew he felt more responsible than he should for Alderon's actions, but there was little I could do about that.

"We have to find him," Bren growled as we headed to the barn with Acaw. "We might even have to kill him. I'm not sure I'd mind, brother or not."

"Finding him is key. If we don't stop him, he will keep up his campaign, letting Goddess-knows-what loose in our Sanctuaries."

"Agreed." Bren sounded miserable and angry, but I knew it wasn't directed at me. "I'm just glad he doesn't seem to be able to open and close entrances like we can."

"That thought is almost too horrible to ponder."

The oldeTowne storage barns loomed ahead. We made for the center one, where we knew the harpy leader to be housed.

The stench in the barn was almost too much for me. How could any creatures smell so unspeakably foul? And why had I thought we could talk to them?

"Perhaps I was in error." I held onto Bren's hand, thinking of pulling him back outside the door. Acaw had entered beside us and seated himself on a bale of hay near the door. His crow-brother remained unusually still and quiet, staring at the staff in my hand.

It was rare for an elfling to loan his sacred staff, but Acaw had always been generous with his, at least as far as I was concerned. The crow-brother seemed to think it wasn't such a good idea.

"We have to do this," Bren said firmly. He was wearing his sword on his left side now that he had to use his right hand, but he made no move to draw it. Instead, he kept his hand joined with mine as we went to work.

One by one, we righted the harpies who were lying on the barn floor, struggling against their bonds. Each one we moved against the barn wall, which had been spelled to withstand their kicks and punches. It took time. There were twenty at least in this barn alone, but finally, we came to the creature we thought we needed to address. The large one. The beast who maimed Bren.

With our magic connected, I felt Bren's disdain and rage as clearly as if he shouted his emotions to the barn rafters. Sensing each other's thoughts and feelings so clearly when we worked joint magic, we hadn't even begun to deal with that complication yet. For now, we were of single purpose.

Using the staff, I pointed and lifted the big harpy and set him on his feet. He towered above us, easily four times our height, with a wingspan that would have toppled the barn if he weren't magically restrained.

Immediately, the creature garbled at us in a guttural, furious way.

Acaw's staff hummed against my fingers, suffused with ancient power plus the combined magic Bren and I brought to the equation. I caught the last few words of the thing's tirade.

". . . witch. Kill. Must."

"He thinks he has to kill you—or us." Bren shook his head. "Acaw, can you ask him why and find out his name?"

Acaw made no response other than to whisper to his crow-brother, who chattered at the harpy with a series of clicks, grunts, and squawks.

The harpy's expression changed from bleak anger to mild surprise. He let loose with another set of sounds, making the staff buzz in my hand.

"Garth," Bren and I said together. It wasn't exact, but that was as close as we could come to the big brute's name.

"Father," was the next word I picked out.

Bren said, "Children."

He grimaced, and I knew his hand was hurting him. I felt twinges in my own fingers through our magical connection, and the low roiling in his belly as he stifled his reaction to the pain. He would rather be anywhere but here, but he was doing this because of his bargain with me, because of his duty to his people.

At that odd moment in the smelly barn, face to face with a monster who had tried to kill us, and had maimed Bren, I realized once and for all how much a king he had become in my absence. He must have caught the rush of warmth and pride I felt for him, because he looked at me.

Not now, his eyes said. *This is a time for hardness, not kisses.*

"Don't be inflexible," I whispered back, then almost laughed at what I'd said.

Garth chattered some more, getting louder, clearly frustrated.

"Free," Bren said as the staff vibrated. "Release. Save."

"He wishes you to release his bonds," Acaw said in a distant tone, listening to the clucks and squawks of his crow-brother.

"That's not happening," Bren said gruffly. "Tell him I'm not willing to take that chance."

The crow-brother and the harpy went back and forth, back and forth. The staff shook and buzzed, but we could tease out little of Garth's meaning.

"Smell, criminal—I think he said criminal deadman, but that doesn't make sense." Bren shook his head. "Acaw, ask him why he attacked us."

The elfling relayed this to the crow-brother, who spoke to the harpy.

Immediately, Garth went still and straightened up. He let out only one stream of careful grunts and whistles.

"Attack . . . save . . . children," Bren said. His eyes widened and he looked at me. "Jazz. He means he attacked us to save his children!"

Incredulous, I glanced at Acaw. The elfling actually looked as shocked as I felt.

"Let me have the staff." Bren let go of my hand and reached for it, and I turned it over gladly. "Keep your hand on my shoulder so we're connected, okay?"

I nodded.

Bren and Garth went to work in earnest then, with Acaw and the crow-brother stepping in less and less. I could barely follow everything they were saying, but the next thing I knew, Bren pointed the staff at the harpy and spoke the words to release his magical restraints.

"What are you doing?" I cried as I felt our power surge toward the beast.

"Turning him loose."

"I can see that! Why?"

"Because he's okay." Bren flicked the staff around the barn. One by one, the harpies descended to stand on the dirt floor. When the last touched down, they surged around Garth, and the big creature clucked and whistled like he was offering them comfort.

"Bren . . ." I squeezed his shoulder. "Don't leave me in the dark like this."

"I won't. Just a sec." He pointed Acaw's staff at the barn door, and it flew open. In seconds, all the harpies except Garth loped out the door and took off into the darkening sky.

"What did you just do?" I whispered, thinking about the hags, the Keepers—all the witches who would now want his blood as much as the beasts he had freed.

Bren lowered the staff and turned to me as Garth settled back on his haunches. "Alderon took their children. He killed them with spells and sent them to Talamadden on purpose—to keep you there!" A light burned in Bren's eyes. I'd only seen it a few times before, and I related it to absolute determination—and a touch of Bren-like madness.

"He told the harpies he wouldn't free their babies until you and I were both dead." Bren massaged his bandaged hand as he continued. "Not until the witches had been torn to pieces, to make it easier for him to take control of the Sanctuaries."

Many things suddenly made sense. How the harpies had come to attack me in Talamadden—and why they were so much smaller than these, why their thoughts and language were so much simpler. They were children. Only little ones, lonely in a strange place, terrified and hungry, and incredibly far from home. Worse than that, Alderon had lied to the creatures. He could no more free them from Talamadden than their parents could, unless . . .

"The Erlking may be helping Alderon," I said, almost to myself.

Bren's jaw dropped. "Where did that come from?"

"Yes," Acaw said as he came over to us and retrieved his staff. "It's the only explanation. Basic creatures such as harpies would sense falsehood. Alderon could not have convinced them he would retrieve their offspring unless he truly could. For that, he would need a powerful ally in the Sacred Lands."

The crow-brother politely translated our conversation to Garth, who spoke back suddenly and sharply. The bird's head whipped back to Acaw. It let out a shrill bunch of cawing that made my skin tighten.

"What?" Bren and I both asked at the same time.

"The harpy claims to have met the Erlking in the Sacred Lands. Alderon took Garth and his mate there to convince them of what he had done."

"So Alderon can open doors on the Path," Bren said before he swore emphatically.

I was too stunned to open my mouth. This was foul news indeed. We had to shore up our defenses immediately. Begin patrols. Discuss methods of detection, and—

And the harpy was talking again.

Acaw listened to his crow-brother and said, "Garth says you are wasting time. He has kept his bargain and sent his kin away. Now you must do as you promised."

My stomach tightened. "Bren? What promise did you make?"

With a miserable expression on his face, Bren ran his bandaged hand across his brown hair, then cursed some more when the bandages hung tight in the strands. After a long minute, during which my stomach began to ache fine and proper, he said, "I told him we would go back to Talamadden with him to rescue the harpy children."

"You what?" Gold and silver sparks blasted up between us, and I knew if I put my hand on him, the whole barn would blow apart.

"You're the one who wanted me to negotiate!" The silver sparks shot higher than the gold ones. "I made peace without another battle. No swords, no magic. That's what you wanted, right?"

"I don't know what I wanted, but it wasn't that. Go back to Talamadden. Have you lost your senses?" Tears pushed at my eyes. "I don't want to go anywhere near death. Not now. Not until my time! Got that?"

Bren's eyes narrowed. "It's the right thing to do, and you know it."

"I don't care."

"Yes, you do."

"Go to hell!" I banged his chest with my fists, and one wall of the barn did blow outward with spectacular force. Boards smacked the ground outside, echoing in the quiet of the oldeTowne dusk.

As Acaw cleared his throat and pointed his staff at the mess of nails and wood, Bren grabbed both of my hands in his good one and held them tight. "You don't believe in hell," he said with that blasted quirky smile.

I had never wanted to hit him so badly in all the time I had known him.

Instead, I leaned forward and kissed him hard on the lips. The stubble on his cheeks and chin scraped against my face. Familiar. Right. Absurdly calming.

Bren looked surprised and confused when I pulled away, and I didn't blame him. That's exactly how I felt.

The glow of our magic gradually settled into a blended, calm light, almost white gold in color, and he sighed. "I didn't know L.O.S.T. was in such danger from Alderon—but even if I had—it's still the right thing to do, Jazz. We have to risk leaving one more time. We have to save those babies."

"Yeah, yeah," I muttered, then recoiled at how much I sounded like . . . like . . . well, Bren. The urge to hit him swelled once more, but I directed my attention to Garth instead.

The giant harpy looked less than patient. His claws clicked incessantly, one to the other, his wings twitched, and he kept opening and closing his mouth, giving me a splendid view of his fangs. Not to mention the fact he was actually starting to stink worse.

Wonderful.

I detached my hand from Bren's and headed for the barn door, since Acaw had so kindly repaired the damaged wall.

"Where are you going?" Bren called as I stalked out of the barn.

"Away from here. Tell the harpy we're leaving tomorrow morning. I need to talk to Mother and Sherise. And some slithers, if Todd hasn't poisoned them all against me."

It seemed like old times on the Path as I stalked through the village, from the ancient-style huts and cabins of the olde-Folke all the way into the modern section of town. Few people were about in the early evening, but most fled as I approached. A few dared to stay close by, but they bowed so deeply they might have been kissing the ground. A finger of guilt nudged at my heart. Perhaps these were some I had turned into daisies when I lost control at the training arena.

I knew I should feel more ashamed than I did, but I didn't have the urge. I didn't have the energy either. How had I spent so much time beating myself up before I died? I don't know how I ever got anything done with all that obsessing. Well, except for cleaning. I was very good at cleaning . . . if a little excessive.

My mother wasn't going to like this at all. Rol would like it less, but Bren and I needed them to stay here, to work with Todd and Sherise to ward L.O.S.T. against Alderon while we were gone.

Goddess, I didn't have the fortitude to deal with Todd and the slithers tonight. Let that wait. A night's rest—that's what I needed. Let me fall asleep, wake up in one piece, and take on the miseries in the morning.

Shoving my hands in my pockets to keep my fingers warm, I turned the corner toward my house and approached from behind, through the adjoining yard. As I stepped into the hedgerow, I heard the sound of nearby voices rising, then falling back to conspiratorial whispers.

Heart suddenly hammering, I slowed down, making my movements through the evergreen branches as quiet as I could.

How could I have been so foolish, to put off what needed to be done?

Had the bastard Alderon already slipped into L.O.S.T.?

Was he preparing to attack my mother and Sherise, thinking I might be in the house as well?

My fingers itched to draw deep on the magic I once commanded all alone, but I was helpless without Bren beside me.

Well, not helpless. I could throw a rock as well as anyone.

I knelt and selected a good-sized stone from beneath the hedge, then resumed my creeping. I inched, then paused. Inched, then paused.

The voices kept up their argument.

When I finally got close enough to hear the words, I could also see the shadowy outlines of a man and a woman sitting on a bench beneath a leafless oak.

"Mac," the woman said, taking the man's hand. "It simply cannot be. There are too many complications. Your sons—my daughter . . ."

The man lowered his head. "Have your feelings changed? Are you trying to let me down easily?"

"No!" The woman's hand fluttered upward, and I recognized the voice and gesture at the same time. My mother.

And a man named Mac?

Goddess. McAllister. Bren's family name. My mother is talking to Bren's father!

The stone dropped from my hand, landing silently in the grass. It was all I could do not to sit right down on the ground in shock. A flush of heat warmed my cheeks, and I knew they had to be three shades of red. I was spying. I shouldn't be spying—but how could I walk away from *this*?

And *this* was heating up just like my face.

As I watched, mouth hanging open, my mother leaned forward and shared a brief, gentle kiss with my boyfriend's father. I didn't know whether to laugh, cry, or be ill.

"You should go now," Mother murmured. "Jasmina will be home soon. I don't know why she's not here already."

"Jasmina is nearly an adult," Bren's father said, hurt evident in his tone.

Mac. Ooh, by the Goddess, she calls him Mac?

"Todd is not," Mother reminded him gently. "He's already disaffected. So angry—and now we have Sherise to deal with as well."

Bren's father let out a slow breath. It was a sound of disappointment, of a heart turning inward to cope with hurt. "Will it always be work and duty and parenting before everything else?"

"I hope not. Mac, I truly—"

"Is it Giles?" he interrupted. "I know he died a rough death, that he was a hero—and—and a king. Do you feel like you're dishonoring your husband's memory with the likes of me?"

"No," Mother whispered. "Oh, no." There were tears in those words, matching my own. "It's the timing, and the timing only. Mac, please tell me you believe that."

After too long a pause, Bren's father finally answered. "I believe you."

A sob threatened to burst from my throat as he stood to leave, but I held my peace.

My mother sat in the shadows, head down, hands in her lap as he silently moved toward the gate leading to our front yard. She didn't look up to see how he stopped, how he looked back, the moonlight catching his face just so, showing the devastation etched in every angle, every line.

I wanted to leap out of the hedge and yell at my mother, shake some sense into her.

That man—Bren's father—oh, all right. Mac. He loves *her. And not just a passing, flirty love. He cares so much, and she sent him away!*

Why? So I wouldn't be upset? So Todd wouldn't get his undershorts in a twist? This was wrong. It was awful.

Long after Bren's father departed, my mother held her same position. She might have been weeping. Goddess knows I was. I sat there under that hedge in the cold night, and I forgot every concern, every goal. Nothing mattered for those endless minutes, except the sight of my proud mother sitting all alone in the dark with her head bowed, letting the man who loved her—a man I could tell she loved in return—walk away.

Duty. Responsibility. Is it worth it? Is anything worth that kind of pain?

The memory of Egidus, of the feather he sent and the message he asked me to carry crossed my mind. In all the chaos, it had slipped away completely—but now it made perfect sense.

Love is never wrong.

That's what he told me to tell her. Give her the feather, and tell her Egidus said love is never wrong. I needed to do it, maybe even right now.

"What are you doing?"

Bren's whisper didn't even startle me.

"I'm crying," I whispered back.

"Uh, yeah. That I can see."

"Sssshhh!"

My mother stood. She dabbed her eyes and straightened her back, then slowly walked into our house without a glance toward the hedge.

I let Bren pull me back out of the evergreen branches and help me up.

"Were you spying on your mother?" he asked, obviously amused.

"Yes." I sniffed. "My mother and your father."

Moonlight showed me Bren's lack of surprise. "Gotcha," he muttered. "Winnie. Jeez."

"Your dad calls my mom Winnie?"

Bren nodded.

I glanced toward the house, wiping away the last of my tears. "She calls him Mac."

"Please don't tell me. I don't want to know."

"When I got here, they were talking. They kissed."

"Jazz!" Bren actually covered his ears. "I'm not hearing this."

I jerked his hands away. "Stop being juvenile and listen to me. Once we do this thing, once we get back from Talamadden, that's it. We're staying here and being the king and queen. No more adventures. No more leaving other people to do our jobs while we're gone. Understand?"

"Yeah. Sure."

He left off the *whatever*, which probably saved his cheek a good slap. Instead, I stood on my tiptoes, brushed my lips against his, then let him go and shoved my way back through the hedge.

As I headed for the house, the cracking of branches told me Bren was following. He was muttering, too. I couldn't make out most of the words, but I caught a few clearly.

"Women . . . never understand . . . crazy."

Well, yes.

That did about sum it up after all.

chapter fourteen

BREN

By the next morning, I realized the whole negotiating-for-peace thing didn't mean we wouldn't need swords. It just meant we couldn't use them.

Jazz and I barely got a quick dinner and a few hours of sleep before the trouble started—at breakfast. With Sherise, Dame Corey, and my dad—just after my dad showed up and woke me up from the living room couch.

"What do you *mean*, you're going back to Talamadden?" Jazz's mom slammed both hands on the table, rattling my pile of scrambled eggs as she stood up. Sherise had covered her mouth and my dad was staring at me with his jaw ratcheting open and shut, open and shut.

Jazz handled herself like a pro, swallowing her bite of biscuit and calmly sipping orange juice before she answered.

"Bren made a binding agreement with the harpies. We have to rescue their children from Alderon's trap."

"You. Deal." Dad sounded like a malfunctioning telephone recording. "Harpies?" He pointed to my bandaged hand. "Didn't you learn—that's still not even healed!"

Sherise wrapped her fingers around her moonstone. She glanced from purple-faced Dame Corey, to Jazz, to me, then to my father, who was pulling on his beard and hair at the same time. Then she got up and fled.

"Sherise!" Jazz jumped to her feet as the front door slammed. "I didn't want to upset her. Damn."

"Do not use that language at my table!" her mother roared.

Jazz actually looked confused.

I crammed eggs in my mouth as fast as I could given my hand problem, anticipating the eggs—or me—getting turned into something I wouldn't want to eat. If I hurried, I might get to leave with a full stomach.

Dame Corey turned the skin-boiling force of her glare at me. I wolfed my entire stack of bacon and reached for a biscuit before sparks flew and the biscuit went running off the table, twitching whiskers and a tail.

I heard a loud *crack*, and I was suddenly staring at everyone's shoes. I twitched my nose and glanced around to see a long, slick rat's tail attached to my backside, which was gray fur now.

"Mother!" Jazz's shout was so loud I cringed, but not before I caught the scent of a nice fat bunch of crumbs near my dad and darted toward them. "We don't have time for this."

The air around me hummed, and my body tingled as my magic joined with Jazz's intentions. One second later, I was licking Dad's shoe.

"Oh. Sorry." I shook off that rat-feeling and managed to get back in my chair before Dame Corey turned me into a slug. This time, at least, I landed in my own plate so I could keep eating.

"Mother!" *Crack!*

I was sitting in my plate, which broke and poked me in the ass.

"I cannot believe—" *Pop!*

Dad caught me against his chest, despite my hideous possum-teeth and claws.

Jazz snarled in frustration. "Stop it."

Pow! I remembered Dad's lap being a lot bigger the last time I sat in it.

"Now, Winnie," this from Dad. Bad move. I would have thought he had better sense.

Zing-snap!

Dad and I wriggled on the floor gazing at each other through lidless snake eyes.

"Sssssssshhhh," I hissed. "Are you nuts or something?"

Thwack! Thock!

Jazz managed to fire at exactly the same time as her mother, leaving Dad and me standing with our heads through a matching set of stocks. We were human, except for what felt like very long horse tails flicking against each other from somewhere behind. The destroyed remnants of the breakfast and the table lay scattered underneath our feet. Well, I had one foot. The other was a horse's hoof.

Horse. Donkey. Hey. It was close to a previous embarrassment I had endured at Jazz's hands, before we fought Nire. That did it.

"Enough!" I yelled. I managed to wriggle both of my wrists, touch Jazz's arm with one outstretched finger, and make a major draw on our shared power as I barked commands. Silver and gold sparks flared. The stocks exploded into dust and swirled out of the kitchen. My tail and Dad's tail disappeared, and both my feet felt normal again. I was about to let go of the spellwork when Jazz's energy surged. The table repaired itself, and the broken dishes and food vanished. In seconds, the entire room was spotless—even my leather shirt, which had taken a beating.

Yep. That's my girl. Some things will never change.

I smiled at her. She rolled her eyes and folded her arms as the gold-silver wave of magic washed down to nothing. My dad cleared his throat, but I popped him a fast elbow to the ribs to keep his mouth shut. Then I evened out my expression and faced Dame Corey.

All in all, after the harpy, she wasn't scary. Much.

"I'm sorry," I said, and I meant it. "If there was any other way, any other choice I could see, I wouldn't have agreed. Saving those kid-monsters from Alderon is the right thing to do, and Jazz and I have to go together—but I swear to you, I'll throw myself into death head first before I let anything happen to her."

Dame Corey's eyes dropped to my bandaged hand. I swallowed hard, feeling my face heat up from shame and a quick flash of anger. Before I could say anything, though, the woman hitched, sniffled, and burst into tears.

Dad muttered, "Wonderful." But he went to her and put his arms on her shoulders.

Jazz was massaging her temples as I turned on her and growled, "Crying's not fair. All you women know it's not fair, but you do it anyway, don't you?"

"Shut up, Bren." She zapped the biscuit-mouse into oblivion as it peered around the kitchen doorway. Then she zapped a whole bunch more stuff. Cobwebs and exploded-stock dust, best I could tell. After a few deep breaths, she added, "I need to pack a few things. You—you—well. Just—deal with them. Then we need to go find Sherise and Todd."

"Me? Why do I have to deal with the parents?" I started to zap something of my own, but Jazz had already left the kitchen, and our connection was getting too weak.

When I turned around, Dad was holding Dame Corey, who was still sobbing.

I sighed. "I am sorry. Really."

Dad nodded. "I know. You have to do what you think is best."

"This is the last time we plan to leave everything in your lap." I frowned, remembering what Jazz said the night before, about how we had to find other solutions in the future. "Our responsibilities are here, to the witches. To the Path. We get that."

Looking at them huddled together, thinking of how much they had lost, of how much they had been having to do for us—how much they *still* had to do while we went off on the rescue mission—I did get it.

That's when the racket started outside. Loud, high-pitched shrieking and hissing and the crackle of randomly exploding spellfire.

It was all I could do not to let loose with a string of words that would have turned Jazz's mom purple again.

From the front bedroom, Jazz yelled, "Bren, could you handle those blasted hags while I find my toothbrush? Crap. I think I hear a Keeper."

I didn't kill her. Really, I didn't. I just waited for her to finish jamming stuff into a canvas bag she borrowed from her mother's closet. When I finally got her out the door, it took almost an hour to calm and disperse the crowd in the main village, and another hour to make our way to the edge of oldeTowne, toward where my little brother headquartered his zoo. We kept having to stop, explain, convince—and we did our best not to use forceful magic on the oldeFolke. I figured Dad and Dame Corey would have enough mess to deal with without adding hard feelings on top of hard feelings.

No sooner had we set foot between the oldeTowne huts than a group of six black-robed and hooded hags confronted us. Their obvious leader, a gnarly twisted sister with long dirty fingernails, shoved back her hood and hissed a challenge to Jazz. So did her cobra-shaped hag-spirit. Then she turned on me.

"How dare you?" she croaked in that gravelly hag voice that always made my skin crawl when I heard it up close. "How can you set loose those murdering sons of a kracken?"

I patiently explained the deal and why I made it, even speaking in the olde language as best I could to be polite. Unfortunately, I could tell right away that this hag could care less. She leaned forward, her snaky hag-spirit leaning with her, bobbing its cobra head.

"Do you think I care about the children of creatures more animal than anything else, boy? Of killers weak enough to bow to whatever evil passes by?" Man, did her breath ever smell like dead onions and deader garlic. "We cast them from our ranks long ago. Let them all perish!"

"We cannot—" Jazz began.

The hag hushed her with a wicked snarl. She raised her wrinkly hand and curled her fingers to hex me, but one of the other hags stepped forward and took her by the arm. "Peace," she pleaded, and I could tell by her sweet voice she was young. "There has been enough death, and I would not choose to see you banished for doing serious harm to another witch—to our king."

"King." The older hag spit out the word like it tasted rotten. "Nigh on thirty dead, scattered through all the clans. We suffered more loss than any, but we had no voice in this—this—accursed *bargain*."

Once more the younger hag spoke up. "Please, *Herzmutter*."

This time, the hag actually lowered her arm. Her expression gentled, but the blaze of disgust still burned in her too-black eyes.

As for the younger one, something was off, something I couldn't quite—wait a minute. Where was her hag-spirit?

"Helden?" Jazz lowered her canvas bag off her shoulder. Her next words came out in German. "I'm glad you survived the destruction of Shallym."

The hag-girl pushed back her hood, and I realized she was human. Around Todd's age, not bad looking for a nutcase who chose to hang out with creepy oldeFolke. She had brown braids and a dimple on her chin. A tiny blue stone glittered at her throat, hanging on a braided leather loop. The color was different from a moonstone, but for some reason, it reminded me of Sherise's good luck charm. Jazz looked at it, too, really hard.

"I am glad you returned from Talamadden, Your Majesty." Helden smiled shyly. "Are you certain you must risk a journey back?"

"Yes. After what you saw of Nire, of evil, you realize the right of this, I hope." Jazz's return smile was hopeful. "We should never turn our backs on truth, on justice, or mercy. If we do—"

Helden nodded. She spoke to the older hag again, and the freaky crone finally sighed and shrugged. I couldn't make out what they were saying, past the hag calling Helden *Herzgreldas* before patting her on the cheek. Then she raised her hood, hissed at the other four hags—who did have hag-spirits—and they slithered away.

"It's a term of affection," Helden explained as Jazz shouldered her bag and we once more started for Todd's zoo. "Before I came here, I was close to a hag named Grelda who died trying to cross the old Path to stay with me. It means, more or less, Grelda's heart."

“Hags have hearts?” It was out of my mouth before I could stuff it back. Jazz popped me a good one on my shoulder, but Helden only laughed.

“They do, *ja.* Hard to find, and the beat sounds a little like hssss-hsssss.” She laughed some more, and it made Jazz and me smile.

“Thank you for helping,” Jazz said. “We’ve never really been able to integrate the hags. They stay to themselves. So clannish.”

Helden shrugged. “They’re easy enough to love once you know them. And you know, one day I’ll be hag in title, even though I wasn’t born to the blood.”

That surprised me. “I didn’t know they—uh—took humans.”

“It’s rare,” Jazz conceded. “But I think Helden is . . . special. You know, Helden, things were so desperate when I first rescued you, I never asked your family name.”

“Hartzell,” Helden answered brightly as we passed beside two big rocks signaling the start of protected slither lair grounds—Todd’s domain. “The spelling has changed across time, but the meaning is—”

“Stag. Yes. A very old line of witches.” Jazz’s expression said, *I should have known that.*

Mine probably said, *What the hell?*

Right about then, I spotted Todd and Sherise sprinkling seeds on the ground to feed his cannibal quails. Seeds and—other stuff. Never mind.

“Hey, Todd!” I waved. Sherise waved back, but Todd barely gave me a look. He did manage a grunt as we joined them, and a second grunt when Jazz introduced Helden. I got the feeling Todd already knew her, but he played that pretty low-key. Looking from Sherise to Helden, I figured I understood at least that much about his attitude. Little sucker knew how to get himself in some major trouble. I thought about grinning, but figured it would get me fed to his bloodsucking birds.

Rol and Acaw made an appearance then, hanging back a little, eying the quail. I could tell by the look on the big guy's face and by the way Acaw's crow-brother hopped around that Garth the harpy was likely losing patience. I whispered as much to Jazz, then turned back to Todd.

"Listen, we have to go to Talamadden—"

"I heard," he said coldly, pitching more seeds and—er—red stuff out for the quail. I tried not to listen as they growled and chomped. "Nobody's too happy about it."

Sherise gave me a nervous smile, almost apologetic.

"Yeah, well, I was hoping I could count on you two to help hold down the fort until we get back."

Once more, Sherise smiled at us, even Helden, but Todd just pitched a bunch of gory stuff all over my shoes. "I'm not your loyal slave. Sherise and I have stuff to do. We can't be running around playing lord king and queenie-poo."

Jazz stiffened at that last word. "Queenie-poo?"

Helden grabbed Jazz's twitching arm just like she had grabbed the hag's. I swear the girl exuded some sort of calm potion through her skin or something, because my brother didn't get turned into one of his psycho-gamebirds.

"Dame Corey and Mr. McAllister will do most of the work, I'm sure." Sherise was holding Todd by the elbow, looking more desperate. "Rol will help. It'll be fine."

"Whatever," Todd muttered.

I so wanted to grab the little snot and take him out behind the storage barns. We'd either beat each other to death or I'd figure out what was bugging him—but we just didn't have time.

"We need a couple of slithers so we can travel quickly," Jazz said through clenched teeth. "A large one for Bren and me, and a smaller one for Acaw."

Todd's glare could have lit a fire when he looked up. "No. You're not getting one of them slaughtered just to save a little time and effort."

"Look, asshole, get a grip." I pointed my bandaged hand at his face. "I'm the king and Jazz is the queen, and we need the lizards." After a pitiful look from Sherise, I added, "Please."

"No!" Todd threw down his bucket of bloody seeds. The quail fell on it, snarling and flapping. Todd looked like he was about to do the same to me.

Sherise made a nervous grab for her moonstone. "Wait! Please, Todd?"

My brother seemed to halt in mid-lunge. His face rearranged into something calmer—still sulky and sullen, but lots more relaxed. He cut Sherise a sharp look, then let out a sigh. Helden sighed, too, and I realized she had her hand on her necklace. Jazz was glancing from Helden to Sherise, looking puzzled—and a little nervous.

"Fine, okay." Todd stuck his clean fingers in his mouth and gave two different whistles. One was long with two beats, and the other short with three. When he finished, he added,

"If they get hurt, I'm taking blood for blood, and I won't be soft on you because of that bad hand. Got it?"

It was my turn for the "Whatever."

All three girls lowered their eyes and shook their heads as the ground gave a few rumbles and a shake. From the sound of the thundering footsteps, our rides were on the way, none too soon for my preference.

Todd didn't bother with a goodbye or a good luck or anything. He just stalked off with his mob of man-eating quail matching him step for step. Sherise gave me a quick kiss on the cheek, which earned her a brief glare from Jazz. But then Sherise gave Jazz a quick hug and hurried after Todd.

"I think I'll see what I can do," Helden offered. She lifted the cowl of her black robe and glided in the direction they went. For a human, she looked awfully hag-like when you couldn't see her face.

"Not sure that's a good idea," I said, watching her go as Rol and Acaw made a beeline for us—along with a huge blue slither and a much smaller golden specimen.

Jazz was rubbing the sides of her head like she already had a headache. "Neither is this, but sometimes the choices suck. I mean, stink. Damn. Did I say any of that? I *have* lost my sanity."

Whatever came to mind, but I wasn't stupid enough to say it.

Instead, I spent my energy on giving Acaw all the proper commands so the Erlking couldn't fry him or stick him in elfling jail once we reentered his realm. I definitely wasn't looking forward to running into that guy again.

chapter fifteen

JAZZ

"It's colder. And darker." I stood inside the Path with Acaw, hugging myself as I shivered. I was tired from having to disassemble and reassemble the walls of the general store to get the harpy and slithers to the point of contact in L.O.S.T. So far, we had Garth and the small golden slither through the opening we had created, and Bren was busy shoving the big blue in from behind. Garth was helping by tugging on the creature's neck, keeping alert for sudden blasts of fire.

"It smells bad, too!" I shouted to Bren.

"Probably our guests," he shouted back as the blue one came slowly onto the ribbon through time.

True enough, the harpy did reek, and both slithers smelled of lair dirt and droppings. Still, there was something else. Something wrong in the Path's energy. The bright silvery walls I had seen on my return from the dead had faded to an unpleasant shade of paste, and I swear I saw faint dark patterns flittering past. When I turned to try to get a better look, they vanished as if they were never there.

Was this my fear of Shadows?

I doubted that.

The look of discomfort on Acaw's face confirmed my fears.

"The Path has . . . changed," he agreed, as if hearing my fears.

"But not like when Nire invaded."

"No," the elfling agreed. "However, you experienced more of Nire's patterns than the rest of us. We were shielded from the worst of it."

Remembering the attack on Shadowbridge, the way Acaw and his crow-brother nearly surrendered their own existence to preserve mine, I couldn't accept that. Still, arguing with an elfling was about as useful as arguing with a witch from Bren's family.

At last, the blue slither fully entered the Path, and Bren and I closed the fissure behind us.

Bren was sweating and breathing hard, and I could see a little blood on his bandaged hand. He steadied himself and glared at Acaw. "Have you thought about how we're getting this brute into the Sacred Lands? There's no way it's fitting through that little hole."

Acaw's only answer was to turn his back and start down the Path, the charms on his staff giving a little music to the faltering hum of the magical energy.

"Why does he talk to you and not me?" Bren asked grouchily as we herded the smaller slither, leaving Garth to lead the larger beast.

"Because he's an elfling male."

"So if you had hired an elfling female servant long ago, she'd talk to me better than you?"

"Of course. Right before she poisoned you, wrapped you up, and left you in a cave to feed her young."

Silence. And then, "You're pulling my leg."

I didn't answer him, but I couldn't help laughing. The sound was strange in the increasingly silent Path. It was like the longer we walked it, the worse it got.

"Something *is* off about this place," Bren muttered. His hand dropped automatically to his sword, but he grimaced when bandage met hilt. "As soon as we're through with this rescue, I'll bring Todd and figure it out. Maybe it needs repairs."

The mere thought of the magnitude of the next problem before we finished tackling the mess at hand—it was enough to render me silent until we finished the hike to the entrance to the Sacred Lands.

When Acaw tapped his staff against the Path, two hinged gates appeared, well taller than the largest slither, and twice as wide.

"So why did I have to climb through a hobbit hole the first time?" Bren groused.

"The entrance was as large as necessary," Acaw allowed as he used his staff to open the gates.

Bren snorted. "Necessary for whom? A gnome? I thought maybe it was so little to keep the Erlking from squeezing through."

Acaw greeted this with a sigh as he escorted the harpy through the gates. I grabbed the smaller slither's lead rope and tugged. "Bren, the Erlking is a shapeshifter. He could assume the form of a cockroach and skittle through a bolt crack if he chose to do so."

"Yeah, yeah, yeah." Bren dragged the blue slither through the gates, which swung shut behind us. "I knew that."

"Once the oldeFolke managed to stop his killing of humans and ward him into this realm, they set spells to keep him here. All magical beings were then charged to stay clear except in extreme need—and never to bring through a host who would be vulnerable to the bastard's tricks." The little slither finally cooperated, which was more than I can say for Bren's charge. "Witches are immune, and oldeFolke, and natural magical beasts like the slithers and harpies—so it's not a problem for us."

Bren held his hand out to help me mount our slither, but he had a funny look on his face. "I'm a halfblood, remember? Is that a problem?"

"Don't worry." I took his hand, then kissed his cheek. "Your blood is strong, half or not, and we're together. Our magic will be enough to defeat him if he dares challenge us."

A few hours later, my cheeks were warmed from the sun, and I felt refreshed from the fresh air. If possible, the Sacred Lands seemed even more beautiful than I remembered from my first trip through.

The harpy made a series of fusses and clicks I had heard before.

"Fly faster," Acaw translated Garth's instructions with his usual composure, even though we were sailing above the ground at a blistering pace.

"What a pain in the ass," Bren muttered in my ear. He was sitting behind me, arms wrapped around my waist, holding me close, reminding me of when we first flew on a broom together. Our slither called himself Firestorm, and Acaw's dragon called himself Ironblood.

Using our combined magic, we had fashioned an aerodynamic shield to deflect the cold and the rush of wind, and to keep communications easier. For our efforts, we were treated to a non-stop dose of Garth's dissatisfaction with how long it had taken for us to leave L.O.S.T. and how slowly slithers flew.

We were all being patient. After all, if our children were on the line, we would be in just as big a hurry as he was.

"So what's the deal with Sherise and Helden?" Bren's question sounded casual, but I could tell he had been pondering it right along with me.

"I'm not sure," I admitted. "All I know for certain is that they are both heirs to very old, very powerful witching lines with unique gifts. Sherise is the Ash of Ash, a family known for prophecy and clarity of sight. Helden is the Hartzell of Hartzell, a bloodline famous for grace amongst conflict, one of the few groups of witches welcome amongst almost any clan or tribe, olde or modern."

Bren snuggled me a little closer, making me smile. "They seemed to handle Todd well. I think he has his hands full with the both of them."

"I think its Helden and Sherise who have the handful. Your brother needs work, Bren."

He let out a breath, warm against my ear. "I know. After the rescue, after the Path, he and I need some serious guy-time. I think he's still really bugged about Mom. Nire. You know."

"Has he always been so difficult?"

"Nah—well, a little. High-spirited, impulsive, big-mouthed. Don't say it."

I leaned my head against Bren's shoulder. "You're living proof that boys like Todd can grow up to be kings."

He coughed, and I wondered if he might be embarrassed by the compliment. I would have expected a smart remark about his incredible prowess, but his silence was quite endearing.

"So, back to these two girls—do you think it's a fluke that we've got two witch mini-queens around the same age, showing up in L.O.S.T. about the same time?"

"Goddess, Bren. Let's keep to one problem at a time. You're getting as obsessive as me."

"Hey, I resemble that remark." He kissed the side of my head.

"The answer, by the way is no. I don't think it's happenstance, but I can't figure out the significance either."

"I'm heartbroken. You really *don't* know everything."

"Shut up."

The harpy made his fusses and clicks, a little differently this time.

"You are annoying humans," Acaw translated smoothly.

That night, after our dinner, the harpy retired to sleep with the slithers, saying he felt more comfortable with beasts closer to his own design. Briefly, I felt sorry for Garth, and for all creatures who were neither truly human or truly animal. I couldn't begin to understand how confusing life must be for them. When he started snoring, I forgot most of that pity, wondering instead how I would ever get to sleep.

Acaw, who had agreed upon third watch, wasn't exactly sleeping silently either. He breathed in and out, and on each exhale, his crow-brother made bizarre bird grumbles until I wanted to bang my head from the sound.

But instead I relaxed into Bren's arms. Stars glittered through the tree canopy and moonlight gave everything a silvery glow. We were sitting before a small campfire that crackled, hissed, and popped. Flames flickered before us and I watched them, almost mesmerized by their magical dance. Despite the snoring from the nearby beasts, the night and everything about it felt romantic as I snuggled into Bren's embrace. I was back with my champion, my love, and this was truly the first real time we'd had alone.

"Where do they live, anyway? The harpies." Bren's voice was low, as if not to wake anyone, as he nodded in the direction of the snoring Garth, who was topped only by the snoring slithers.

"Harpies live everywhere," I whispered, leaning into Bren as he tightened his arm around my shoulder. "They just keep to themselves, usually in the oldest of the older Sanctuaries. As time has moved on, they have become more scarce. Their caves and hunting grounds have been laid waste—and they aren't exactly popular, even amongst the oldeFolke. Most of them live here, in fact. In the Sacred Lands. It's the best place for them."

"So, when we rescue these kidlings, Garth and his can just . . . go? Find their own way home?"

"Yes."

Bren relaxed a fraction. "At least something is easy."

"Hush. You're teasing the Goddess."

He gave me a tighter squeeze. "Guess I shouldn't mention that I think it's weird we haven't seen the Erlking?"

"Stop it!" I elbowed him.

"I'm serious." He bit the top of my ear.

I shivered at the same time I threw him another elbow, firmer this time. "Me, too!"

"You *are* annoying humans," Acaw said sleepily, then turned over and covered both his own head and his crow-brother's with his blanket.

Bren leaned toward the fire and stared at the elfling. "Was he translating?"

"Uh, no," I whispered, doing all I could not to break into loud laughter.

Resting my head against his shoulder, I sighed. "I can't believe we're going back to Talamadden."

Did I say that out loud?

Bren tensed. "I can't believe I'm letting you go back there. I won't leave you, Jazz. This time if you get stuck there, you're stuck with me, too."

I tilted my face up to smile at Bren, but caught my breath when I saw the look in his warm brown eyes. He was studying me with a gaze so intense, so filled with longing, and something more, that it took my breath away.

"I wish . . ." His voice trailed away for a moment, but his gaze never faltered. "I wish we had more time together. Just you and me. Alone."

"What about now?" I whispered. "We're alone."

Bren's gaze cut to the snoring slithers, Garth, and Acaw, then back to me. "It's not the same." He shook his head and his silky hair brushed my cheek. "We're heading into danger again . . . to death's haven and God knows what we'll have to face. I want you home. Safe. With me."

I reached up and cupped one of his cheeks, and the light stubble tickled my palm. "Wherever we are, whatever happens, I will always feel safe with you."

I drew him to me, and his mouth gently took mine. That kiss—that kiss was unlike any kiss we had ever shared. A tingling sensation expanded deep in the pit of my stomach and my arms trembled as I wrapped them around Bren's neck. He tasted of the honeyed sweetcake he'd eaten after dinner and his scent of man and the outdoors surrounded me.

It struck me then, full and completely . . . Bren was no longer the boy I had trapped and taken onto the Path. He wasn't impulsive or irresponsible, or any of the things I used to yell at him when I was angry. He was a true and great King of the Witches. He was a man now.

And what was I?

I had survived death, turned loose of so many obsessions, and come back to embrace life. Along my journey I had become—what? A true queen? A woman?

The thought sat strangely inside me, terrifying and exciting, wrong and right all at the same time.

When Bren pulled away from our kiss, I felt the resonance between us. By the look in his beautiful eyes, I knew he'd felt it, too. For all we had been through together, this one moment outshined the rest.

Somehow, everything had just changed.

"Jazz . . ." He hesitated, and his throat moved as he swallowed. "I know we're still young. But we're not too young to be king and queen." Bren reached up with his good hand and brushed his knuckles across my cheek. "I mean to *really* be king and queen."

My heart pounded so hard my chest ached. I swallowed, too. "Exactly what are you trying to say?"

I asked, even though I knew, knew it with everything I had. Hearing it out loud, hearing it from him, felt so important.

He stroked my cheek again and gave me that crooked smile of his that made the fluttering in my belly intensify. "You know what I'm saying, Jazz." He brushed his lips softly over mine then whispered. "When we finish this, when everything is back to normal . . ." He paused again and gave a soft laugh. "As normal as it can be for the King and Queen of the Witches."

"Then what?"

"I want you to be my real and true queen, Jazz." His gaze deepened as his lips hovered above mine. "I want you to marry me."

I swear my heart skipped two, three beats. He'd said it, he'd really said it. I tightened my arms around his neck and buried my face in his tunic. The leather smell of his shirt mixed with the smoky odor of the fire made my eyes ache. No, they ached because of the tears that hovered at the back of my eyes. At that moment I was so confused. I wanted with all my heart to say *Yes!* when my head told me *No*. I had barely turned seventeen, and Bren was just eighteen now. We were too young, there were too many journeys lying ahead of us.

But why couldn't we take them together, bound to each other for all times?

Because this time you might not make it out of Talamadden, Jasmina Corey. You'll likely not survive a second traveling in death's haven. And Bren . . . No matter what, he must live.

"Oh, Goddess," I said aloud, without meaning to, and this time a tear did roll down my cheek.

"What's wrong?" He brushed my hair behind my ear. "You love me, don't you?"

Even though I wanted to keep my face hidden in his shirt, I forced myself to release him and to draw myself away. I wanted to cling to him forever, but that couldn't be. Not now. Not yet. Maybe not ever.

"Hey." Bren reached up and wiped away the single tear with his thumb. His brown eyes searched mine, and I saw both love and confusion in his gaze. "You do love me?"

"With all my heart." I brought his good hand to my chest so he could feel the pound of it beneath his fingers. "But right now we're facing too much to make such a big decision. Let's wait until we're back in L.O.S.T., and everyone is safe again. Then we'll talk about . . . about permanence. About marriage."

For a long moment he was quiet, then he gave a slow nod. "All right." He slid his hand from where it rested above my beating heart, up until his fingers were wrapped in my long hair, and he drew me to him again. "But when we do get back, just realize that I'm not taking no for an answer."

The coolness of the forest wrapped around me and I snuggled against Bren's chest. We were still sitting beside the fire, and the flames drew my eyes like an irresistible force. Warmth in the cold, light in the dark. My eyes drifted closed. I didn't want to sleep, I wanted to stay awake as long as Bren did, but . . .

Helden and Sherise sat in the clearing Sherise and I used for her training. They looked tired, rumpled—hair out of place, clothing askew, as if they had been hard at work. There were shadows all around them, including a particularly large lump heaped on the ground. I tried to focus on the lump, but I couldn't make it out.

"She said it might have power," Sherise said, holding up her moonstone.

Helden lifted her chain, letting her own heirloom jewel swing back and forth. It was an ancient starstone, of that I felt certain. "Grelda said the same of this. That if I learned the proper gaze, how to see through it and hold my intent, I could be stronger."

"Magnify the gift! Yes, that's it." Sherise cupped the moonstone. When she looked up at Helden, her eyes burned with startling intensity. She seemed more than powerful. Almost frightening. "We have to try it."

The clearing filled with nervous clucks and tuttings. Some of the dark shapes shifted, and I realized they were hags. Six or seven at least. But where were the hag-spirits?

The bundle on the ground shifted, and one of the hags hissed, spreading out gnarled fingers and muttering a warding incantation.

This seemed to startle Helden into action. She cradled her own stone and stared into it with a grim, disturbing frown. Very hag-like. Very menacing.

Sherise did the same.

The two stones flared, pitching light through the darkness as the girls turned their sharp, unnatural gazes toward the bundle.

It shrieked and flailed against its bonds even as the hags worked containments. I realized with sick dread what those bonds were. Snakey hag-spirits, clinging tight, trying to strangle the life out of their captive. A human. A boy.

Dear Goddess.

It was Todd!

I woke with a gasp.

"What is it?" Bren pulled me even closer. "You're shaking."

"A dream." I coughed. Yes, it was a dream. A nightmare. Obviously, I had drifted off to sleep in Bren's embrace, feeling safe, and loved, and happier than I remembered ever feeling. The fire had burned low, and Bren had been too much of a gentleman to wake me by drawing on our combined magic to build it up again.

The way his arm gripped me, and the slight movements he made, even the rise and fall of his chest told me that he hadn't fallen asleep like I had. Certainly it was nearing time for Acaw's and his crow-brother's watch.

"So?" Bren kissed the top of my head. "What did you see?"

"It was Todd." I sat up and pushed back from him, studying his handsome face in the firelight. "I dreamed Sherise, Helden, and some hags had taken him prisoner."

Bren frowned. "What, because he did something asinine?"

I shook my head. "I—in the dream, the girls—I think they were using their stones to hurt him."

"Damn!" Bren jumped up, wild-eyed.

I got up with him, totally at a loss for what to say.

At that second, low and beautiful singing began to filter through the forest in a mesmerizing cadence.

"Oh, shit," Bren muttered as I turned a full circle, looking for the source of the sound.

My heart pounded a little faster. I blinked sleep from my eyes and listened intently to the eerie song that was growing stronger, winding around us like a serpent coiling around its prey.

A few feet away, Bren shivered as if taken by a strong and sudden chill. "The Erlking's daughters." He gripped the hilt of his sword with his right hand, then slowly drew the weapon from its sheath. Metal scraped against leather, loud to my ears and almost harsh against the beautiful, but certainly deadly song.

"Enchantresses," I murmured as I moved closer to him. My fingertips crackled as our power flowed between us, and his sword glowed a light silver. "Best to never be caught unprepared with the likes of them."

"Not to mention their bastard of a dad." Bren shivered and stomped his feet as if to warm himself. I pointed to the dying fire, drew on our combined power, and it leapt into a full and proper blaze.

The singing was louder now, the music both eerie and menacing. Why hadn't the harpy woken? Even the slithers and the elfling slept. Or did I see a twitch beneath the blankets? Ah, yes, my good and faithful servant was merely feigning his sleep, if only to surprise the enchantress if need be.

Bren shivered so much now that his hand tinted blue against the hilt of his sword, and I could tell he had a hard time maintaining his grip on his weapon. Why was he so cold? With his injured hand he rubbed behind one ear and winced from the pain it must have caused his hand.

The singing was so loud now that my ears ached with it. Even I was not entirely immune to the power of their song. I had to fight to maintain my senses.

Now the music was coming from every direction, surrounding us.

I sent Bren a burst of heat through our magic and he jumped. "Thanks." He looked less chilled now as he held up his sword and slowly turned to look at the trees around our small clearing. I turned, too, my back to his, our magic flowing between us, ready the moment we needed it.

Ghostly forms appeared in the trees, wavering, as if made from moonlight. In the next moment, four—no, six—beautiful women melted from the covering. Their forms became stronger and clearer the closer they came to us. I sensed their hatred and their desire for our demise. Except one—the blonde one who gazed at Bren with a seductive look to her eyes. At once I knew she was the enchantress who had touched Bren's essence, and I balled my fists to keep from zapping her and knocking her on her backside.

"Stay back," Bren ordered the enchantresses, his sword flashing a sudden silver brilliance. The women hesitated and their singing faltered as they shielded their eyes and gave soft whimpers. "What do you want? Where's your father, the Erlking?"

A redheaded enchantress took a brave step forward. Immediately I sensed she was the eldest of the sisters, their spokesperson. "Our most powerful and noble father sends you a message."

"Noble, my ass," Bren muttered, then louder he said, "What does the bastard want?"

The redhead hissed, and her eyes glowed a vicious green. The other sisters moved closer, their eyes glowing, too, their nearly sheer robes billowing in a sudden breeze, and their ethereal forms becoming more solid the closer they came.

I grabbed Bren's bandaged fingers and felt him flinch with pain. I flinched, too, but focused on our power as I held up my hand and shouted, "Cease!"

Nothing happened. The redhead merely laughed, showing delicately pointed incisors.

"It doesn't work on them," Bren grumbled. He raised his sword and brilliant silver light flooded our small clearing. The enchantresses whimpered and drew back, shielding their eyes. "But for some reason my sword does."

The redheaded enchantress hissed again. "Our father sends word, whelp."

"Get on with it." Bren's grip on his sword never wavered. "Deliver the message and get the hell out of here."

"If you do this unnatural thing, if you enter Talamadden to attempt to bring back the harpy young," she said in a voice that slithered through the night like the deadliest serpent, "the Erlking will make you pay."

"I'm so scared," Bren muttered where only I could hear him. Louder, he said, "Whatever. Now go before I use you to send my own message."

His sword throbbed with our joint powers, and the air around us lit up like high noon.

The enchantresses let out clamorous, furious wails. Clawing at the sky, they melted back into the forest, then vanished, like low-hanging fog in a wind.

chapter sixteen

BREN

We didn't talk about Todd.

We didn't talk about L.O.S.T., or risks, or the Erlking's daughters.

We just broke camp, mounted up, and flew like hell, which was fine by me. I couldn't believe how fast we were moving. The journey that had taken days before—it would be so much shorter this time. Good. I wanted this over as fast as possible.

Jazz seemed to understand how miserable I felt. Acaw, his crow-brother, and Garth didn't ask any stupid questions, either.

The enchantress's words rang in my ears, louder and louder with each passing minute, each new hour. It was still fresh in my mind when we reached the summit, landed, and disembarked to stand before the gateway between worlds.

The land of the living . . . and the land of the dead.

Damn. Todd. Was that a nightmare or a vision? If my little brother was in trouble, why didn't I *know? Are we that far apart now, that Jazz would get the vision and I'd get zilch?*

It tore me in half to keep flying away from him when I wanted more than anything to turn around and lay tracks for home.

Brother, son, boyfriend, king—trying to sort everything out sucked big time. How could I do everything I needed to do? Be everywhere I needed to be, and be responsible for everything I needed to be responsible for? It didn't seem possible.

Focus. One thing at a time . . .

We had come to help the harpies. We had to finish that in a hurry, then get home and figure out what was going on.

And speaking of the harpies, what was the Erlking planning, anyway? Last time he tried to kill me with a push. This time, though . . . it just seemed weird we hadn't seen him. I kept looking left and right, expecting to see something, or feel it—but I didn't sense a thing. Finally, I centered myself and got back to business.

The slithers landed smoothly in the now dark clearing I remembered from my first journey, and sure enough, there was the gateway.

Jazz and I bailed off and ran to it, both breathing hard, like we'd run all the way. Acaw and the harpy double-timed over, too.

For a long moment we all studied the black monolith, the doorway to a place the living should never be able to enter, and most of the dead couldn't leave. We didn't touch it, just stared at it. This time the sun wasn't shining, wasn't giving us at least some warmth from the snow beneath our feet. Moonlight lent an eerie glow to the doorway, and every noise made me want to jump. The hoot of an owl. The scurry of a mouse through the brush. And a sound like something slithering over branches . . . I didn't even want to think what that might be.

The slithers snorted and stamped, and Garth gave an impatient growl. Close by us, Acaw and his crow-brother remained silent.

Todd. What's going on? I sent the thought like my brother would actually hear me. *I'm worried about you. Just hang on. I'm going to take care of this thing, then I'll be right back to help you. Whatever you need, okay? I promise.*

I couldn't believe I was trying to talk to my brother in my head. Or trying to open the gateway to Talamadden to save a bunch of big, stinky harpies. And I still couldn't believe I'd asked Jazz to marry me. But at least that felt good. It felt right.

Focus, focus, focus . . .

Jazz shivered beside me. When I put my arm around her and my remaining fingers gripped her shoulder, I realized my hand didn't hurt—much—anymore. The magic and herbs the healers had used, and Jazz tending to my fingers with our magic each night, had made the skin heal over and the scabs were pretty much gone. I wondered if any of the pain I still felt in my hand was simply the pain of loss.

Yeah, maybe I didn't have all my fingers anymore, but I still had my magic—as long as I was with Jazz; still had my instinct for battle—as long as I was paying attention; and I'd learned to keep a cool and calm head—most of the time. I'd been a switch-hitter on my baseball team, I could sure as hell learn to be a switch—er, swordsman.

Jazz's trembling increased, and when I looked at her she was biting her lower lip. "Shadows," she whispered, then shook her head. The fear in her expression turned to one of resolve. "*No.* I will not let my fear draw them to me. I will not fear them any longer."

"Hey," I caught her chin in my hand, forcing her to look at me. "You don't have to cross over. You can stay here and wait. I'd be happier knowing you're safe anyway."

She frowned and elbowed me. "As if you could do it without me."

I clasped my hands to my heart. "You wound me, madame."

Jazz rolled her eyes and shoved me away. "You've been watching too many old human movies. Or reading too many ancient scrolls."

I winked, even though I was worried as hell.

We both turned our attention back to the wall. Jazz audibly inhaled and I rested my hand on my sword hilt. It felt all wrong with the sheath being on the opposite side of my hips, but maybe one day I'd get used to it. Yeah, one day I would. I just hoped it was *soon*.

The slithers raised their heads and snorted again, louder this time. Garth flapped his wings and gave a startled cry. Acaw's crow-brother squawked, but the elfling simply stated in his matter-of-fact voice, "Twilight grows in the land of the dead while midnight approaches on this side of the passage—as do many dangers. If you do not find a way to cross over now, I fear we may not have the opportunity to do so again."

Jazz and I looked at each other, and that's when the singing began.

"Damn," we both said at the same time.

"The weird sisters," I muttered.

The singing was louder this time, more intense. I forced myself to concentrate and tried to block the sounds from my mind like I'd learned to do with the klatchKeepers. But it was harder, so much harder. My head swam and my body chilled until my teeth chattered. Jazz sent me a stream of warming energy, and I straightened my stance, waiting for the freaky combo to come creeping up in their eerie way.

That was just about the second when everything went nuts.

Shadowy forms flew at us from every direction, so fast I barely had time to raise my sword and send a burst of power through it. Shrieks rent the air and I saw the enchantresses in the sword's silver glow. This time they barely flinched from the light. Instead it seemed to attract them, bringing them straight at us.

And this time the women were wielding daggers.

Sparks sizzled at Jazz's fingertips and I felt her draw on our mutual power as she shot a bolt of pure energy at an enchantress bearing down on her. The enchantress squealed, fell on her side, and rolled down the snowy incline.

At the same time, the redhead came at me, tiny fangs glistening in the moonlight, her hair flaming in the silvery light of my sword. Jeez, I didn't want to hurt a woman, but she was out to kill me.

Instead of slicing her head off with my weapon, I gripped the hilt and slammed the blade broadside against her shoulder. The impact jolted my teeth. The sword slipped in my off-hand, almost tumbling into the dirt.

The redhead cried out, dropped to her knees, and leaped back to her feet again in a flash. Shit, could that chick move! I could barely bring the sword around in time to drive her back a step. Each thrust, each parry, I was sure I was going to drop the blade and get my head bitten off. Literally.

While keeping my attention on fang-woman, I was aware of Jazz, fingers blazing, battling an enchantress or two, while the slithers and the harpy were also under attack. Acaw and his crow-brother were doing their Kung-Fu kickass thing, keeping more of the enchantresses away from me and Jazz.

There were so many! Or was it just that they moved so fast they seemed everywhere at once?

How could I fight them off? The sword felt like it was ripping my wrist off.

The redhead dove for me again, her face twisted with rage, her teeth and dagger coming straight at my neck. This time when I tried to block her with my sword, she dodged it and flung herself against my chest like a lioness. Woman or not, I fisted my hand and started to punch her jaw.

Before I ever landed a blow, something ripped her off me like she didn't weigh a thing.

"Get away from him, bitch!" Jazz had the redhead by the hair. Golden eyes blazing with fury, Jazz landed a swift kick to the enchantress's belly, then flung a fireball at her red curls.

That's my girl!

The redhead screamed and rolled in the snow, trying to put the fire out at the same time the other enchantresses continued their attack. The air smelled of burnt hair, blood, and battle. I could taste it on my tongue—could hear it roaring in my ears.

The slithers flapped their massive wings, knocking at least two enchantresses down the hill and almost sending Acaw after them. The elfling barely ducked in time, while driving away another one of the vicious women.

Garth was screeching, clawing at the enchantress who had given me that burst of healing and energy after I'd fought the Erlking. For one second I felt sorry for her. After all, she had healed me and gave me something extra. But when I saw her slice her dagger across the harpy's hand, my hair prickled on my scalp. I was seriously pissed. The bastard might have taken my fingers, but he'd done it for his children, and he'd become one of us on this long journey.

Sword in hand, I ran toward him and stumbled over a fallen enchantress. When I reached Garth, I braced myself and sent out a firmly planted side kick to the one who'd sliced the harpy. She went tumbling into a snowy bank, but she still got up. After she slowly pushed herself to her feet, her icy glare froze me down to my gut.

"You will regret that," the blonde said, just before she faded and vanished into the treeline.

I braced myself for another attack, but when I looked around, not an enchantress was to be seen. Only a piece of glimmering ripped cloth here, glistening strands of hair there, and blood glowing silvery black in the snow beneath the moon's light. I couldn't tell if the blood was theirs or ours, or both.

My breathing came hard and fast as I assessed the damage to our little troupe. Acaw and his crow-brother were already attending to the slithers, calming them, and placing balm on their wings. I swear the elfling had everything in his knapsack, including a whole magical first-aid kit. I smelled marigold and comfrey, and the sinus-clearing scent of tea tree oil that he was using to treat the slithers' wounds.

I turned my head and had the ridiculous urge to laugh, and at the same time felt a swell of pride when I saw Jazz. Her knees were bent in a battle stance, a dagger in each hand, obviously taken from an enchantress or two. Jazz's long black hair was wild around her face, her golden eyes blazing. Daggers at the ready, she looked like a warrioress who could kick some serious enchantress ass—which was exactly what she'd just done.

A soft cry jolted me from my thoughts and I turned to see Garth holding his human-like hand to his feathered chest. It was bleeding like crazy, and pain and misery twisted his ugly features—and something else. *Gratefulness*, I thought. He was grateful to me.

"Jazz," I called out, needing her healing energy to join with mine so that we could help the giant harpy.

The wild-haired woman with the flashing golden eyes dropped to her knees and let the daggers fall to her sides. She softened at once. "He's hurt."

"I need your help," I said, and as one we reached for Garth's hand. He mewled and cradled it closer to his chest.

"We're going to help you, heal you." Jazz's voice became soft, reassuring. "Let me see it."

Garth's hand trembled as he held it out and I felt light-headed at the sight of all that blood. Just like me, the harpy had lost fingers in an attack, only he'd had three whacked off with the dagger, where I'd lost only two.

"*Only* two," I muttered.

While we used our magic to seal the wounds and stop the flow of blood, I was intensely aware of all that was going on around us, and ready for any bitch-attack that might come out of nowhere. Acaw's crow-brother kept on constant lookout, while Acaw finished administering to the wounded slithers.

Apparently we'd won this round, but I wasn't waiting around for them to show up again, or their no doubt very pissed-off father. When the Erlking saw his hair-snatched, cut, beaten up, burned, and bruised daughters, there was going to be hell to pay.

When we'd done the best we could to ensure everyone was taken care of, Jazz and I once more stood before the monolith. Cold air found its way through every opening of my clothing, and Jazz shivered beside me. "Let's do it," she said.

We quickly took candles from out of one of the slither's saddlebags—big ones this time. We placed them farther from the black door so that Garth would also be encompassed by the circle. The slithers, Acaw, and his crow-brother were staying behind. Showing their displeasure at being abandoned, the slithers snorted and stamped. They melted the snow with a blast of flame, and almost singed my butt in the process.

Jazz took Acaw's staff and dug the circle in the trampled snow, large enough to surround us all. She chanted aloud,

Close this circle, to the Goddess we pray.
Bind us in safety and show us the way.
Bless our task and guide our hands.
Help us to cross between the lands.

I mentally crossed my fingers. We had come here to do a good thing. A right and true thing. Surely the universe would shine on us for a second, give us a little help.

Jazz pointed her finger at each candle and the wicks burst into flame. When she finished, she came to me and gripped my good hand. Raising our arms together, we tilted our faces to the moon and Jazz chanted,

Bless us with mercy, help us to cross.
Help right this wrong, reverse this loss.
Help us bring balance, give life its due.
Open this gate and lead us through.

Warmth flowed through me and I felt it like I had been plunged into the strongest current in the ocean, as if it would suck us under, or through that black door. Our magic swirled between us, silver and gold glowing like a glittering aura. The moon blazed above us, bright white, brighter than the sun.

Was the Goddess listening?

Something was.

More light. More power. Rising. Rising like waves, like tides, like a force we couldn't resist.

We drew down the power of the Goddess, and I felt it in my body stronger than when I'd drawn down the sun. More tangible, like I could grab onto it and draw the moon right to me—or run to it and wrap my arms around its warmth.

As one we lowered our gazes and our arms, and stared at the doorway. From inside the circle behind us, Garth let out a long, slow breath. The slithers, Acaw, and his crow-brother remained completely silent.

My heart beat as I studied the blackness of the stone, trying to see some sign that it was open.

Nothing happened.

I gritted my teeth and our powers blossomed together, growing brighter and brighter until it encompassed the whole circle of protection we had cast.

This is right. Open the gateway. Let us do what we came to do.

The moon blazed in the flat surface, seeming larger, deeper.

Slowly, so slowly, the surface of the black monolith seemed to shift under that moon.

The glowing silver orb faded, but the black remained.

And it moved.

Through it I could see the top of a mountain. It had spindly trees at the edge of a treeline much like the one behind us.

And then I saw them. I could almost hear their cries—the baby harpies.

Behind us Garth gave an excited roar, followed by what sounded like a reassuring call.

The smaller harpies answered with hysterical chattering.

I took a deep breath and heard Jazz inhale beside me. Together we placed our palms against the black doorway, leaned, and began to tumble forward.

Jazz let loose with a shout as we entered the darkness. I grabbed for her hand, tried to reach her, but she was too far away.

Black, so black. Shadows darted around us, cold and dark. I wanted to whack at them with my sword, but it was still sheathed and my arms were too heavy to move. Behind us I sensed Garth was close, right by the gate. Acaw was shouting at him. The slithers were shooting streaks of fire, making the whole passage wink and flash.

Vaguely I could make out Jazz's outline, thought I heard her scream, ordering the Shadows to leave. My heart pounded and I struggled to move my hand to my sword hilt. I would not lose Jazz to the Shadows again!

In the next moment, a gray half-light and cool air hit my face, and I slammed onto the hard ground. A rock dug into my reopened cheek scar. Pain flamed through my fingerless hands and my face. I started to scramble to my feet when something smacked into me from behind, knocking me back to the ground and causing air to whoosh from my lungs. Acaw's staff rolled by, charms banging together. Arms wrapped around me and I realized it was Jazz.

M first thought was, *Thank the Goddess I'm not a bird.*

My second thought was, *If Jazz landed on me, then Garth will turn us both into a super-sized pancake.*

"Hang on!" With all the strength I had, I pushed to my feet with Jazz's arms still fastened around my neck, her legs clamped around my waist. I leapt up and dove forward, as if sliding into home base, getting us as far away from the doorway as I could. My mouth and eyes filled with dirt, rocks scraping whatever bare skin I had.

A huge *thump* sounded just inches behind us and Garth gave a cry of pain. Jazz and I untangled and scrambled to our feet, just barely avoiding his slide. I spit dirt and wiped it from my eyes as I looked up. Then I saw them.

Above us in the gathering twilight, huge shadowy figures shrieked and dove straight for us.

Jazz took on her warrior princess stance. Her fingertips sizzled while I yanked my sword from its sheath. The gold and silver light from our combined powers caused the figures to cry out, and Garth gave a shriek in his garbled language.

"Oops," Jazz and I said as one. I lowered my sword and the glow from it and Jazz's fingertips went out. The dark figures weren't Shadows. They were the little harpies.

As the enormous "babies" began landing around Garth, Jazz and I took cover in a little alcove that looked like a natural altar. From our spot we watched the reunion in Talamadden's eerie early evening.

The smaller monstrosities retracted their talons and cooed and bumped one another, trying to get as close to Garth as they could. With his incredible wingspan, he almost encompassed all the babies in his embrace. His face looked very human now, very father-like, as he spoke in what must have been a gentle, reassuring tone. It sounded more like bleeps and squeaks to me.

Wiping dirt from my mouth with the back of my hand, I looked down at Jazz. Tears streaked her dirty face. "It's so beautiful." Her voice was hoarse as she blinked more tears from her eyes. "They're together again."

I hooked my arm around her shoulder and she leaned into me. I have to admit I got a little choked up too, to see all those ugly babies being comforted by that big old harpy. They were going home, where they belonged. I'd make sure of that.

I leaned down and brushed my dusty lips over Jazz's and she smiled up at me. "I love you," she said, and my heart did a somersault.

A grin spread across my face. "I love you, too. Now let's figure out how to get our asses back to the land of the living."

"Time isn't in sync on both sides, so we might have to wait until midnight—" Jazz began, then went stiff. Her terrified gaze riveted on something behind me. At the same time I realized the harpies had gone deathly silent. Garth gathered the babies under his huge wings, and he stared at the same place Jazz was looking.

With the tiniest cry, Jazz grabbed that place on her arm—the place where she had taken the fatal wound from the Shadows.

I whirled, sword in hand—only to see the biggest Shadow I'd ever seen in my reign as King of the Witches. Something stirred inside me, an instinct, a thought I seemed to share with Jazz.

This is the one. This is the one . . .

And I knew.

This was the Shadow that had taken Jazz from me before. This was the Shadow that killed my girl.

Behind the foul, hateful bastard, a whole host of other Shadows shrouded the early night sky.

chapter seventeen

JAZZ

I had no breath.

I had no feeling but the pain in my arm. The old pain. That last, final pain.

I had no thought but the truth.

This is the one . . .

Darkness was falling too fast, even for the land of the dead. But then it wasn't darkness, was it? The Shadows had come to reclaim what was theirs.

Bren moved up beside me, sword drawn. As if from a great distance, I felt him draw upon our joined magic. Silver whirled into the flat, motionless air—but no gold moved to join it. I had gone dead inside. I had no magic.

"Jazz?" Bren whispered as the killer Shadow advanced. Slowly. One step. Another step. Closer. Coming for me.

I couldn't focus on anything but my approaching death.

"Jazz!" Bren seemed to be yelling. Was he still beside me? I couldn't tell. The night was so dark.

Miserable, cold, empty . . .

I sank to my knees.

The Shadow kept coming, only it didn't seem real. Nothing seemed real.

Something brushed past me. A sword lifted in the darkness.

If you touch her, I'll cut you in half.

The words echoed as if across a chasm. My brain could barely process the meaning, but the picture gradually made sense.

Bren, standing between me and the Shadow that killed me.

Bren, facing down an army of Shadows with no magic, with his sword held off-hand.

He was ready to die for me. In seconds, he *would* die for me.

Rise, Jasmina.

This time, the words drifted up from my past.

"Rise," I whispered, pushing against the cold ground. "Rise."

The second time I said it, another voice joined mine.

A brilliant blue bird landed beside Bren. Feathers shimmered as his wings settled, drawing Talamadden's moonlight even through the surging Shadows. Light seemed to radiate around the bird—but I realized it was Bren's sword, slowly flaring into life.

Screaming, wanting to run, I lunged forward instead and wrapped my hands around Bren's. Silver twined with gold, striking the blade like lightning. Suddenly, it seemed all of Talamadden caught fire. Silver-gold flames shone and danced around us. Overhead, the moon flared in response, pulling the magical fire into a circle around us, stretching all the way to the Glorieuse. The younger harpies chittered, but Garth calmed them, silenced them with a masterful cluck.

Outside the warding of the lights, the Shadows screeched with frustration—all but the largest. It sidled crabwise, closer, closer, until silver-gold tendrils nearly bit into the darkness that formed it.

Its maw opened.

Instead of the usual discord of Shadow sounds, out came very human-sounding words.

"Surprise, bitch," it rasped. "Do you really think any of this matters?"

Even inside the warmth of the moon-fire, a chill reached my spine. That voice sounded all too familiar.

Bren recognized it too.

"Alderon," he growled.

"Not in actuality," the peacock Egidus, my spirit guide returned, said quietly. "This is a true Shadow, but Alderon is using it to mirror his thoughts."

The Shadow—or the voice speaking through it—laughed. "So, you take the counsel of pompous birds now, little brother. How pathetic. Have you spoken to Mother lately? Oh, that's right. You can't. You hurt her, drove her away, sent her into some life-forsaken wilderness of time. What kind of son are you?"

In the sword's light, Bren's stern expression never changed. I felt a surge of pride, of compassion and love. The blade's light grew even brighter as we held it together, fending off the pain of the creature's words.

"Not worried about Mother? Figures. But maybe you care about Todd. You do care about Todd, don't you Bren?"

Bren's breathing picked up. In, out, in, out—I could tell he was struggling.

"You abandoned him, didn't you? Well, I won't leave Todd hanging like you did. I'll treat him like the king he is." The Shadow laughed, but still hovered outside flames that flickered higher every time it neared the circle. "He'll be much happier with me, and so much more appreciated."

A bit of moisture glittered in the corner of Bren's eye, but he made no movement.

"Silent treatment." This time, the Shadow made a noise like a man spitting on the ground. "You've been around the bitch too long, I can tell."

Still, Bren gave no response. I didn't either. Words couldn't do us real harm in a circle powered by love, by the Goddess herself. They could only worry us, hurt our feelings, which was certainly bad enough.

"No matter." Alderon's tone grew more sarcastic. "I absorbed as much of Mother's power as I could—and let me tell you, it's plenty enough. The Shadows are more than happy to follow my lead, and this lot, well, it's less than half of my true strength."

Bren's eyes narrowed. So did mine. Through the connection of the sword, probably through the connection of experience itself, we were both thinking the same thing. If these weren't all of Alderon's Shadows, then where were the rest?

"Steady," came the quiet intercession of Egidus. "Do not let it break your resolve."

"Do you want to know where I sent the rest? Where I am right now?" The Shadow dipped in and out of the circle's flames, careful to avoid the dancing light. In that second of revelation, I could have sworn the horrid thing had some of Alderon's weasel-look to its features.

"Come now," the Shadow hissed. "Surely you're curious."

Bren and I both tightened our grips on the sword hilt. Our gaze shifted to one another, his pained reality meeting my pained reality. We knew the answer before Alderon spoke it through the foul lips of his minion.

L.O.S.T.

Alderon and the Shadows were attacking L.O.S.T.

"Todd is proving to be an interesting catch," the Shadow said conversationally. "As for that puny human you call a father, well, I pity you that bit of heritage."

The sound of Bren's grinding teeth made me cringe inside, as did the Shadow's next taunt.

"And your mother—how she cries. She remembers her own captivity by Nire. Returning to such a prison would be a personal hell for her."

Other names and faces reeled through my thoughts, no doubt passing through Bren's mind and back to mine. How could this horror be happening again? I couldn't bear it. Not a second time.

We had to get back, right now. Faster than right now. But how? My throat tightened with the force of my frustration.

"You can't hold that circle all night." Alderon's silky voice felt like cold oil sliding down my neck. "Don't you feel weak already?"

"The Goddess never weakens," Egidus replied, loud enough to make Bren and I stare down at him. "Begone from this place, at her command."

The big Shadow's response was a sneer.

Bren's expression in the sword light communicated my thoughts.

Laughing at the Goddess is never a wise idea.

Egidus fanned his tail with an audible pop and rattle.

"Be ready," he commanded—to me? To Bren? The harpies?

It didn't matter.

My peacock spirit guide was doubling in size. Tripling. He was rising above the moon-fire, moving into the flames, *becoming* the flames.

Brilliant golds and silvers spread in all directions, laced with iridescent blue.

Our little corner of the land of the dead became so bright even I wished for sunglasses.

Shadows screamed with pain and fury. The air swirled with the hateful things, shrieking and keening. All at once, I felt the circle's warding give way.

Dozens of Shadows fell dead and vanished in the outward rush of energy.

Those that remained fell on us with a vengeance.

For a split second, Bren and I thought about pulling apart and fighting with sword and dagger. Then I saw in his eyes the resolve to stay joined with me. If we died, we died together.

As one, we lifted the sword and swung it like a club.

Shadows exploded on contact.

More attacked—and more fell.

I could see stars now as Shadows perished, as the overpowering light of the Goddess waned.

Bren and I moved like dancers in an ancient ballet, dipping and swaying, looking at each other, letting the sword find its own targets. Only a handful left—then two or three—then only one—the worst one of all.

At the sight of it staggering forward, Bren did pull away from me. He pushed me backward before I could protest. Then he hoisted the sword in his off-hand even as its magical light began to fail.

Sensing weakness, the Shadow snarled and charged, but Bren didn't change his stance.

"I've been waiting a long time for this, you bastard!"

As the Shadow slammed forward, Bren pivoted and brought the sword down harder than I imagined possible. Darkness tore in half, top to bottom.

With the weakest of pops, the murderous Shadow disintegrated.

Bren dropped the sword and staggered until he regained his footing.

"Damn, that felt good." He laughed. "It felt *real* good!"

I jumped to my feet with half a mind to slap him senseless for taking such a chance, but instead, I threw my arms around him. He was still laughing, gasping and laughing, and then he was holding me so tight I could barely get a breath.

Behind us, near the Glorieuse, I could see Garth rocking the harpy babies, eyes closed. The big beast had been willing to die like that, holding the children of his people as close as he could get them. I understood his sentiments completely.

Egidus, back to his normal size, came flapping softly down beside us. He landed with a bob of his head, then ruffled and settled his feathers. They still shimmered an unearthly blue in the brighter-than-bright moonlight.

I settled Bren down with a kiss on his cheek, then let go of everything but his hand. When I looked down at the bird, he was staring steadily at us, his black eyes reflecting what seemed like a thousand stars.

"Jasmina," he said gravely. "I may have been hasty in my judgment of your young man."

To his credit, Bren kept his mouth shut.

"Thank you." I smiled at my spirit guide. "For that, and for helping me once again."

"Now as always, that has been my charge, to guard you and help you. To teach you and to love you." He quirked his head sideways. "Go now, and see to the harpies. Send them through the Glorieuse quickly, as we haven't much time."

Immediately, Bren and I started toward them, but Egidus said, "Not you, boy. You stay where you are. I need a word."

Bren shrugged. "Sure. I definitely owe you that much for the giant-expanding-light-bird routine. What was that, anyway?"

As I approached Garth, it seemed like a curtain of silence fell between their conversation and my ears. I could barely even see them. Bizarre. But I couldn't dwell on it.

The harpies, both huge and less huge, were more than willing to do as I told them. On my command, the young ones linked arms with each other, forming a chain. I anchored one end, while Garth took the other.

On my count, the giant harpy plunged into the Glorieuse, pulling his children with him. I held on to the last baby, making certain the entire chain followed in his wake. It took a few moments, and a lot of repositioning and finally shoving, but I got them through, just as Egidus had instructed.

As if in protest, as the last harpy vanished into the passage, the stone grew a little milky. By the moon's position, I figured it was nearing midnight on this side of the gateway between life and death. Bren and I would need to leave soon. I had a suspicion it would be bad for us—perhaps even fatal—to have to wait another full day to make the crossing.

When I turned to call to him, he was already standing right behind me, a slightly annoyed expression on his face. "That bird is a pain in the ass. Sort of."

"Um, yes. I do remember. What did he say?"

"A lot of stuff about protecting you or facing things in life far worse than harpies and hags." Bren shrugged. "The rest—well, it was private."

"Bren—"

"He wishes to speak to you now," Bren mimicked, nailing the bird's haughty tone with perfection. "Go on. We don't have all day."

I had to laugh. "Okay. Okay. Wait here. I'll be right back."

Mindful of the moon's relentless journey overhead, I hurried over to the peacock and knelt down beside him.

For a few seconds, he said nothing. He just looked at me, stars still shining like tears in the black pearls of his eyes. When he did speak, he had no attitude of arrogance, no tone of reprimand or condescension.

"You have done well, Jasmina. Few could have mastered the fear of returning here, coming so close to death, even to do the noble task you and Bren set for yourselves."

"Thank you. We couldn't have done it without you."

"You are wrong in that." He sounded both proud and sad. "The help I gave, I drew from the strength you brought with you, the strength you and Bren wielded together. The Goddess could not help but bless such an effort." The stars in his eyes seemed to multiply as he bobbed his head, then turned away, sighed, and turned back. "You do not need me any longer."

"That's not true!" I leaned forward, until I was almost nose to beak with him. "What if I lose my way again?"

"You have it within you to find your way back to your true path, your destination–and your destiny." He pecked my nose gently, almost like a bird kiss.

I started to protest, but he cut me off with a rustle of his splendid tail feathers. "Did you give your mother my message?"

"Oh." I slapped my hand over my mouth, then lowered it. "In the commotion–I'm so sorry, Egidus. I forgot."

"Remember this time," he said earnestly. "For me. Please."

"I promise. Love is never wrong–I'll tell her."

He bobbed his graceful head. "That's it. It would do for you to remember that as well."

"I will." I gave him my best smile even though I really wanted to cry. Impulsively, I grabbed hold of the bird and hugged him to me. He didn't resist. In fact, he brushed my cheek with his crown feathers.

"Go now," he whispered. "Before the passage closes."

I let him go, running my fingers across his silken feathers. "Will I see you again?"

The night played a few tricks on my eyes, but I was certain the peacock winked at me. "For certain, when the time comes. Goodbye, Jasmina Corey."

As ridiculous as it seemed, despite the fact that I once wanted to cook him, I actually did start to cry as he took flight. "Goodbye, Egidus!"

I waved, and kept waving, until his shape faded into the moonlit night of Talamadden.

Thankfully, Bren elected not to pick on me about crying when I joined him at the Glorieuse. I could tell he wanted to know what we talked about, just as I wanted to know what Egidus had said to annoy Bren. These were topics for another time, though. We had pressing matters ahead of us.

We located Acaw's staff and held it between us, our hands locked together around the ancient magical wood. Together, we spoke a quick word of thanks to the Goddess, and leaped into the passage without the slightest hesitation.

Instead of the horrible Shadows and fears I had faced before, I felt only the slightest tug in my belly. Bren let go my hand, taking the staff with him, but I could still see him, fuzzy, almost a doubled image, as we slid through the cool blackness, back to the land of the living.

With the sound of wind through rushes, Bren slid out ahead of me. I came right after him, but the world looked strange to my eyes as I emerged into the first light of dawn. The snow-covered ground of the Sacred Lands stretched below me, but it seemed too far away.

Had I landed in midair?

I flapped my wings.

Wings? Wings!

When I looked down at myself, I saw golden-red feathers and talons. But—wait. There was my body, sprawled on the ground in the snow. Acaw was standing over me chanting, staff in hand. On the elfling's other side lay Bren.

"Hey, phoenix-girl," squawked a close-by voice.

I jerked my attention to the right, only to see Bren's hawk form hovering in the air beside me.

"What were you saying when we did this before?" he asked in a tone entirely too calm. "About *ba* essence getting pulled apart from *ka*?"

chapter eighteen

BREN

"Damn it!" The phoenix burned a few of my tail feathers with the force of her answer. The smoke would have made me sneeze, if I weren't a bird. "We don't have time for this. Come on."

Jazz-Phoenix folded her wings and plunged toward the ground.

"Hey!" I folded my wings and shot after her. "Slow up! Be careful!"

She wasn't listening, but I was gaining in a hurry. We were still about twenty feet up from our bodies. Then ten. I caught her around eight feet from the ground, grabbing at her brilliant red midsection to break her fall just in case it might hurt her.

My talons never touched her. Instead, they went right through her.

I went right through her!

It was a total, dizzying rush, like being smacked with an electric wire, right in the brain.

Both of us shrieked, bird-style, as we plummeted the rest of the way into our bodies.

With a jolt I opened my eyes—my human eyes. I wiggled all eight of my fingers, my toes, arms, and legs, just to confirm that I was a guy again and not a bird. Skin, no feathers. *Right on.*

By the position of the sun I could tell it was a little later in the day. When I sat up, I saw Jazz perched on a rock next to Acaw and his crow-brother, and the slithers lumbering around behind them. It looked like the beasts were pacing.

I made a quick visual check just to be sure I had legs and arms instead of feathers, then got to my feet. I stumbled a little, then regained my balance.

Jazz pointed her index finger at me. Gold light with a few silver sparkles crackled outward, straightening my clothes and hair.

She grinned.

"Wait a minute." I started to step toward her, then stopped. "You're too far away."

Another spellblast cleaned the snow off my butt and dried it at the same time. With a bit of a scorch.

"Witch!" I shot back with a bolt of my magic, missed, and knocked Acaw off the rock into the snow.

"Oops. Sorry about that." I clenched my fist and brought my elbow down to my side in a quick motion of victory. "But, yessssss! My own magic!"

"And it seems to be stronger," Acaw growled as he pushed himself up with the aid of his staff.

I looked around. Nothing but slithers, an elfling and crow-brother with serious attitude problems, and a witch who had just singed my butt. And the smells—snow, fresh air, and pine. "Where are the harpies?"

"They departed," the elfling grumbled, but looked a little relieved.

Jazz stood and held out her hand. "Come on. I think I've figured out a spell to speed us along. We need to hurry, just in case Alderon was telling the truth about the Shadows and L.O.S.T.—just in case there was any truth to my nightmare."

All of that came rushing back to me in one nasty stream of images, and that was all it took. I ran toward Jazz and Acaw, and we mounted the slithers.

As if sensing our fear, our need to get home, and following their own need to make sure Todd was okay, the big lizards snorted, then took off like they'd been fired out of magic cannons.

Jazz and I made our shield against the wind, then tried out her spell for speed. She handled Acaw's little golden slither while I worked on our big blue ride.

It worked—big time. The Sacred Lands turned into a blur underneath us. If the Erlking and his daughters wanted to pick a fight, they'd need supercharged flaming branches to catch us—or something. We were really booking.

The magic didn't seem too big or too draining, either. It was weird, but I still felt a touch of Jazz's energy inside me. I wondered if she felt the same way, but as usual, there didn't seem to be any time for us to talk about it. Our lives weren't leaving much room for . . . well, us.

Frustration and worry curled in my chest, and the slithers started slowing down.

Jazz leaned back against me, resting her head on my shoulder.

"Focus," she whispered, as good as any medicine.

I wrapped my arms around her, and I did exactly what she said.

We flew without stopping. We flew without sleeping. Acaw and the slithers seemed to understand the need, to be willing to go until we all dropped.

Time lost all meaning. Hours ran together into a day, maybe more. My legs ached. My throat felt like a desert. And still we flew. I felt like we were blazing across the sky on one big burning branch ripped from a live oak.

There was only the shield and the spell, the sky, the wind and the wings. And somewhere, seemingly forever away from us, our families, our friends, our people.

L.O.S.T.

"Goddess help us," Jazz said as the exhausted slithers banked in for a landing at the edge of the brighter section of the Sacred Lands. Yet somehow the brilliant landscape seemed shadowed, not so cheerful and sunny. The dwarves toiled without spirit and the fairies weren't buzzing around the flowers.

I forced my attention to our goal. We had reached the doorway to the Path—but I could tell immediately how wrong things had gone.

The outer walls were a dusky gray, lifeless, and without their vibrant hum.

This looked more like the Path I had first crossed with Jazz, what seemed like a century ago.

Jazz let out a soft cry and slid to the ground, hugging herself. "How can this be? Nire is gone!"

"It's Alderon," I slid down beside her. "You heard him back in Talamadden. He's got some of Mom's powers—and he's got the Shadows."

"Indeed." Acaw came up beside us, thumping his staff on the ground. "This will be a tricky passage. I have communicated with the slithers, and they have reluctantly agreed to remain here until we can fetch them."

"Todd won't like that," I said without thinking, then wanted to shout and hit something. Todd. My brother. Would he even be in L.O.S.T. when we got back? And if he was there, would I find my kid brother or some hag-strangled corpse?

Jazz gripped my hand, holding me to reality, to the next step.

Acaw did his part, tapping the side of the polluted Path walls. The round door I remembered from before appeared. A hobbit hole, but . . . it looked like live black moss covered the whole thing. I didn't want to touch it in the worst way, but what choice did I have?

Clenching my teeth against the disgusting, slimy feel of the stuff, I grabbed hold of the portal and swung it open.

Out rushed a black fog of rot that turned my stomach.

The slithers stomped and snorted behind us, and from somewhere, I thought I heard fairies screaming and the sound of dwarf footsteps scrambling away.

"Quickly!" Acaw plunged into the unnatural darkness.

Jazz whimpered, but she followed, diving through head-first.

"Todd, this is for you." I jumped in behind her.

My guts seemed to stay in the Sacred Lands, along with half of my head. I couldn't see a thing. I couldn't smell anything but funk, death, and sour dirt. Coughing, I lurched around, but couldn't get my balance on the moving floor until hands grabbed my shoulders.

Jazz.

"Draw your sword, Bren!"

I didn't hesitate.

It still felt heavy and wrong in my right hand, but I got the blade out of its scabbard and held it up, sending a burst of magic through the well-worked steel. Light flared.

Shadows hissed and recoiled, flowing in and out of the Path walls.

Jazz, pale as a ghost and shaking so hard I didn't know how she was standing, slammed the portal shut. Acaw tapped it, making it disappear.

The three of us turned as one. Acaw used his staff to defend himself, sending pulses of energy at any Shadow that got too close. Jazz shot blazing gold light from both palms, fingers outstretched. I led the way, swinging my brilliant silver sword back and forth.

Retching and staggering, we made slow progress, pushing the limits of my blade's silvery light. Falling more than walking, refusing to surrender to the madness around us, we headed for home.

By the time we reached the entrance to L.O.S.T., I felt like I had hacked my way through the base of a huge mountain. My shoulders burned. The cut on my face had opened. Blood spilled down my cheek. My hand was bleeding, too, as the healing seemed to go in reverse. So much pain. Agony. Fire.

"Jazz!" My clenched teeth bit off the shout, but she heard me.

Screaming, shooting at Shadow-fingers that swiped at her ankles, she fell past me and thrust her hands into the Path wall.

A fissure opened–more like cracked.

She got sucked through immediately, and I felt the pull, too. It was all I could do to hold off the Shadows until Acaw got past me. As he slipped into the fissure, the elfling reached back and hooked his small–but very strong–hand behind my knee.

With a big yank, he jerked me through the opening.

I pitched off, flying more than falling, and belly flopped onto the floor of the general store. My sword skittered out of my hand. I sucked air into my flattened lungs, wishing I had enough breath to yell.

It was just as dark in the store as it had been inside the Path. Not good.

"Closing," Jazz gasped from behind me. "Closing now."

Golden light flared, and I knew she was sealing the gash she had opened to get us home.

Acaw helped me to my feet and handed me my sword. I didn't sheath it.

Jazz stumbled toward me, collapsing into my one-armed embrace.

"I don't want to do this," she whispered.

"Me, neither." I kissed the top of her head, allowing myself two seconds to enjoy the feeling of holding her, the way her hair smelled. Whatever happened, at least I'd lived long enough to tell her how I felt about her. She was my girl, my queen.

And I was king. It was time to do my job.

I straightened up as best I could, gave Jazz one more kiss, then sent a spellblast up my sword to light the store—which had been destroyed all over again, by . . . something. And not just destroyed. The place was mostly dust and fingernails and glass, scattered between big, burned holes in the floor.

Acaw let out a soft cough of dismay.

I lifted the blade a little higher as Jazz stepped out of my embrace and grabbed the wrist of my injured hand. "Let's go."

We marched forward, looking straight ahead at the door.

Outside, through holes where glass should have been, we saw unnatural flashes of black light, mingled with silver sparks and gold bolts of power.

I reached the door first, yanked it open, and strode into the madness, sword raised. One step. Two. I didn't get a third.

A force slammed into me. My muscles seemed to wobble and turn to nothing, along with my bones. Jazz's hand tore out of mine. I dropped the sword, plunging myself into darkness as I was swept up from the ground.

What had ahold of me? What was yanking me into the air?

I couldn't see anything. I couldn't even struggle against the force.

Sharp, burning pains lanced my chest. I looked down. Light flared out of a bunch of holes, right around my heart. The beams joined, forming what looked like a bird.

A hawk?

My experiences with Talamadden flew through my thoughts.

Ba and *ka.*

Some evil magic was tearing apart my spirit and my physical body!

Thinking fast, thinking like Jazz, I centered myself. With every bit of my will, I wrapped my magic around the silvery hawk-spirit. My lips and voice came to life as I touched the shimmering apparition.

"No! I'm not ready to die!"

Just as fast, I realized what Jazz would do. In a big hurry, I muttered wardings and containments, all of them I could remember, binding myself and my spirit into that one space, into that one time.

But I couldn't pull the light to me, couldn't get it back into the holes around my heart.

We just hung there, suspended above the world, seemingly outside it, my body and my spirit, staring at one another with wide, desperate eyes.

chapter nineteen

JAZZ

Bren was gone before I had a chance to react. He was swept upward in the foulest cloud of dark magic I had ever seen. Shadows flew up and ringed the cloud, making what looked like a solid, pulsing tornado over the general store.

Acaw dropped his staff and reeled away from me, slicing Shadow after Shadow as his crow-brother took flight, doing the same. There were so many. Too many. The elfling fell in seconds, covered by the ravening darkness.

With a scream of rage and grief, I threw myself toward Bren's sword and snatched it off the ground. Shadows closed in to swallow me. Icy teeth chomped near my ears, my eyes.

I raised the sword and screamed "Cease!" in my most commanding voice.

Nothing happened. Something was binding my power! Or at least pushing it back. Nullifying me just enough to ruin my intentions.

From above came a hideous bunch of screeches, different from the rest of the noises.

The Shadows drew back from their attack, chittering darkly.

From overhead, huge winged shapes plunged into the fray. I couldn't see them, but I knew what they were.

Harpies.

The beasts had come to pay their debt.

I whirled around to join the fight—and found myself face to face with Alderon, separated only by a few feet and Bren's sword between us.

"Welcome home." He grinned his nasty grin, and those disturbing electric blue eyes gave an equally nasty flash. As he had been during his tenure at Shadowbridge, he was filthy and oily in his brown tunic and breeches.

"Like what I've done with the place?" He gestured toward the town I had so lovingly constructed, the hope I had given myself when all other hope had failed.

L.O.S.T. was nothing but a collection of smoldering support beams and rubble. Shadows clogged my vision, darting up and down, harrying witches who tried to fight back. Dark lumps lay in every direction.

So much death!

I couldn't gather my wits, but I kept Bren's sword between Alderon and me.

When I called to a group of nearby hags, Alderon laughed.

"Don't be stupid. They're on my side. Something about sacrificing their clans to the harpies, then setting their murderers free."

That I couldn't process. Hags, gone over to serve Shadows. How could we fight Alderon, Shadows, and the hags, too? What if all of the oldeFolke had defected?

We would never have peace again.

Likely, human witches—and in time, humans themselves—wouldn't even survive.

Focus, I told myself, just like I would have told Bren.

Bren.

"What have you done with Bren?" I shouted at Alderon.

"What do you think?" He nodded to the tornado, which was gaining in size, pushing toward us. "I killed him."

Pain lanced my chest, bringing instant tears. "I don't believe you, you lying bastard. If he's dead, show me the body!"

"In due time." Alderon drew his own sword. It flashed a blinding white-silver, laced about the edges with Nire's all-too-familiar purple. "First, I'm going to cut out your heart. It'll help me with a few potions I'm brewing."

With that, he charged toward me.

I met his downswing with a two-fisted upswing of my own, pulling on everything Rol had ever taught me from the time I was a small child.

Purple lightning crackled around gold fire. My teeth slammed together. Both my arms went numb. I staggered, but so did Alderon. As he wheeled on me, he looked a little surprised.

"You never were much with a sword," he growled, lifting his blade again.

"Things change." I lifted Bren's.

We circled each other, step for step, pacing, searching for any weakness in stance or strategy. I tried to think like Bren, see the situation through his sharp eyes.

Alderon was bigger, but I was faster.

He was stronger, but I was smarter.

He was insane and evil. I was determined and pissed.

Purple sparks fired from his sword.

Gold sparks fired from mine.

They met each other and canceled with a flash, dropping away to ash and nothing.

"Don't think to fight me with magic," I goaded. "You know better."

Alderon snarled and lunged at me. Impulsive. Unbalanced.

I parried him easily, turning him, almost ripping his tainted blade from his hands.

That's my girl, I imagined Bren saying. *Kick his ass.*

Had I ever been afraid of Alderon? Of the Shadows? I couldn't remember. I couldn't remember being scared of anything at all.

Alderon surprised me with a quick feint, drawing his blade across the arm where the Shadow had once attacked me.

Cursing, I spun away, but the damage was done. The wound opened and bled freely, and I felt the cold of Shadow poisons trickling into my flesh. Alderon's blade was as deadly as any viper—maybe more so.

I muttered a spell, doing what I could to bind the damage and slow its progress. I would die again, but that was okay. *Been there, done that*, as Bren would say. Death didn't scare me anymore. Besides, I had the satisfaction of knowing I was taking this bastard with me.

Sweat broke across my forehead. I felt sick in the pit of my stomach. Weakness spread through my limbs at an alarming rate.

"Do you like the feel of the grave, bitch?" Alderon feinted, then withdrew, laughing when I flinched. Still, I kept my eyes on him, watching his patterns, his rhythms. I had more of Bren in my mind and heart than I realized.

"It's cold, yes?" Alderon feinted again.

I slashed down hard, cutting him from shoulder to waist.

He swore and leaped backward. A line of blood welled outward, staining red against the brown filth of his tunic.

"Very cold," I agreed. My teeth chattered. "You'll know soon enough."

Pointing my sword, I sent a shower of energy into the wound I had opened. He parried with a volley of purple sparks, but some of my gold won through. I saw it strike him, saw him bend and twist from the spelled pain and instant weakness. My energy was as poisonous to him as his was to me.

He roared and came at me again, seemingly in slow motion. I could see it in his face, in those hateful, wicked blue eyes. His arrogance wouldn't let him believe I could win this fight. He couldn't fathom that I wouldn't yield to his onslaught.

Up went his fearsome purple blade. He intended to take off my head with one powerful blow.

I kept my approach simpler.

With a roar of my own, I used all of my strength to ram Bren's blade right into Alderon's vulnerable gut. At the same time, I threw the force of my magic into the steel.

Gold fire spread up, up, up, and out, turning Alderon bright from the inside out.

Sparks shot from his eyes, his ears, his open mouth.

His own energy came rushing out like a white and purple cloud of rabid bats, swirling around the two of us. From the hilt of my sword to the tip of his still-raised blade, it crackled and sparked, moving between us. I felt a cold-beyond-cold plunge into my very essence. It tore at my heart, clawing at the life, the beat, the force that made me who I was.

Instead of fighting, of being afraid, I drew it in, just as I had drawn Alderon into his fatal charge. His magic couldn't hurt me. It couldn't take anything away from me. I knew this as sure as I knew my own name.

"I am Jasmina Corey, Queen of the Witches!" I shoved my sword deeper, all the way through the vermin who had thought to take something from me he could never understand. "This is my magic. My heart. My home! In the name of the Goddess, in the name of truth and love, I cast you out!"

The husk that had been Alderon shattered like an image in a smoky mirror, falling away from my blade.

His sword, still flaring purple, tumbled toward my head.

I caught it easily with my free hand and held it up along with my own.

Golden fire burned away Alderon's remnants, then surged back through the steel of both swords. From tip to hilt, hilt to hands, then all through me, battling the darkness, containing Alderon's final murderous strike.

My hair lifted from my shoulders as I yelled with triumph. Light seemed to boil from every cell in my body, purple, and white, and silver, and gold as the sound of my shout filled the entire Sanctuary.

I felt a binding inside as I absorbed Alderon's evil intentions and crushed them to nothing.

Shadows parted and fell out of the sky. Sun blazed from a suddenly clean, cloudless sky.

The tornado over the general store cracked, then split open, revealing Bren, full of Shadow arrows but alive, locked in a struggle to keep his life force from departing.

I sent my energy swirling toward him, bringing him slowly down to the ground at the same time I was fighting for his life.

The shadow arrows fired out of his flesh as if I had pulled some mighty bowstring. In seconds, his silvery hawk form flowed back into the holes in his chest, which closed before his feet ever touched the ground.

All over L.O.S.T., fires went out. Somehow, I could see them all. I could see everything.

Witches struggled upward as Shadow poisons drained from their wounds. My mother. Bren's father. Rol. Acaw. Harpies, hags, Keepers, elflings, moderns . . .

My own wound cleansed and bound itself, taking with it that terrible cold.

As my awareness settled back into my own mind, I realized that many Shadows had not died. They had taken more human form, and they were scrabbling toward me, knees bent, heads lowered, collecting before me like a pathetic sea of ink and misery. The meaning was clear.

Nire was defeated. Alderon dead. I was their ruler now.

I had become the ShadowQueen.

"Rise," I shouted.

The Shadows obeyed me.

Sparks from my swords showered them like flaming rain.

The creatures moaned and wailed, catching fire and burning, burning, darkness blazing away from them until . . .

Until they were flesh again.

Hundreds and hundreds of naked, shivering witches stood before me, human and oldeFolke alike. I saw all the magical races I knew, and some that had been naught but legend for centuries.

As one, they once more went to their knees, as did the survivors of the battle of L.O.S.T.

"Bren?" I called, my voice so loud every beast and witch covered their ears.

From behind me, I heard a laugh. Then, "Damn, baby. Could you dial it back a notch?"

I turned around.

Bren, at least, wasn't naked.

He was walking toward me, slowly. A little carefully.

"I killed your brother Alderon," I said, my voice still abnormally loud, but waning. My hair was calming down, too, settling back around my face and shoulders, though sparks shot here and there in random colors.

Bren raised both hands. "I've got no problem with that. Really."

He stopped a few feet away. Opened his arms.

Without hesitation I threw down my swords and ran into Bren's waiting embrace.

chapter twenty

I didn't remember passing out, but when I woke up in the healer's hut, I knew I had.

Cursing, I sat straight up. My father was there at the foot of my bed. His left cheek sported one massive bruise, but otherwise he seemed okay.

"Jazz?" I croaked.

"She's fine." He jerked his thumb to the west of us. "She's in the hut next door, sleeping it off. You were both so exhausted you just fell where you stood—you kids must have been to hell and back."

"Something like that." I took a glass of water he offered and killed it. The liquid felt cool as it went down, clearing my thoughts a little. I made a quick tally and to my relief everything was intact—arms, legs, toes, ears, fingers—well almost all of them. Yep. This time, I hadn't left any of myself on the battlefield.

"How long have I been out?"

"Three days." Dad took the water glass and refilled it from a nearby pitcher. I blinked because he did it without touching the pitcher.

He saw my open mouth when he turned around, and he shrugged. "Whatever happened there at the end, it turned loose the little bit of magic I have inside. The little bit of magic every living thing in L.O.S.T. possesses. Did you know trees get pissed off when you pick an apple without asking?"

I took the glass of water and tried not to think about it. Dad, however, kept going. "Grass makes you feel good when you touch it, and water—it's so refreshing now. Do you think there's a living force in water?"

The gulp I had taken tried to come up in a big snort, but I managed not to choke to death.

"Oh, sorry." Dad grinned. "It's just so new and wonderful. Except the fish. They're just downright disrespectful, not to mention the crows and the bluejays."

He must have seen that I wanted to pass right back out and stay asleep forever, because he added, "But don't worry. It seems to be fading away, except for humans and olde-Folke. I think we may get to keep the—ah—gift."

"What about Rol? Dame Corey?" I put down the glass of . . . of whatever magical alive water was called and swung my legs over the edge of the bed.

"Everyone's fine, Bren. We lost a few, but the healers did amazing work with the rest."

"Todd," I whispered, unable to avoid it any longer, but not wanting to ask.

At this, Dad's shoulders sagged.

Dread spread through my chest and I got up too fast. My knees gave, but Dad caught me by the arm.

"He's gone, son. No—wait." He doubled his grip to keep me from tearing away from him. "I don't mean dead. I mean gone. As in not in L.O.S.T. Not in any Sanctuary."

I took a few seconds to process this as Dad turned me loose. He shook his head, and a little of the spark left his eyes. "We've done a thorough search, though Rol still hasn't given up. He and the harpies are poking through different Sanctuaries, convinced they'll find something. Acaw's gone back to the Sacred Lands to get the slithers and see if those, um, folks know anything. So far, there's no trace. Except. . . ."

He broke off and looked at the floor.

"Dad." My jaw already hurt from clenching my teeth. "Tell me now. You know I'll find out anyway."

Dad sighed and studied his fingernails. "It's just that Sherise and Helden and those hags Helden runs with—the ones who didn't defect—they have this wild story. I want you and Jazz to hear them out, see what you guys think."

"Sherise and Helden?" The memory of Jazz's nightmare on our way to Talamadden shoved all my other thoughts to the side.

She had dreamed that Todd was a prisoner. That Sherise and Helden and the hags had trapped him for some reason.

"Take me to Jazz," I told Dad. Then, remembering I was both king and son, I added, "Please."

A few hours later, in the late afternoon, I sat on a bench in Jazz's favorite forest clearing, waiting with my arm firmly around Jazz's shoulder. She had been talking to me about keeping my temper all morning, in between kissing me and telling me how glad she was I had lived. We had come to the forest outside of what used to be oldeTowne, because the main town was too noisy, what with all the Shadow-people getting clothes made and the spelling, building, and repairing—and the fact that all the animals were running their mouths, too.

Who knew dogs laughed so much? And the cats. Never mind. They were just a bunch of royal snots with British accents. It was too weird. At least out here in the forest, all we had to deal with were whispering plants and gossiping birds. The plants and trees I couldn't understand at all. They were speaking fern-Martian, for all I knew. Jazz didn't get them either. As for the rest of the wild animals, they thought we smelled bad and stayed away—or so the bears informed us before marching off toward Todd's zoo.

Todd's zoo.

My gut tightened all over again.

Dame Corey and a bunch of the oldeFolke had been seeing to it. Todd, apparently, had been letting it go to hell for a while. Some of the slithers were half-starved, and the man-eating birds had started eating things they shouldn't—like each other.

"You've got to give them a chance, Bren. Sherise and Helden may have had good reasons for what they did." Jazz's voice was soothing. So beautiful and relaxing it made me want to kiss her every time I heard it, no matter what was going wrong around us.

It might have been an enhancement from her moment of totally wild magic, like the water. Whatever. I didn't want it to stop.

"I know," I grumbled. "I'll try. But I should have been here."

She patted my leg, sending a golden burst of comfort straight to my heart.

My girl had a lot of new abilities we hadn't even begun to explore, stuff we figured she absorbed from Alderon, which included remnants of Nire, and converted into her own strong, good energy. There was no way to know if it would last, or if I would still be able to share it just by touching her like we did when our magic was joined. We'd just have to figure that out over time, along with what we were going to do with the newly restored Shadow-people. They just kept showing up in droves, from the Path, from other Sanctuaries, from places we didn't even know existed. They didn't need our help to use the Path, either. They could open and close doorways to Sanctuaries, and they could escort other Witches, just like Jazz and me. It took a lot of pressure off of us, but still. I knew that could turn out to be a problem. A serious one.

The trees started whispering in their low Martian tree-voices, and my head snapped up.

Dame Corey and Dad entered the clearing. Behind them came Helden, Sherise, and a small clan of hags who had supposedly remained loyal to us in the Battle of L.O.S.T.

The two girls clung to each other, obviously nervous, as they approached and sat down on the bench across from us. The hags crowded behind them, hag-spirits wary and swaying, keeping beady black snake eyes trained on Jazz and me. Dame Corey seated herself next to Helden, while Dad sat next to Sherise.

"I'm glad you made it home safely," Helden said to Jazz.

Sherise said the same thing to both of us with her wide, sad eyes. She seemed too intimidated to speak, so Helden got us rolling.

"I know Queen Jasmina had a vision of what occurred in your absence—of our capture of Todd McAllister."

My good fist clenched, and I nodded. "You've got some explaining to do. Why would you go after my little brother like that?"

A hag put her hand on Helden's shoulder and hissed, but Helden just patted the gnarled fingers and said something in German that sounded very sweet. For a potential kidnapper.

Sherise raised her hand and gripped her moonstone, fidgeting. "Just after you came back from the land of the dead the first time, Todd . . . *changed.* He started acting so weird, so different and all wrong—he didn't even talk like himself. I finally realized the animals were just as nervous with him as I was, and that's when I knew we had a huge problem. So, we tried to look into his heart through our stones."

She took a centering breath like Jazz did when she was really upset. "He sensed our probing and attacked us, and the hags had to help by tying him down, and we found—well—" She managed to meet my gaze. "It wasn't Todd."

"What?" Jazz sounded as confused as I felt.

Sherise looked at Helden, who took hold of her blue pendant. Starstone, Jazz said it was called.

"Show them," the hag behind her urged in a not-very-friendly voice.

Dame Corey nodded, and my dad took a deep breath.

The two girls kept one hand on their stones and laced their other fingers together. They both sighed, like they were relaxing, or sinking into some kind of meditation. Dame Corey kept up a comforting touch on Sherise's knee, while Helden's pet hag offered freaky hisses that probably passed for encouragement amongst their kind.

The stones started glowing.

Little by little, on the ground between our benches, a wavering image formed. It reminded me of lame movies we used to watch in school, but I could tell who the star was right away.

My brother. There was no mistaking it.

He looked like a combination of Alderon and Nire, the resemblance stronger than ever. And he looked totally furious as he struggled against the things that tied him. My skin crawled. Hag-spirits. That's what had him all wrapped in a knot.

My whole body went stiff. I wanted to stand up and blast the girls and the hags into some other Sanctuary, but Dame Corey's voice cut through my anger. "Keep watching."

I did. I didn't want to, but I did.

And Todd started to change.

It was slow at first, but definite, as if fighting the hag-spirits was draining away some magical energy that allowed him to hold his shape.

Jazz grabbed my hand. Her fingers dug into my palm as Todd gradually morphed into what looked like a snarling child covered with long, tangled hair.

Red hair.

The image thrashed, turned its mean little eyes in my direction, and let out a maniac laugh I knew all too well. Then it roared, flashed reddish black light, and vanished, knocking down hags and leaving the hag-spirits limp on the ground.

"Son of bitch." I stood, pulling Jazz to her feet with me. "That was the Erlking!"

The bastard had come to L.O.S.T. and shapeshifted into my brother. But when? And what had happened to the real Todd?

The image flickered and went off like an old-time film breaking right in half. Helden and Sherise released the image, then drooped like flowers who hadn't had enough water. Hags knelt and gave them vials of blue and green liquid I wouldn't have touched for all the money in all the banks in the world, but Dame Corey helped them both drink the stuff.

As they recovered, the lead hag turned her wrinkled, pinched-up face in our direction. "Someone set that heinous monster free from the Sacred Lands."

It sounded more like an accusation than a statement.

Jazz reacted with a flare of golden light across her shoulders. "Listen," she snapped. "If you're trying to say that Bren or I would do something like that—"

I took her elbow, very glad that neither of us had worn our swords. I had taken mine back, and she had kept the one she won from Alderon, but on my dad's advice, we had given them over to the healers for safekeeping.

"Stop," I said, loud enough and firm enough to get her attention.

She shook loose from me and turned, eyes blazing. "I won't have them accusing us."

"But it might be the truth." I grabbed her by the shoulders before she could start yelling and blasting things. "Remember what I asked, about whether my half-and-half blood might be a problem? Well, obviously it was. I was really afraid of that."

She gaped at me. So did the hag.

"I don't know how he used me, but—oh, wait. Yes I do, maybe." I glanced at the hag, and at Dame Corey. "Jazz said the Erlking could shapeshift into something as small as a cockroach if he wanted to."

They nodded. So did Jazz.

I let her go and reflexively reached up to rub behind my ear. The spot which had itched so badly the first time I left the Sacred Lands. "What about a flea?"

At this, Jazz sat back down on the bench, clearly horrified.

Dame Corey went pale, and the hag's ugly mouth twisted into an even uglier frown.

That was all the answer I needed.

The Erlking had used the weakness of my half-and-half magical blood and ridden me out of his prison like a common mule. Then he turned himself into my brother until Sherise and Helden caught him and forced him to change back to his normal shape. Which brought me back to the original questions I had.

"When? And what happened to the real Todd?"

Silence wrapped around the clearing, except for the trees, who were still muttering to each other.

I wanted to yell at the lumber to shut up, but Helden turned her head sideways, like she might be listening.

After a few seconds, she said, "The pines tell me the Erlking came during the attack of the harpies. And they say you should be more careful about snapping off their branches. You are clumsy."

Jazz nudged me in the butt before I could make any cracks. "Can you get them to tell us more about what happened to Todd and the Erlking?" she asked. "The trees–any of the plants? The animals?"

Sherise looked thunderstruck and frustrated, like they should have thought about that before, but Helden just nodded.

I didn't doubt her. If the chick could get the hags to love her like they did, in my book, she could do just about anything.

"It may take some time," Helden said as she stood up. "If Sherise will help me, and my clan sisters?"

Sherise stood up immediately. To my great surprise, the hags assented quickly and gathered their spirits close.

"I know you might wish to hunt for your brother and interrogate the flora and fauna," Helden said to me as she lifted her black cowl. "But please, refrain. You have an amazing ability to anger the plants."

"Um, okay. If you say so." I jammed my hands into my breeches pockets. Jeez, but it was hard to have to wait. No matter what, that was my little brother out there, somewhere, and he needed my help.

"We'll meet you at sunset," Helden called as she and her non-plant-pissing-off crew fanned out and departed. "Sherise and I will come to Dame Corey's house."

I gritted my teeth. Okay, so I'd learned to respond, not react. I'd learned to plan and not charge straight into whatever mess might be going on. I'd learned to listen and compromise.

But this. This was tough. This was my little brother we were talking about.

Jazz turned to her mother. "We still have a house?"

Dame Corey nodded as we all started back for the main town.

"Is it still, uh, yellow?" Jazz asked in a tone of voice that said she hoped it wasn't.

Despite my heavy heart, I had to bite my lip to keep from snorting out a laugh and getting turned into something unpleasant.

We spent the day helping clean up and repair, build, rebuild, and catch a few of Todd's carnivorous escapees. The harpies were still there lending a big, smelly hand, and by late afternoon, Rol and Acaw had returned from their trips.

As sunset approached, Jazz and I sat with Dad, her mom, Rol, and Acaw, drinking tea and lemonade on Dame Corey's porch, which was yellow now, too, after the repairs. Wall, roof, shutters—the whole thing—yellow. Jazz muttered something about sunglasses, but I reminded her that she was lucky. After all, it could have been purple. That shut her up.

A cat went by, gave us a stuck-up look, and meowed instead of saying something rude in British slang.

Dad, still experimenting, pointed his finger at the lemonade pitcher. It lifted up a few inches before he smiled and set it back down. "We've outlasted the animals."

"I think the changes to human and oldeFolke are permanent," Dame Corey said for the fifth time in the last hour. She didn't shoot Dad an annoyed look, but I could tell she wanted to. She probably wanted to straighten his goofball hair, too.

Rol cleared his throat. "Let us hope that's a good thing."

Acaw and his crow-brother, wise as always, said nothing at all.

A flicker of movement down the road caught my attention. I got to my feet. Dad stood up too, and Jazz, as a cluster of hags approached with Sherise, Helden—and another girl, much younger, wearing a hag robe that had been spelled down to her size. The little girl, who seemed to be around eight, was holding Sherise's hand. She had the wide-eyed look of one of the newly recovered Shadow-people.

"This is Kella," Helden said by way of introduction. "The Grainne of Grainne, keeper of the sunstone."

As if in proof, the little kid pulled out a silver chain to show us a smooth, bright yellow rock. When I narrowed my eyes to see it better, I could have sworn I saw flames dancing around inside.

"Three of the old charmed families," Dame Corey mused aloud. To the hags, she said, "Do you think the legacy bearers of the other nine will turn up?"

"I have no doubt," one of the hags answered in a low, gravelly voice. The hag-spirit curled around her arm hissed its assent.

"Will you be keeping Kella under your care?" Jazz asked.

"Yes," another hag replied. "Sherise has a home with us as well."

Surprised, I looked at the girl who had gotten my little brother's attention. "Is this what you want?"

"For now," she said softly. "There are things I need to learn—and fast."

"The news is not good," Helden offered by way of explanation, "but neither is it terrible. We believe Todd is alive, Bren. Before they lost speech, the trees told us the Erlking took him hostage almost the very moment you returned from Talamadden with Jasmina."

"The first time you came back," Sherise clarified. "The Erlking intended to lay in wait for you here and murder you, but the harpy attack caused him trouble. He kept the form you trusted, waiting for his chance, but you and Jazz were almost always together or with lots of other witches or oldeFolke. After you left the second time, we caught him, so he never got his chance."

"Todd was kept bound and gagged in a vacant slither day-lair." Helden's eyes shone with new tears as she addressed Bren. "Your brother struggled so hard to free himself, using magic and cunning over and over, he forced the Erlking to spend his energies attending to his captive. The foul creature had little time to make mischief in L.O.S.T. The oaks said Todd was the bravest human they have ever seen." She hesitated, wiping a tear. "The maples also noted that unlike you, Todd is not clumsy with trees, and they wished very much they could have helped him escape."

"The dogwoods told us Todd knew what he was doing, that he fought like that on purpose," Sherise whispered. "Todd was trying to keep us safe by nearly killing himself to get loose, taking up all the Erlking's time."

"And now?" Dad sounded tense, unhappy.

I totally understood. I would have asked myself, but I couldn't get the words out.

"When the Erlking escaped us that night, he left L.O.S.T. and took Todd with him on a quest." Helden sighed. "The hawthorns say that with Todd's powerful magic, the endeavor can hardly fail."

"Todd would never help that bastard." Those words came out well enough, in a major hot rush. I folded my arms even as Jazz stood up and rubbed my shoulder. "That part the trees got wrong."

Sherise stared down at her feet. "He doesn't have to do it willingly. The Erlking has ways of persuading him."

Even Jazz's powerful calming energy couldn't untie the knot from my guts then. "I'm pretty sure I don't want to know, but what are they after? What is the Erlking trying to find?"

All three girls looked away from us, even the little one. It was the hags who lifted their heads to answer.

One word.

One tiny little word, hissed by a chorus of ancient voices.

It wound through my mind, rubbing harsh against my ears, filling my heart with a heaviness I didn't think I'd ever be able to escape.

"Nire . . ."

epilogue

JAZZ

The weeks after the Battle of L.O.S.T. were amongst the bleakest I had known beyond my death and imprisonment in Talamadden. Bren was absolutely lost to me as he worried over his brother and railed against the reality.

We had no way of tracking the Erlking, no way of figuring how the wicked dwarf planned to go about traveling to a Sanctuary no longer connected to the Path. The ancient scrolls offered no clues, the oldeFolke had no inkling, and the girls the hags were training could not see possibilities, even with their powerful legacy stones. Acaw was beside himself. I had never seen the elfling at a loss for answers, but he had no more ideas than we did.

Thus, the painful truth: Bren and I could not mount a rescue to save Todd from his fate, or stop the Erlking in his mission to release Nire. We had no choice but to wait for them to come to us.

That was the consensus amongst all who had experience with the Erlking, hags included. He wouldn't be able to resist gloating if he succeeded. He would have to taunt Bren with his brother, since Bren had bested him once before. It was the only way he could feel superior again. It was the only way he could win. As for Nire, the Shadowmaster was his ticket to vengeance against the rest of us, all of the witches, whatever race or strength, who had kept him contained in the Sacred Lands.

Waiting for the bad guys to come to him—well, obviously, that didn't suit Bren's style at all. He spent his days alone, pacing, thinking, reading scrolls, quizzing oldeFolke, and traversing the Path and the Sanctuaries. He wanted to find a clue so badly, needed to find a clue so much, that he lost sight of most everything else in life.

Me included.

I understood. I really did, and I wasn't angry. Just . . . lonely. And perpetually out of sorts, as Rol often remarked during our endless hours of sword training. I had mastered the blade that once had been Alderon's, and Nire's before that. It obeyed my physical and magical commands without question, and I felt confident I could wield it if I had to, without risking any loss of control.

As late fall plodded toward winter, there came a time when I began to wonder if Bren still felt anything at all for me—for anyone. But much as I couldn't find Todd when I didn't know where to look, I also couldn't find Bren. He would have to come to me when he was ready.

On the positive side, with the combined and enhanced magic of the L.O.S.T.'s many inhabitants—old and new—rebuilding went faster than I would have believed possible. A few families of harpies decided to make their home with us, and Garth and his three offspring took charge of Todd's zoo. Even better, I did not have to encourage the recovered Shadow-people to get along, even with races who would have normally declared war upon seeing longtime enemies. After living through Nire's attacks, spending years as tortured half-alive creatures, they were all too aware of the price of hatred.

They were also all too aware of what we would face if . . . when . . . the Erlking and Todd succeeded in freeing the Shadowmaster.

At the Yule feast toward the end of that year, I stood in the great hall of L.O.S.T., an addition made to the general store during the time of repairs. It was a huge banquet hall, with many fireplaces and even more tables and seats for hundreds upon hundreds. It even had an open-air section to permit the ongoing growth of a huge and ancient cedar. Helden had chosen the direction and the tree, and we had followed her instructions in building so that we honored the tree to her satisfaction.

This night, the tree had been decorated in splendid fashion, with candles of many colors glowing warmly along every branch. Bren's father and dozens of children were busy covering its finery with endless ropes and chains, which Helden,

Sherise, and Kella spelled to change color and shape across the night. Garth and his were flapping up and down the length of the cedar, stretching chains and hanging candles wherever the children pointed. My mother was making ready for the lighting of the candles, and bells had been positioned at every possible location for a strong and powerful ringing.

As I stood toward the back of the hall helping to tidy after the feast—an endeavor well suited to calming my mood and nerves—I sensed rather than saw Bren's approach.

I turned to find him standing against the edge of one of the massive hearths where Yule logs crackled and flamed. By the bulge of the muscles beneath his black tunic, he had not neglected his training. His right arm now looked of equal size and strength to his left, and I knew he had likely regained most of his skill with the blade. The stubble I had grown so accustomed to made his face more handsome.

He looked . . . older.

As for wiser, that remained to be seen.

He held up his hands by way of greeting, and I saw that he had sprigs of holly fisted in his left, while a small box rested on his right palm. The box had been wrapped in bright reds and greens.

Rol, who had been making sure I didn't zap away anything of consequence, managed to make himself scarce faster than a witch of his size had any right to do. Acaw, who had been setting his crow-brother on scraps and sweets, took himself away in equally rapid fashion.

Despite the enormity of the crowd, we were suddenly very much alone.

Bren still said nothing. He came to me slowly, stopping only a few inches away. Then he turned to the fire and threw his dried holly into the flames.

"The year's almost gone, and I'm saying goodbye to sad things I can't control." His voice was so rich and deep, so very quiet. His brown eyes, captured in the flame, seemed equally rich and deep. "Are you almost gone, too? Because I don't want to say goodbye to you."

I just stood there like an absolute dolt, feeling too off-balance to speak.

"Well." He sighed. "At least you didn't tell me to go to hell. That's something."

Before I could find my voice, he knelt before me and offered me the box. "This is so you know how much I love you, and how much I meant what I said in the Sacred Lands."

My hands started to shake, which made me infinitely angry. Bren must have seen the rage flash in my eyes, because he gently covered my hands with his before I could tear into the paper. "Later," he murmured. "When you're ready. I want you to have all the time you need to think. Goddess knows I've taken my time lately."

He stood. Humoring him but planning to rip into the box the minute he took his attention elsewhere, I tucked the small package into the pocket of my green Yule gown.

"Do you know how beautiful you are?" He smiled at me, his face warm and open in the fire's ever-dancing light.

"I—I like your tunic," I finally managed. Okay, so it was pathetic, but it was all I could muster at the moment.

He grinned, then leaned down and kissed me.

The feel of his lips pushed away the pain of his long emotional absence, at least for that one special moment. I was vaguely aware of the giant circle of candle-holders forming around the hall, capturing us inside. Even less aware of the blessings, the lighting of the red candles, and the singing. Bren held me so close, and he kissed me again and again, until the Yule bells started pealing, until they stopped ringing, until the shouts of "Happy Solstice!" and "Good Yule!" rose around us like an endless cheer.

When he finally let me catch my breath, I stroked the rough stubble covering his chin and said, "If this portents our next year, I'm very happy."

His look went from soft to amused, finally settling on serious. "Consider it a portent. And I'm glad you didn't turn me into an ass, even though I deserved it."

In the early hours of the morning, I sat in the living room of my mother's house with only a Yule candle for light. Reminding myself to breathe, I ran my fingers over the paper of the still unopened Yule gift from Bren.

Mother had turned in for sleep long ago—alone—still distant from Bren's father, no matter how I encouraged her otherwise.

Now isn't the time, Jasmina . . .

After we find Todd . . .

He has too much on his mind . . .

I had heard each excuse, over and over.

Right that second, with my own nervousness at what the box might hold, I didn't blame her for her anxieties and insecurities. It was very frustrating to discover that there were still *some* things in life that scared me silly.

The paper crinkled as I slid my fingers inside and pried it up to find a small, felt-covered box within.

Hands shaking once more, just as they had when Bren handed it to me, I opened the box to find a glittering silver and gold band. I knew immediately what it was.

A promise ring.

For a moment, I just held it, tears streaming, wondering if I could bear to discover the promise he intended to make solemn with such a gift.

When I got control of myself again, I once more focused on the bright piece of jewelry. Exquisite Celtic knotwork comprised the outer ring—an endless knot, woven of silver and gold threads. Our energies, our magic, blended together into one perfect work of art.

The inner ring, a smooth silver band, carried the simple promise, etched in gold.

I will always be yours.

"Oh, Goddess." I stood up, dumping wrapping paper and box onto the floor. Damn him!

I palmed the ring and zapped box and paper into the netherworld.

When did he learn to make exactly the right choices with my heart? Say exactly the right words?

He was offering himself to me with no demand that I do the same. He was saying he was willing to prove himself for as long as it took, for whatever it took.

Damn him!

Unable to zap anything else without facing my mother in the morning, I paced back and forth, holding the ring tight in my fingers. If I put it on . . . how could I accept such a vow?

Now isn't the time, Jasmina . . .

After we find Todd . . .

He has too much on his mind . . .

My mother's words blazed in my thoughts as I blew out the candle and walked in darkness to my room. I would sleep on my decision. That was the only sane choice, after all.

With a snap of my fingers, I lit the sconces on my wall, and my eyes fell immediately upon my bed.

The beautiful blue feather was laying there, as if placed oh-so-carefully by graceful elfling hands.

The feather was so bright, so long and lovely—there was no doubt this was the train feather my spirit guide had given me before I escaped the land of the dead. Along with the message I had so completely forgotten to deliver.

Feeling outside of my own body, I drifted toward the feather, reached for the hollow tip, and lifted it as gently as I could.

Then I turned and ran down the hall to my mother's room, snapping on lights as I went—snapping on every light in her yellow, yellow house—adding more lights with each step I took. By the time I burst through her door and threw myself on her bed, she was sitting up wide-eyed, clutching her covers to her chest. Her silver and black hair looked wild and out of place, and her yellow gown was rumpled all over her arms.

"Jasmina! Are you all right? What is the meaning—what is that feather—what are you doing?"

"He told me to tell you." I sat up and thrust the feather into her hand. "He told me, but I forgot."

"Who told you what? Did you get into the Yule wine?"

"In Talamadden, I had a spirit guide. A peacock. His name was Egidus, and he told me to bring you this feather and give you a message." I caught my breath and finally spit out what I needed to say. "Egidus told me to let you know that love is never wrong."

"Egidus . . . ?" Mother's eyes blinked rapidly. Her mouth worked, but her voice seemed to fail her.

"That last time, he said I didn't need him anymore, but not to worry, because I'd see him again, and he *reminded* me but I forgot. I'm so sorry, Mother. Egidus wanted you to know that love is never wrong."

I was about to tell her about Bren's promise ring when I realized she was clutching the feather and laughing and crying all at the same time.

"Egidus," she said between sobs and bursts of giggles. "Peacock." She laughed some more.

"Mother?" I leaned toward her. "Did I miss something?"

"Land of the dead," she gasped. "Spirit energy—bird—true form!" She laughed some more.

I thought about how Bren had turned into a hawk, and how I had briefly found my spirit in phoenix form when we came back through the Glorieuse. "So, in life, Egidus was somebody who deserved to be a peacock on the other side!"

"Yes!" Mother's shout was full of pain and joy, laced together like Bren's silver and my gold. "Jasmina. My sweet girl. Don't you see? True form, root form, root name. Egidus. In modern times, in our times now, the name would be—"

"Giles." I cut her off, stunned.

Egidus was the ancient form of Giles. As in Giles Corey.

My father.

We gazed at each other, my mother and I, the feather clutched in her hands, drifting between us like the miracle it was. A gift from the Goddess. A gift from my father!

We both cried then, and I opened my clenched fist to the welcome sight of Bren's promise, shining in the bright, bright candlelight.

With no hesitation, I slipped the band onto the ring finger of my left hand. I was on my feet in a flash, running, running, out of the yellow house, off the yellow porch, down streets barely illuminated by the first dawn of the new year.

I ran all the way into L.O.S.T. without slowing down, determined to find the man I loved—and my mother ran almost as fast, heading for her own new beginning.

To Write to the Authors

If you wish to contact the authors, please write to them in care of Llewellyn Worldwide, and we will forward your letter. Both the authors and publisher appreciate hearing from you and learning of your enjoyment of this book. Llewellyn Worldwide cannot guarantee that every letter written to the authors can be answered, but all will be forwarded. Please write to:

Debbie Federici and Susan Vaught
℅ Llewellyn Worldwide
2143 Wooddale Drive, Dept. 0-7387-0827-5
Woodbury, MN 55125-2989, U.S.A.

Please enclose a self-addressed stamped envelope for reply, or $1.00 to cover costs. If outside the U.S.A., please enclose an international postal reply coupon.

Many of Llewellyn's authors have websites with additional information and resources. For more information, please visit our website at:

www.llewellyn.com

Sign of the Crescent

DEBBIE FEDERICI

Teenagers are mysteriously disappearing in Tucson, Arizona, and other cities. One night, seventeen-year-old Taryn nearly becomes one of them when a revolting, unearthly creature attacks her. The touch of a Zumar warrior should render her unconscious, but Taryn has the strength to fight until a young man with a sword comes to her rescue.

This is how Taryn, an orphan with Ménière's disease, meets Erick, a Haro Knight from another world. His job is fighting the Zumar who are kidnapping and enslaving oldworlders (Earth people). It is forbidden for Erick to socialize with oldworlders, but he can't ignore the strong attraction between them . . . and Taryn seems different from other Earth people. When she's abducted by the Zumar and taken to their evil sorcerer leader, Taryn is confronted with shocking truths that explain her strange dreams and special powers.

0-7387-0808-9

312 pp., 5³⁄₁₆ x 8 **$8.95**

L.O.S.T.

DEBBIE FEDERICI & SUSAN VAUGHT

Is Brenden the Shadowalker who could save the world? Seventeen-year-old Brenden is happily on his way to San Diego for a short summer vacation. Stopping to use the restroom in a small town changes his life forever when everything familiar disappears and he finds himself in L.O.S.T.—one of many witch villages from different times (ranging from medieval to modern) and magically disconnected from the rest of the world. The golden-eyed teenage girl responsible for taking Brenden to this land of witches, hags, and sirens is Jazz, Queen of the Witches. She recognizes an inner power in Brenden that could save her people. Throughout their adventures, Jazz and Brenden share an irresistible attraction, yet they must devote their strength to defeating Nire, an ancient evil threatening both of their worlds.

0-7387-0561-6

312 pp., 5$\frac{3}{16}$ x 8 **$9.95**

Blue Is for Nightmares

LAURIE FARIA STOLARZ

Sixteen-year-old Stacey Brown isn't the most popular girl at her boarding school, or the prettiest, or the smartest. She has confidence issues, a crush on the boyfriend of her best friend Drea, and she has painful secrets. Stacy is also a hereditary Witch. Now she's having nightmares that someone is out to murder Drea.

Guilt plagues Stacey because a series of dreams several years earlier predicted a death she couldn't prevent. Now she is determined to use her skills (including folk magick, dream magick, and contacting her grandmother's ghost) to find the killer before the killer finds Drea. Edgy and engaging, Laurie Faria Stolarz takes her readers on an unforgettable ride with this witchy thriller.

0-7387-0391-5

288 pp., 5³⁄₁₆ x 8 **$9.95**

Silver Is for Secrets

LAURIE FARIA STOLARZ

After graduation, spending the summer at the beach seems like the perfect vacation. All Stacey wants to do is relax; hang out with Jacob, her new boyfriend; and enjoy the ocean with her friends. But this proves to be impossible when her nightmares return, this time accompanied by annoying nosebleeds and a dreadful feeling that danger is lurking.

Stacey senses that Clara, a fifteen-year-old visiting the same beach as them, is in deadly trouble. Cute, flirtatious, and rumored to be a boyfriend-stealer, Clara is not exactly popular with the girls. And Stacey is finding it difficult to help Clara when she's obviously hiding something. What is her mysterious secret? Why is she telling lies about Jacob and Chad? Can Stacey solve the mystery before someone gets hurt?

0-7387-0631-0

312 pp., 5$\frac{3}{16}$ x 8 **$8.95**

Red Is for Remembrance

Laurie Faria Stolarz

Since Jacob's disappearance, Stacey has been trying to move on with her life. With a full scholarship, she begins classes at Beacon University, which her best friend Amber is also attending. But Stacey still misses Jacob and can't quite accept that she'll never see him again.

The president of Beacon introduces Stacey to his fourteen-year-old daughter Portia, who is struggling with her own nightmares that foretell murder. The two become friends as Stacey helps the young girl cope with her frightening premonitions. They work together to find the boy in Portia's dreams—locating him in a cult-like community. Despite their innocent goal to live peacefully without technology and material goods, there's a dark side to this community. And one of the members, Shell, looks remarkably like someone Stacey used to know . . .

0-7387-0760-0

288 pp., 5³⁄₁₆ x 8 **$8.95**

Don't Die, Dragonfly

LINDA JOY SINGLETON

After getting kicked out of school and sent to live with her grandmother, Sabine Rose is determined to become a "normal" teenage girl. She hides her psychic powers from everyone, even from her grandmother Nona, who also has "the gift." Having a job at the school newspaper and friends like Penny-Love, a popular cheerleader, have helped Sabine fit in at her new school. She has even managed to catch the eye of the adorable Josh DeMarco.

Yet, Sabine can't seem to get the bossy voice of Opal, her spirit guide, out of her head . . . or the disturbing images of a girl with a dragonfly tattoo. Suspected of a crime she didn't commit, Sabine must find the strength to defend herself and later save a friend from certain danger.

0-7387-0526-8
288 pp., 4 3/16 x 6 7/8 **$4.99**

Last Dance

LINDA JOY SINGLETON

Sabine can't wait to show off her new boyfriend at the upcoming school dance, but she's also worried about her grandmother, Nona, who's suffering from a fatal hereditary illness. The only cure lies within a remedy book, lost long ago.

Determined to save Nona, Sabine goes to Pine City to visit a distant relative who may have clues. But there's someone else clamoring for Sabine's attention: a fifty-year-old ghost named Chloe who's been appearing in her dreams. Celebrated by Pine City every year on the anniversary of her tragic death, Chloe has become a town legend. Despite death threats and missing the school dance, Sabine must use her psychic skills to solve the mystery surrounding Chloe's untimely demise . . . and lay her soul to rest.

0-7387-0638-8

312 pp., 4$\frac{3}{16}$ x 6$\frac{7}{8}$ **$5.99**

Stay on the Path!

Llewellyn would love to know what kinds of books you are looking for but just can't seem to find. Witchy, occult, paranormal, metaphysical, or just plain scary—what do *you* want to read? What types of books speak specifically to you? If you have ideas, suggestions, or comments, write Megan at:

megana@llewellyn.com

Llewellyn Publications
Attn: Megan, Acquisitions
2143 Wooddale Drive
Woodbury, MN 55125-2989 USA
1-800-THE MOON (1-800-843-6666)

And be sure to check out Llewellyn's website for updates on new books from your favorite authors.

www.llewellyn.com